# LIES BETWEEN FRIENDS

## A.A. Abbott

Edited by Katharine D'Souza Editorial Services.

Cover design by Getcovers.com.

Published by Perfect City Press.

This book was written by a British writer in British English.

**PAPERBACK EDITION**

**ISBN 978-1-913395-19-3**

A FEW WORDS OF THANKS

Thanks to my editor, Katharine D'Souza, and everyone else who helped make this book great, especially Amarjit Nar, Andrea Neal, Callie Hill, Colin Ward, David Wake, David Walford, Dawn Abigail, Deb Day, Debbie Young, Dennis Zaslona, Ellie Shepherd, Gary Davidson, Jenny Prosser, Jeremy White, Jill Griffin, Jo Ullah, John Lynch, Marie Wright, Michèle Weibel, Nicki Collins, Nigel Howl, Nigel Messenger, Pete Crawford, and Suzanne H Ferris.

**A.A. Abbott**
England, September 2025

# CHAPTER 1 GAIL

## Day 12 - Friday

Less than two weeks ago, I'd have told you my life was perfect.

Okay, I'd have been lying. True, my husband was rich, clever and handsome. We shared a gorgeous Victorian house in Bristol's best district, and two adorable children. Blonde and blue-eyed like their father, eight-year-old Mary and six-year-old Tom gave me everything to live for. They still do.

But I'm not sure I'll ever see them again.

As I watch the helicopter vanish from sight, cold tears add to the sting of a salty breeze. The beauty of the landscape, with herring gulls soaring gracefully over bright yellow gorse, means nothing to me. This island is one of the bleakest places I've set foot. And even though living off-grid as a child should have equipped me to survive, I face one major obstacle.

My so-called best friend has left me alone with a killer.

# CHAPTER 2 GAIL

## Day 1 - Monday

Nick tackles his breakfast in silence. My husband isn't a morning person. He slept so badly that he stole my concealer before his first meeting. No-one must see the dark circles around his eyes. I pretended not to notice, because why choose a battle about that?

He's hardly said a word to me since he joined me in the hotel dining room. I daren't ask how his pitch went. From his sullen demeanour as he mainlines black coffee, I can guess. But at the sound of a helicopter's mechanical hum, everything changes. There's a sparkle about him. Nick is preening.

Excitement fills the air as the craft lands outside. Eyes are drawn to the windows. The racket drowns out conversation around us, but I sense an air of anticipation. Is a VIP about to emerge? Or do we have a celebrity among us?

Nick is waiting for the moment when the other guests find out the chopper has arrived for him. He could walk to the reception lobby to meet the pilot, asking the concierge to carry the luggage stowed for him. However, that's not his style. He remains at the table, sipping his drink and smirking.

The noise slackens before dying altogether. I spot a pair of men dashing to the side of the steel-grey craft; ground crew, no doubt, rather than aimless bystanders. It's that sort of hotel. While the wood-panelled walls and moulded ceilings speak of a bygone age, residents expect twenty-first century convenience. Helicopters are welcomed. In contrast to the nosy stares of the clientele, the staff are unfazed. Our server, a willowy girl bearing a silver coffee pot, stifles a yawn.

With the rotors silent, chatter begins again. More full English breakfasts are served. Mushrooms are speared, marmalade spread on toast, drinks poured.

An aroma of fried bacon hangs heavy in the overheated room. Nausea forces me to gulp. Stomach curdling, I stare down at my bowl of yogurt and fruit, Nick's gaze following mine.

"You should eat more," Nick snaps. "You're thin as a pencil."

"I'm not hungry."

I can control my food intake, if nothing else. The rest of my life stretches and bends to fit around Nick.

He glares at me, then at his Apple Watch. "Where's the pilot?" he gripes, pushing his plate away. "The man's late."

"There?" I point to the figure being escorted into the room, smart in a black suit. To my surprise, and presumably also to Nick's, the pilot is female.

She's short, perhaps an inch less than me, chubby-cheeked and full-figured. Nick's gaze immediately fixes on her breasts, their swell visible beneath her crisp white shirt. He makes a cupping motion with his hands.

"Nick, stop it," I beg, heat rising to my face. What if she notices?

As usual, he brushes off my concerns. "I don't know what you're complaining about, Gail. I've offered to buy you new boobs, even. Next birthday? It's the big three-oh," he suggests, as if dangling the prospect of Swiss chocolates.

The girl with the silver coffee pot has overheard him. We exchange glances of mutual understanding. It must be more than her job's worth to show disdain.

Nick stands up as the pilot reaches our table. At six foot four, he towers over her. He's still not looking at her face, though. What self-discipline she displays, keeping her smile friendly, holding out her hand to shake his.

"Mr Masterson? I'm Lacey Lewis from Helicon."

"Delighted to meet you," Nick murmurs.

Beneath Lacey's black fringe, shaped in a choppy pixie cut, her violet eyes flick across to me. She looks young for a pilot. At a guess, she's mid to late twenties.

I wish Nick would stop ogling her cleavage.

"I was told just one passenger," Lacey says. "Is that correct? I've room in the kite for another – it's a B206 – but I'll have to agree paperwork with the office first."

"Just me," Nick purrs. He blows me a kiss. "Wish me luck, darling."

"They'll love you. You're a star fund manager."

Nick nods, clearly satisfied with my response. "See you on Friday."

The kids don't rate a mention. I miss Mary and Tom terribly, even though they've been staying with friends for only one night. To Nick, they're out of sight, out of mind.

I must remember he's hoping to pull off one of the biggest deals of his life. Of course he's on edge. His new investment product is crucial, he told me; his business depends on it. That's why he's broken with his usual Monday morning routine. Instead of travelling to London by limousine, he's already seen a foreign investor holidaying in this opulent hotel. Next, he'll fly to a billionaire's country house in Surrey.

It's the only way he could get airtime with both of them. Anyway, Nick is always saying he must look the part. He's selling a success story. The City offices, swish Thameside pad and huge house in Clifton are chapters in his tale, proof he's living the dream.

So is our marriage.

On our wedding day, I believed we were marrying for love. After all, I was. Barely a week later, though, I overheard him tell a friend that he'd proposed because I could stick 'The Honourable' in front of my name. He believed it would lend him cachet within the investment community. No doubt he was right. Even his father approved. It may have been the only time that Nick impressed the old monster.

Ironically, I rarely use the title. My dad, a viscount, has never bothered with his. He taught me to regard such labels as an accident of birth. Only Nick and his chums seem to place any weight on them.

He's in his element now, revelling in the attention from other guests as he swaggers past them. They'll be wondering if they should recognise him; if he's a Netflix actor or reality TV star. Nick has the looks for it. Wheat-coloured hair hugs his head in waves. His jawline is strong, with a cleft chin, regular features dimpling into a smile.

He's kept a muscled rugby player's figure too, but it's hidden under business clothes. When we met at his cousin's art show, he was convinced his physique had lured me to his side. After all, girls threw themselves at him to test his fitness. He was wrong, though. Nick's eyes drew me to him, sky-blue and unshakably confident. Nick believed in his right to rule over others. And, young and timid, I was willing to be dominated.

I've grown out of it.

Nick no longer piles on the charm, either. That stopped long ago. He doesn't waste time glancing back. The rotor's cacophony begins again, and the spinning blades spirit him away.

Still queasy, I push aside my food and black coffee. This sick feeling could be a bad omen, a sign that my husband won't secure the investment contracts he craves. After all, the day hasn't begun well for him.

I stand up and stretch, hoping to quell my fears with movement. No-one takes any notice when I creep past the buffet, almost retching at the spread of meat, cheese and fruit. The wood-lined walls close in. Portraits of ladies and gents in Elizabethan garb stare disapprovingly at me. I recoil at a full suit of armour lurking in an alcove, as if a ghostly knight is poised to jump out.

In the garden, I clear my head with huge gulps of fresh air. Only the tang of aviation fuel hints at the departed helicopter. Feeling a little better as I wander across the velvety lawn, I take in the stone walls and mullioned windows. While it's not my style, it would be my dream to work on a design brief for a place like this. The hotel is a genuine Tudor castle, grand and luxurious. A night here is a treat even for Nick, who believes in spoiling himself. My friends will want to hear all about it.

I return to my bedchamber. No other description does justice to this room, with its Elizabethan maximalist vibe. Windows and four-poster bed are swagged and curtained, the carpet ornate, the ceiling's plasterwork intricate. The girls will have to see it to believe it. Smoothing the bedcovers, I snap a couple of photos. The elegant bathroom, quietly understated in a monochrome palette, deserves a picture too. But when my gaze hits the black granite counter, my throat tightens.

A scattering of white powder glares at me from the polished surface.

It won't be sugar or talc. I know that for sure.

Nick has started early this morning.

# CHAPTER 3 NICK

## Day 1 - Monday

Nick slams his office door and slumps in his executive chair. Despite being ergonomically designed with high-end carbon fibre, it gives him backache. He is not happy. His nose is running, and the adrenaline that kept him upright has evaporated. As soon as he closes his eyes, promising himself it's just for one second, his landline rings.

Tamara.

What is wrong with her? Okay, so he stormed past her as he arrived just now, but he has a lot on his mind. She's only a PA, with no right to demand his attention. It's her job to serve him, not the other way around. She's developed an entitlement complex since they started sleeping together. He should let her go.

Images of her shapely breasts swim into his mind. They stir a craving. Not yet, he decides. He'll keep her for a while longer. Anyway, the phone's jangle has stopped.

It begins again. Perhaps he should pick up. Suppose she's trying to put through a VIP? An investor could have changed his mind, deciding to put in cash after all. Nick's eyes narrow at the memory of his latest humiliating dismissal. All that effort to arrive in style, and he's kept waiting for thirty minutes. Curtly rejected inside another ten.

Even the pilot laughed when he suggested she could make an investment. She flat out refused to give him her number.

What is he going to do?

He reaches for the phone, hoping. "Who's on the line?"

"Nick," Tamara says, unexpected steel in her tone, "we need to talk."

"Now's not a good time." Outraged at her insensitivity, he cuts the call. Puts his head in his hands. Takes a deep breath. He must phone his friends.

Harry's the first, his trusted wingman among the Bristol Boys, now a bank manager in Reading. There's plenty of money in Berkshire: rich farmers, light industry, head offices. Harry could recommend Nick to his clients. In fact, now he thinks about it, Nick reproaches himself. He should have asked Harry before.

Harry answers on the first ring.

“Nick! Not like you to call on a Monday morning. Thought you’d be sleeping off the weekend.”

“I’m a family man these days. You know that.” He omits to say that Gail parked the children with one of her pals. Nick can’t even recall who. She takes care of the domestic side.

“Anyhow, Hazard, I genuinely love my job. And today’s special. I’m rolling out a new investment line…” He uses Harry’s school nickname, which was well-deserved. Put it this way, you wouldn’t stick Harry in charge of a chemistry set.

“Well, I’m pleased for you, mate. Glad you’re living up to your old man’s legacy.”

Harry sounds as if he means it, but what’s with ‘mate’ and ‘old man’? They didn’t teach the boys to speak like that at Markham’s. Still, even the Prince of Wales doesn’t use the King’s English.

“I’ll cut to the chase,” Nick says. “We’re looking for new investors, fifty K minimum…” Inwardly, he sighs. At that level, he’ll need a hundred of them to get close to the five million pounds he’d expected to secure earlier. “…and I wonder if I could set up a presentation for your clients? And cut you in, naturally. We’re looking at tasty returns. Twenty per cent, although I can swing a sweet deal for you individually. Drop the management charge on your share.”

There’s a long silence. Nick wonders if he’s overplayed his hand. “Hazard? You still there?”

Harry coughs. “I wish I could go for it, mate, I really do. But you wouldn’t believe the red tape I’d have to navigate even to get your outfit on an approved supplier list. Then the product — well, our bean counters would have to crawl all over it. Scared of the taxman, the FCA and who knows what else. You’d have to disclose proprietary information. Tell them how it all works. You don’t want to do that, do you?”

“I can bear the risk.” A cold sweat grips Nick. His collar itches. He must agree to whatever the bank demands: anything to make the deal. “How long will that take?”

He can practically hear Harry counting on his fingers.

“Six months,” Harry says.

Nick resists the urge to fling his phone across the office. At this very moment, it’s looking like he can’t afford to replace it. He mustn’t hint at his troubles to Harry, though. Gradually, he stills his quickening breath. The product wouldn’t pass scrutiny by Harry’s bank in any event. He’s dodged a bullet. “How about a personal stake?” he asks. “My offer stands. You’re my buddy, and I’ll reduce our charges.”

“No can do, sorry,” Harry says. “Cost of living, right? I’m in debt to my eyeballs.”

That resonates with Nick, but it means Harry is no use to him. “Got to go, I’m afraid. My PA’s just come in.” The lie slips easily off Nick’s tongue.

Next, he tries Michael Gill. The lawyer’s pension fund is already under Nick’s control. Surely Mike can stump up a few hundred K more. He’s a Magic Circle partner; he must have earned just shy of a million last year. But no.

“You can’t imagine the school fees with quads,” Mike moans. “And I’m doing up the chalet in Sauze d’Oulx. Jessica insisted.”

No doubt, as she insists on every aspect of their expensive lifestyle, down to the private IVF they had when she decided Mike’s sperm wasn’t up to snuff. Mike is firmly under the thumb. He was always easily led. Nick should have taken him aside before, should have explained about women. You treat them mean and keep them keen. Now, it’s too late to put him right.

He calls several more of the Markham’s lads, but success eludes him. Either they don’t pick up, or they’re broke, or they’re risk averse. So much for the old school tie. Why couldn’t his father have sent him somewhere better? Eton or Harrow would have provided a higher quality network, for example. He imagines the old sadist scowling at him, jeering that he’d never have passed the entrance exams.

Nick swipes through his contacts.

A jolt of hope straightens his shoulders. Jonno. He came from Bristol too, although not a member of Nick’s inner circle. A hopeless nerd. That won’t have changed. When Markham’s held a reunion ball three years ago, gauche Jonno annoyed even Gail, who’s meek as a mouse. Nevertheless, Jonno runs a huge corporation. He’s making money hand over fist. Convinced from their first day at Markham’s that Jonno would never amount to anything, Nick is glad he was wrong.

He hesitates before phoning, though. It’s not like they were best buddies. Jonno used to remind Nick of his father, with that perpetual glint of contempt in his eye. Then there was the time Jonno hid Nick’s insulin.

Nick’s hands ball into fists, memories overcoming his panicked desire for cash. He could have died. As a Type 1 diabetic, he must inject insulin to survive. That's why he had a mini fridge in the dorm. He still recalls his terror at finding it empty, his rage when he realised who was responsible.

Only four boys had access to that room. He obviously hadn't stolen his own insulin. How about Mike and Harry, then? Unthinkable. That left Jonno, the sly worm.

Sure enough, the insulin reappeared after they gave Jonno a beating.

Nick wonders how Jonno winds him up so easily. He shakes his head, releasing a long breath. Then he chuckles. That fridge came in handy for gin later on. They hid the spirits in Evian bottles. It was a Saturday night routine in the sixth form: shots with Nick.

He's smiling when he finally makes the call.

"Yes?"

Jonno still has that Bristol accent. The lads used to mimic it. Better not do that.

"It's Nick Masterson. How are you?"

"All the worse for speaking to you."

"I beg your pardon?" Nick recoils an inch or two. Did he hear right?

Jonno swears, adding, "I don't have the headspace, Nick. Leave me alone."

Headspace?

Nick's mouth settles into a sneer. That's the kind of inane comment Gail would make. At the ball, Gail expressed her disdain for Jonno forcefully, but now Nick wonders. Was it a smokescreen? She's all alone during the day in that big old house in Bristol. Who knows what she gets up to? Rage builds, straightening his shoulders, sparking a wave of energy.

About to smash his fist on the desk and tell Jonno to go stick his headspace, Nick stops. Thinks. It's vital to get Jonno onside. Nick needs the man's cash. He pulls his focus back to the conversation.

"I'm sorry you feel that way," Nick says. "I've got a tremendous opportunity for you, twenty per cent guaranteed returns. As your old friend, I'm giving you first dibs."

Jonno curses again.

The phone pings.

Nick's schoolmate has cut the call.

Nick throws the device onto the floor. It hits the velvety carpet with a soft thud. Sighing, he picks it up and prepares to pitch again.

His office door swings open. Tamara sashays in, Barbie-pretty. Ash blonde curls tumble to the waist of a high-necked, figure-hugging black dress. He can't suppress the surge of desire at the sight.

"Tamara," he says, holding out his palm to stop her. "I have to ring people."

"They can wait." Tamara pouts, lower lip wobbling.

With a start, he spots the hand she has placed on her board-flat stomach. He swallows, mouth suddenly dry.

"We need to talk," Tamara repeats.

# CHAPTER 4 JONATHAN

## Day 1 - Monday

Jonathan flings a volley of curses at his office wall. Solid and unblinking, it offers no reaction. There is more integrity in a square inch of plasterboard than in the whole of Nick Masterson's miserable existence.

He can't say the phone call came as a surprise. Nick inherited an investment fund, didn't he? Naturally, he'll push his financial products. The arrogant prick already tried at the reunion ball three years ago. Jonathan's shoulders tense at the memory. Why did he bother going? He works out regularly, he looks good and has absorbed that public school polish, but he's still the odd one out. It took all of ten minutes for Nick to get under his skin. First, there was the sales pitch. Then the hand on his girlfriend's bum. Nick claimed it was an accident at first. Not later, though, when he took it further. Cornering her, squeezing her breasts, and asking why she bothered with such a loser.

Jonathan should have hit Nick then. Or walked out. But he didn't, and how he regrets it. Already drinking heavily to hide his discomfort, he knocked back half a bottle of whisky and made a play for Nick's wife.

She slapped his face.

His girlfriend dumped him.

Jonathan doesn't blame either of them.

Of course, he hadn't met Tilly at that point. Since he did, Jonathan couldn't care less who Nick married. It's typical of Nick to choose a girl who could be a supermodel, though. And not just stunningly beautiful, with her curly brown locks and sultry eyes, but an aristocrat. The Honourable Gail Masterson.

Nick wasn't just born with a silver spoon, he's had an entire gilded cutlery set thrown in his direction. Even if he could understand what it's like to be the only child of an alcoholic single parent, he wouldn't give a monkey's.

Jonathan recalls his first day at Markham's. He'd expected to find a place of safety when his scholarship catapulted him into boarding school. No more living on his nerves, hiding behind bins, walking the long way home. As a puny geek on a council estate, each day held dangers. Markham's would be different.

He learned otherwise. Quickly. Escorted to the four-bedded room that they were to share, Jonathan met Nick and his two followers.

"Oh my word. What's that?" The sneering voice belonged to a boy with cropped red curls. For years afterwards, Jonathan imagined Mike Gill's ginger hair gave him a chip on his shoulder. Now he understands the truth is more complicated.

"You mean that," Nick Masterson, handsome in the style of the Hitler Youth, prodded Jonathan's chest, "or that?" He kicked Jonathan's shabby suitcase.

The lock sprang open, disgorging Jonathan's carefully folded garments in a rumpled heap on the floor. Harry, the third boy, giggled. Tall and skinny, he'd stretched out full length on the window seat, feet up on a cushion. Clearly, he hoped to enjoy a show.

"Get off there," Nick ordered Harry. He opened the sash, scooped up armfuls of Jonathan's clothing, and threw them outside.

"Stop it," Jonathan begged. He grabbed Nick's arm, tussling as the strapping blond boy moved to repeat the process.

"You going to make me?" Nick swatted him off like a fly.

Jonathan tried not to cry, still tugging uselessly at Nick's sleeve. The garments fluttered onto the lawn below, some landing in a bed of thorny bushes. They were clean, new things, as specified in the uniform list. Mrs Henderson had taken him shopping. There was a grant, apparently. She'd given him the case, too, an old one of hers, aware he'd be lucky if his mother supplied a bin bag.

"Want them back?" Nick asked.

Jonathan nodded.

"Then go for it." Nick shoved him onto the window seat, keeping up the pressure.

Jonathan felt himself tip backwards, the frame's lip biting into the nape of his neck. Sky loomed above him. "No!" he shouted into the breeze whistling past his ears.

Harry raised an eyebrow. "Defenestration, Nick? We don't need the drama."

Nick cursed. His grip slackened. "All right, Hazard."

Jonathan wriggled from Nick's grasp, only for Mike to grab hold and frogmarch him to the door.

"Get out," Mike said, with a rough push.

Even their laughter, ringing in his ears, sounded upper crust. They belonged to a different world and were eager for him to know it. Cheeks flaming, he scuttled outside to retrieve his soiled clothing.

It went downhill from there, despite Jonathan's attempts to win Nick over. He tidied the room, fetched snacks, and stopped Nick making crass mistakes with his homework. It was never enough. If Nick's icy stance appeared to thaw, an obstacle soon presented itself. Insulin vanished from the mini fridge. Muddy shoes were flung carelessly on the floor just before a spot inspection. A frog sprung out of Nick's bed as he pulled back the covers.

Jonathan wasn't responsible, but Nick didn't believe him.

Who set him up? He suspects Mike. Because Nick needed a victim. Mike, less comfortable in his skin than he appeared, must have feared he was next in line.

Jonathan shakes off the memories. None of it matters now. He's exacted revenge on most of the Bristol Boys, especially Mike, who he holds in boundless contempt. Not Nick. Not yet. Maybe never, as Tilly has changed his mind in so many ways. She has become his whole world.

He glances around the office he used to share with her. These days, it's his alone. He can choose from the twin white standing desks, ergonomic chairs and blisteringly fast laptops. Jonathan appreciates their simplicity. The magenta walls, ornately framed artwork and leopard print sofa are less to his taste. He adores them all the same. They carry Tilly's essence just as much as her perfume. She wears Opium by Yves Saint Laurent. In his desk drawer, he's secreted one of her silk scarves infused with the scent. At stressful moments such as this, Jonathan retrieves the scarf. It's thin and silvery, insubstantial as mist. He buries his nose in it and feels her presence.

Memories of school bullies melt away.

Two smart raps on the door signal Stan Voyze's arrival. The CFO waits outside until Jonathan calls for him to come in. Tilly's scarf has been hastily stowed out of sight.

Grey-haired Stan is more Tilly's age, at least two decades older than Jonathan. He stands tall and straight, like a soldier in a sentry box. His military bearing is accentuated by the way he marches in. Jonathan always expects him to salute and bark, "Suh!", but it hasn't happened yet.

Instead, Stan asks, "How's the lady boss?" He sniffs the air, his expression curious. "Has she actually been in? I swear I can smell her perfume."

Jonathan won't admit to the hidden scarf. He tuts. "Must have got a trace on my shirt when I left the flat."

Stan shifts from one foot to the other, although his face shows no discomfort. Perhaps it was tactless to hint at conjugal bliss. The CFO is going through an expensive divorce, triggered when his wife discovered he'd visited a strip club. That seemed out of character for a stolid, dull accountant. Still, a midlife crisis can hit anybody.

"How can I help you?" Jonathan asks. "We don't have a meeting in the diary, but I assume this isn't social."

Stan exhales. "Just stuff to sign." He brandishes a plastic wallet.

"What are they?"

"A new photocopier licence. An employment contract for my purchase ledger temp. Forms to open a money market account. We can get a better interest rate. Then there's a letter to HMRC about their investigation."

"Anything to worry about?" Jonathan thought Stan had answered all the taxman's questions. He doesn't need the hassle right now.

"It's all routine," Stan says, his tone bored. He removes a wodge of papers from the folder, placing them in front of Jonathan on his desk.

Jonathan flicks to each neon-coloured tab indicating where a signature is required. He pens a quick scrawl without even skim-reading the documents. Stan has been with the business for years. He's trustworthy and meticulous.

Handing the paperwork back to Stan, Jonathan grimaces to hide a yawn. "Can I pick your brains?" he asks the CFO.

"Go right ahead." Stan meets Jonathan's gaze.

"All this." Jonathan sweeps his arm around, gesturing at the obviously feminine office. "Who did it?"

Wrinkles deepen on Stan's forehead. "Bloggs & Co. They handle our maintenance, remember?"

"It's before my time. Did they sort out the colour scheme and the furniture as well?"

Stan's brow clears. "Oh, I see. The overall concept… Tilly's own idea, I believe." He pauses, screwing up his eyes. "Wait. It was her daughter's friend. She's an interior designer. A nice girl. Pretty, if you go for the anorexic look."

"What's her name?" Jonathan decides he owes Stan an explanation. "I want to make our flat a bit more homely for Tilly. It's too minimalist. We didn't get round to redecorating…"

"Say no more." Stan's face softens. He adores Tilly. "I'll dig out her invoice."

He leaves the room. By the time the phone rings ten minutes later, Jonathan is engrossed in his work.

It's Stan.

"I've found that designer's name," the CFO says. "Gail Masterson. The Honourable, would you believe?"

# CHAPTER 5 GAIL

## Day 1 - Monday

The foyer's grand stone walls close in on me. I am small, dislocated. Like Alice in Wonderland, I am in uncharted territory.

Folding my arms and clutching at them, I repeat stupidly, "The card's been declined?"

The receptionist's name badge informs me she's called Lyra. She has the smooth skin of youth. At twenty-nine, I could be nearly twice her age.

She nods. "I'm afraid so, Mrs Masterson. Do you have another card?" Her voice is clipped and professional. She doesn't smile.

I retrieve the Amex Gold from my purse. It's attached to Nick's business account, of course. Butterflies swirl in my stomach as I slip the card into the chip and PIN machine. Why couldn't Nick have settled the bill before he left? Too focused on Lacey's assets, no doubt.

Luckily, I chose an easy PIN to remember: my wedding anniversary. Seconds after I punch it in, the transaction is approved.

Lyra folds the bill and places it in a thick cream envelope. "Thank you, Mrs Masterson. I hope we'll see you again."

"I'm sure you will." The next time Nick wants to impress somebody.

Let's hope the helicopter trip to Surrey paid off. Wheeling my case to the car, I decide to wait for him to tell me. If his meeting went well, he'll be more than ready to boast. While he's in a good mood, I'll broach the subject of his drug use. I owe it to our kids to try. He might even agree to a stay in the Priory. Anywhere exclusive will appeal to Nick, rehab unit or not, especially as his fellow patients will be loaded. He'd use it as a networking opportunity.

In the privacy of the Tesla's driving seat, I check my banking app. My light-headedness, the feeling of existing in a parallel universe returns. It's no wonder that my debit card was declined. Our joint account is ten thousand pounds overdrawn.

Have we been scammed?

Does Nick know?

Trembling, I tap his number on my phone.

His mobile seems to ring forever, until there's a click and he picks up.

"Darling." My voice wobbles. "Oh Nick. I think we may have a problem with our bank."

"Gail, it's Tamara."

Heat rises to my cheeks. If only I'd remembered how often his calls bounce to Nick's PA. She's as efficient as a robot. Nick says she has to be: her face is not her fortune.

"Nick is tied up, unfortunately. I'm in a meeting myself, but I know you wouldn't ring him if it wasn't important. How can I help, Gail?"

"Well, I need Nick, really. It's a bit personal…" I catch myself. It could be hours before I can speak to my husband. Nick might not even have arrived in the office. He could be agreeing on details with his big investor. If we've been robbed, the sooner it's reported, the better. And Tamara will know what to do. She always does.

"Look, Tamara, I'm worried that our bank account has been compromised. That's my joint account with Nick. It's gone massively overdrawn, and I can't use the debit card anymore."

"How awful for you." Is there a hint of tension in Tamara's voice? "I take it you've been through the transactions. Are there any you don't recognise?"

"Um, no, I haven't looked." I wince. Fancy skipping such a basic check.

"Do that and call straight back, all right? I'll sort it out."

"Thanks." Although aware she can't see it, I manage a weak smile.

That vanishes when I scrutinise my banking app. Usually, Nick transfers money into the account. This time, he's taken ten grand out.

Why?

# CHAPTER 6 NICK

## Day 1 - Monday

Nick glares at his PA as she ends the call.

"Why the hell did you answer her?" he demands.

"Because you didn't. It's my job."

Her eyes flash. Nick is used to viewing them up close, ice-blue and adoring. This new, argumentative version of Tamara doesn't appeal. He knows she's right, though. Since Tamara began working for him, he's congratulated himself on finding a PA with both brains and beauty. The south London accent winds him up, but she's quick and effective at her job. Too many of his City friends employ decorative girls who turn laziness into an artform. They think it's enough just to show up and shake their boobs. Depressingly, they're often right.

Tamara has more about her, but his gaze is still drawn to her chest.

"What did Gail want?" he asks.

Tamara frowns. "Her debit card was refused. The account is overdrawn. I've told her—"

"I heard what you said." Nick face-palms. He meant to top up the joint account again with cash from the business, but to his horror, there isn't any. If only Tamara would leave him alone. He could sniff a little Charlie, clear his head. His stomach heaves as he recalls there's no Charlie left either.

He hears his father sneer, "Screwed up again, haven't you, son?" Instinctively, Nick flinches, although his logical brain tells him the blow will never come.

"Nick." Tamara smiles, pretty and amenable once more. "Cheer up. There's good news too. I'm pregnant."

He gapes at her, the absolute horror of it sending a chill down his spine. "That's good news?" he spits. "Get rid of it."

He'd usually make soothing noises about paying for a private hospital, taking her on a trip to Paris as a treat. It's what he did for the others. But he can't be bothered to tread the same line with Tamara. His house of cards is tumbling down. What money he can lay his hands on, Nick needs for himself. And he has enough stress to deal with. As Jonno would say, he doesn't have the headspace.

“You said you loved me. We would get married and be together forever.”

“No way,” Nick says, his voice as cold as the shivers engulfing him. “I would never have told you that.”

A niggle of doubt freezes him even more. Nick works hard and plays hard. He has a lot to drink on occasion. Sometimes it’s more than a drink. But he keeps a grip on reality, doesn’t he? Women go to bed with him on his terms. He doesn’t need to lie; his good looks and fat wallet charm the pants off them. And he’s taken care of Tamara well. She earns a salary above the market rate. He’s splashed out on a company flat where she lives rent-free. It’s in the same block as his, although hers isn’t a penthouse and it doesn’t have his glorious view of the Thames.

The smile has vanished. Beneath the false lashes and heavy makeup, Tamara’s eyes are flinty. Hard. It occurs to Nick that she’s been playing him, or at any rate, trying to.

His lip curls.

“You’re an adult,” he says. “You shouldn’t believe in fairy stories. Lose the brat, and I might just pretend this never happened.”

# CHAPTER 7 GAIL

## Day 1 - Monday

"Come on through." The morning sun highlights Daisy's flame-red ringlets. She stands at her threshold, smiling.

A refreshing spring breeze catches her floaty skirt. As it spritzes my face, I'm sorry I brought the car. I could have dropped it at home and walked the mile or so. The stroll would have helped clear all the uneasy thoughts churning through my mind. But I'll need the Tesla later to collect the kids from school.

"Thanks for having the children," I gush. "I hope they weren't any trouble."

"Not at all. Mary persuaded me to make flapjacks with her. She actually knew a recipe. Impressive."

"She'd be baking every day if I let her. And Tom would eat the lot."

Daisy laughs. "He demolished three before my boys took him off to play video games. I heard not a peep from them."

That's one worry dispelled at least. I release some of the tension in my shoulders.

"I encouraged them to pack their own clothes this morning, so their bags are ready for you," Daisy says. "Now, how about a coffee?"

Her kitten heels clatter across the hall's marble floor. I follow her to the open-plan kitchen and dining room at the back, with French doors overlooking a wrought-iron veranda. A clematis has covered the white-painted tracery in powder-pink flowers. Three candyfloss tufts of cherry blossom draw my eye in the distance.

"Magical, isn't it?" Daisy says. "I wouldn't change a thing in the garden. The house, well, that's different."

"Why don't you give me a tour? Then you can say what you like and don't like."

"Coffee first. I know you often take it black, but I've discovered skinny caramel lattes. Want to try one? Sugar-free syrup, hardly a calorie in sight."

"Go on then."

Daisy waves me to sit on a high stool while she gathers paraphernalia. Pods are popped into a machine, hot milk and sweet flavourings swirled into bone china mugs emblazoned with roses. She hands one to me. "How was your night of passion?"

Heat flushes my face. "It's a nice hotel. Here, I'll show you a photo of our four-poster."

Daisy gives me a knowing look. "That's not what I asked. I don't want to see the bed—"

"No? The style is so you. And we are supposed to be talking about your décor."

"Later. I'm interested in what happened in that bed. You said you and Nick needed alone time. Did he exceed your wildest dreams?"

Why does she care? "We made good use of it," I lie, pasting on a smirk. Nick was satisfied by his lovemaking, anyway. It's been years since he paid attention to my pleasure, if indeed he ever did.

"Well, let's see the photos," she says.

I scroll through them. Daisy coos over the lavishly appointed bedchamber. The simple black and white bathroom attracts less praise.

"I think we already know you go for a romantic look," I point out. "In your last place, you had moody florals, velvet, mirrors…"

"Gordon grumbled about it. Too feminine for him. I tell you what, though, we made a fortune selling the place. He was quick to boast about that."

"You have a blank canvas here." My gaze skims the old wooden units and peach tones. It screams 1980s throwback. On the plus side, plenty of original features remain. "You'll keep the Aga, won't you? Really, you can do anything with this house. It has good bones."

"That's what Gordon said." Her eyes narrow. "He sees it as a fixer-upper. You know, stay a year, move on, never mind the upheaval. Remember how long my kitchen took last time?"

"Three months, wasn't it? Stunning, though."

"And the fitter was hot." Daisy grins. "Go on girl, find another like him."

"No promises."

"Anyway," Daisy huffs, "bearing in mind Gordon's plan, I'm after a lighter feel this time."

"Say, nets on a four-poster instead of heavy drapes?"

"Perfect. And when we sell, I'll finally move to Clifton rather than Redland. We can be neighbours. Clifton is where I wanted to live, but Gordon couldn't resist a bargain."

"He certainly got one."

Outwardly, our houses could be twins: detached, constructed three storeys high from rough-hewn red sandstone, sitting in sizable plots. Gordon and Daisy must have saved a million pounds through buying in Redland, though. It's an upmarket district, but Clifton is pricier. Everyone's heard of it thanks to the famous suspension bridge. DFLs – buyers down from London – all seek property there.

For once, it wasn't Nick's strategic thinking that led us to Clifton. Our family home had been Nick's when he was a teenager. On my first awkward visit to Nick's parents, his mother told me she bought it as a bolthole. I considered the comment odd at the time, especially as she repeated it later. She was just starting to become forgetful. Her husband was in denial, although by then, they were virtually living separate lives. It was too late. He'd already pounded her brain into mush. That's what Nick hinted, anyway.

He would never become like his father, Nick said. Yet, more and more, I wonder. He certainly adopted the old man's work ethic. When his mother was widowed and Nick suggested I stay with her for a few weeks, he remained in London to manage the business. And I never left Bristol. Newly-wed and pregnant, I became the carer for a woman whose mind drifted in and out of reality. It was only two years ago that we moved her to a nursing home.

Nick never sees her when he's back at weekends. I can't take the kids either. They'd be upset when she invariably failed to recognise them, even though they used to love her anecdotes and her child-like delight in their company. But I often visit while they're at school. When I can, I take her out in a wheelchair to the green spaces and coffee shops of Clifton. Surely the odd treat, like a cappuccino on the hill overlooking the suspension bridge, will perk her up? Perhaps I'm kidding myself.

As if on cue, Daisy asks, "How's your drink?"

"Lush." I take a final sip, calculating how much I should cut back on lunch. Glancing at my phone, I see a Starbucks tall skinny latte is eighty calories. This one appears roughly the same size. "Do you want to take me round now?"

Daisy giggles when I gasp in horror at orange fittings in the downstairs cloakroom and an avocado bathroom suite on the first floor. However, apart from that and the dated kitchen, there's nothing a lick of paint can't put right.

We finish up sitting in the kitchen again. I power up my MacBook and show her pictures of a study alcove and a library wall. "These would work well for you, and they'd add buyer appeal."

Daisy nods. "Amazing. You have an eye for possibilities."

"Thank you. I'm so glad to do a job I love." Not to mention a career that Nick judges socially acceptable; one he can brag about to his cronies. When I told him I wanted to sew curtains for other school mums, he hit the roof. I still run them up for my clients, though, and pretend I sourced them elsewhere.

Daisy squints at the screen again. "Not sure on that creamy colour scheme," she says. "I'd prefer more drama."

"Don't forget you're flipping it. This isn't about your taste, or Gordon's, it's about your buyers'."

"Gordon won't care as long as it's cheap. Will you do mate's rates?"

I had an inkling she'd ask. It takes an effort not to sigh. "I can't speak for the builders — whoever you choose — but I'll knock ten per cent off my design fee. It'll be higher than last time, though. That was a taster rate, because I needed to get a portfolio up together."

Daisy's lips tighten. "And you landed a few projects with it, didn't you? Mama's office, for instance. You're my bestie, too. Couldn't you go to twenty-five per cent?"

"Okay." Darn. It can be difficult working with friends. I'd never treat a so-called bestie the way Daisy just pushed me.

In my head, I have a conversation with Nick about her. It's unlikely to happen in real life, as Nick is so focused on himself. But I imagine my hard-nosed husband advising me to show her a higher rate card and deduct the discount from that. I make a mental note to do it.

Daisy's expression relaxes. "Staying for lunch? It's quiche and salad. There's a nice chilled white to go with it."

"Yes please to lunch. No day drinking for me, though — it never ends well."

"Fine, but I will."

Daisy produces a bottle of Soave with a screwcap. She pours at least a third of it into a glass.

"What would you like? Elderflower fizz?"

That hints at sugar. Calories. "Water, please."

Daisy pulls a face, but fills a pink crystal tumbler from the tap. Passing my glass to me, she clinks hers against it. "Cheers."

"Here's to a transformation."

"And a move to Clifton." She takes a swig, then turns her back to remove food from the fridge.

"The quiche is salmon, from M&S — Ocado did a delivery this morning. Is that all right?"

"Absolutely. A small slice would be lovely." Smarting from the discussion about fees, I wonder what Gordon thinks of her Ocado deliveries and Boden wardrobe. It's not as if Daisy contributes income to their household. My guess is that her late father left her a big inheritance. Plenty of the school mums are trustafarians.

When they learn I have a title, strangers assume I was born into money. They couldn't be more wrong. My father's family may have been wealthy once, but the riches had slipped through their fingers by the time he came along. With Mum, he travelled around the country, picking up odd jobs. They home-schooled me and my two sisters. We had the kind of education that taught me to repair a VW camper van, not get into Cambridge like Nick.

I've lost track of my parents' whereabouts. The last I heard, they were off the coast of Tierra del Fuego. They sank their life savings into a boat and sailed off with my sisters. I was madly in love with Nick by then, so I refused to go too.

They didn't care. I doubt they ever cared. Although Dad had made it clear he detested Nick, he simply smiled and said I was old enough to make my own decisions.

My family were thousands of miles away when we married. I bought into Nick's claim that our whirlwind dash to Gretna Green was romantic. It's honestly the tackiest thing I've done in my life. But was it really such a big mistake? I have the lifestyle I yearned for: children, friends, and a home that doesn't move around. Whatever his faults, Nick is generous. Look at Daisy, forced to justify all her expenditure to Gordon.

"How's this?" Daisy brings me back to the present, setting a plate down in front of me. She's warmed a tiny portion of quiche and arranged it prettily on a heap of rocket. The dressing sits in a bowl to the side, where I can ignore it.

"Mmm, thanks." I chew slowly.

Daisy stares at my untouched salad dressing. She says nothing, finishing her glass and sloshing more Soave into it. The bottle is almost empty, and I've had none of it.

"Do you always drink at lunchtime?" I ask.

"Doesn't everyone?" She laughs. "Apart from you."

An icy shiver creeps between my shoulder blades. It was kind of her to take Mary and Tom, but I won't leave them here again.

Daisy takes a swig, creating enough space for the dregs of the bottle. She helps herself. "It's amazing wine. You don't know what you're missing."

"I'm in the car, remember?"

She drives too, but I question whether she should be collecting her boys from school. I could offer to do it.

A faint sheen coats Daisy's olive skin. Her face reddens. The effects of alcohol are beginning to show. "Gail, I worry about you. You're absolutely obsessed with calories…"

"I don't get hungry easily," I protest. "Or thirsty."

"Don't think I didn't clock you checking your phone. Look, you're super-slim. You can afford to let your hair down a bit. Have a chocolate truffle on me. Or a G&T. Both if you like."

My stomach flips at the thought of the combination. "You're as bad as Nick. He tried to fatten me up this morning. And pressed me to accept a boob job as a birthday present."

Daisy's eyes sparkle. "He's paying? Take him up on it. It'll suit you."

"It's not like buying a new dress."

Daisy shakes her head.

"What are you like?" she asks. "If I had a sexy husband, I'd make the effort to please him."

My jaw drops. I had no idea she viewed Nick in that light. With luck, he doesn't feel the same about her. A glance at Daisy's well-endowed figure doesn't reassure me, though.

"What's wrong?" Daisy asks impatiently.

"Isn't Gordon sexy?"

"Heck, no. Way too serious. Know when you're well off, girl." Daisy sighs, gulping down what's left of the wine.

For my own sanity, I need to change the subject. Picking up my MacBook again, I open my portfolio folder. "Can we look at a gallery of my previous work? You can tell me what you like and what you don't."

"Good shout," Daisy says. She points. "Look, there's my old kitchen."

"And your mum's office. She loves that magenta shade, doesn't she?"

Daisy skewers me with a glare. “I can’t say. I feel I don’t know Mama at all, anymore. We’re not speaking.”

“Oh. I’m sorry, I didn’t realise—”

“It’s okay. I haven’t broadcast it.” Daisy notices her glass is empty. She pouts. “Mama married a toy boy. It’s disgusting. No fool like an old fool.”

I recall the tall, elegant woman whose office I redesigned. Matilda Gill wore her sixty years well. She could easily have been two decades younger. A whirlwind of feminine energy, she impressed me as anything but foolish. After all, she was running a successful company single-handed. I grin, remembering her throaty laugh, and the humour with which she charmed everyone.

“Why don’t you approve?” I ask. “Doesn’t she deserve her happiness?”

“It’s a bit sensitive.” Daisy squirms, face a deep shade of pink.

“Oh?” I press, sensing a boozy revelation.

“Well, he’s kind of an old flame. One of my brother, Mike’s, school pals. Like Nick.”

“You didn’t go out with Nick, did you?” My mouth twitches at the corners. He hasn’t mentioned a romance with Daisy.

“Don’t be silly.” Daisy huffs. “We didn’t mingle when we were single. You honestly think I’d have let Nick get away?”

Nick might have a different opinion. She’s not Honourable, is she? However, I’m hardly keen to admit why he chose me as his wife.

Daisy leans forward. Her voice is a conspiratorial whisper. “It all started at the supermarket. Can you imagine? An afternoon last summer. I’d packed away the shopping and put my trolley back.”

Only a year ago? I’d imagined their romance pre-dated her marriage. This gets worse.

“A gorgeous guy tapped my shoulder. I mean, you should have seen him, Gail. He wore shorts and a deep tan. Ripped muscles and a big smile. He told me that my car had a flat. Then he asked if he could help. And he was brilliant. Had a jack and a toolkit, and the spare wheel was on inside ten minutes. A white knight riding to the rescue…”

I gawp at her, refraining from saying I’d have changed the wheel myself. Nick wouldn’t thank me for letting that slip. It’s hardly the image he wants his wife to project.

"… and the least I could do was invite him back for coffee," Daisy says.

My mouth continues to gape open. I don't want to hear more, but there's no stopping Daisy now.

"Well, one thing led to another. I saw his private toolkit, put it that way." She glares. "You're judging me."

"I'm not," I lie.

Daisy switches off her death stare. "I know you won't tell. Look, I didn't mean to cheat on Gordon. It just happened."

"Was wine involved?"

"Might have been. Gin, actually. We moved on to the hard stuff after coffee. I'm not proud of it, but it was so worthwhile. The best sex ever."

I feel my cheeks blush to match hers. Hoping she doesn't notice, I ask, "So… this man ended up marrying your mother?"

Daisy grimaces. "How stupid was I? He had it all planned. We met every weekday for a fortnight, then he finished with me. Said we had no future. But you know what? He was looking for a meal ticket. And I'd bared my soul to him."

Not just her soul, though. A chill runs through me. "He blackmailed you."

She twists her face, as if the notion hadn't occurred to her. "No," she says slowly. "It wasn't like that. But he'd won my silence. You see, he knew I'd never leave Gordon. And of course I'd talked about Mama. How lonely she'd been since Dad died. What a hassle it was to run their business by herself. Well, he saw a rich widow and started chasing her."

"A gold-digger."

"If it's a guy, he's a gigolo, I think. Same difference. And guess what? They met in a car park." Daisy contemplates the empty glass, clearly wishing it was full.

"I wouldn't have any more if I were you. Unless you're walking to pick up the kids."

"Can you run me over there? I can walk home with them."

"No problem. Are you okay?"

"No. I'm still angry," Daisy says. "Mama was full of it; how her tyre had a puncture, but then she'd crossed paths with this wonderful man. I wrote it off to coincidence. Then she wanted her children to meet him, and it had to be in London, because Mike is always so busy with his law job. Mike and his stuck-up wife booked afternoon tea at the Ritz. Of course, I twisted Gordon's arm, so he came too. Little did I know. My God, it was awful."

I picture Daisy in a state of high alert, gaze darting between husband and lover. Evidently, the crisis was averted. She's still living here with Gordon in Redland, committing him to home improvements.

"You got through it. Good on you," I say, patting her arm.

"That time, yes. Mike wasn't impressed either. You should have seen him when he realised who Mama's new squeeze was. I mean, this is his schoolfriend, half her age, right? We made the best of it, hoping she'd enjoy a fling and move on. But instead, she married him. She didn't listen when I hinted he was after her money."

"And you couldn't tell her because…"

"Too risky. Suppose she let on? Even if Mama hadn't breathed a word to him, just broken it off, he'd have stuck the knife in. Once Gordon found out, my marriage would be over." Daisy dabs her eyes.

"Oh Daisy." I reach for her hand.

Mascara runs from Daisy's lashes. "We're besties," she sniffs. "You won't say anything, will you?"

"You can rely on me," I promise. But her secret weighs heavy on my shoulders. Daisy's infidelity unsettles me far more than the vision of a cougar cavorting with a young man. If it wasn't for the way he'd used Daisy, I'd congratulate her mother on pulling him.

"I guess you're wondering why I did it."

"A moment of madness?" I venture, queasiness making me glad I didn't eat much.

"A flash of excitement, more like," Daisy says. "My existence is boring, you know? You've got an interesting career with your design work. Hey, I bet you've even got an escape fund. Nick knows he can't take you for granted."

Her view of my life is 180 degrees apart from reality. Perhaps I should build an escape fund, though. With Nick's roving eye, a divorce isn't out of the question. He'd only have to meet a well-stacked aristocrat, and I'd be last year's model. And maybe he would respect me more if I had money.

It's not going to happen on the rates Daisy pays me.

Meanwhile, I wouldn't dare suggest Daisy was obsessed with her stepfather, but she can't stop talking about him. "He's a smooth operator," she says. "He got Mama to change her will right away. Mike checked. And she brought him into the family company. He's got his filthy hands on everything Dad built up."

Didn't she just say her mother had struggled to run it alone? Still, she could have hired a consultant.

Daisy's phone starts pumping out an Ariana Grande track. She swipes the screen to reject the call. Seconds later, the ringtone starts again.

"Someone's keen to talk," she says, silencing it.

"Not Gordon?"

She stares at me, lip twisting in a sneer. "No. Wedded to his work. He'd have to be surgically removed from the office before five o'clock."

"Ha, I know the feeling."

Her phone vibrates on the countertop. Daisy glances at it. "They've left a message. Excuse me for a minute."

She wanders out of the kitchen, phone in hand. I overhear a low murmur of conversation. Clearly, whoever rang, they were important enough to merit a call back.

Daisy returns, eyes bright and skin even more flushed.

"Everything okay?" I ask.

"Yes." Daisy plonks the phone down. "Can you do me a favour? If you'd pick up my kids and give them tea with yours, it would help me out."

"Yes, Tom and Mary would love that." A playdate is the least I can do. I owe Daisy for the sleepover.

"Great. I'll message the school so they're aware. Well," she glances at the old-fashioned station clock hanging on the wall, "I'd better shoot."

"Doing anything nice?"

"Meeting my red-hot lover."

As I laugh, I wonder if she can tell I'm faking it.

# CHAPTER 8 GAIL

## Day 1 - Monday

It's too early to pick up the kids when Daisy ushers me out. I head home, releasing a deep breath the moment I cross the threshold. The cool neutral interior exudes calm. Vibrant paintings by Bristol's street artists add just enough of an edge. Pride of place goes to a Banksy, spotlit above the drawing room's marble mantelpiece.

Nick bought the artwork: his choices, along with the colour palette and extreme tidiness. Once he realised we'd be here for good, he insisted on redecorating, and his mother didn't raise objections. To cope with family life, I installed lots of hidden storage and had the floorboards varnished.

If Nick didn't have such strong opinions, I'm not sure what decor I'd have picked myself. As a designer, my tastes aren't relevant. I have to be a chameleon, producing schemes that match my clients' desires. Perhaps that's why the assignments keep coming my way. I'm not established enough to refuse work, though, even from friends who take advantage.

Daisy's disclosure still has me reeling. Her admiration for Nick nags at me. Having had a fling already, she might regard him as fair game. But he's my husband. As a friend, surely she wouldn't touch him? And like Gordon, Nick is always busy at work. He has no time to cheat, and being in London, he's a hundred miles away from Daisy. It's insane to give space to these groundless suspicions.

I make a cup of Earl Grey (slice of lemon, no milk) and empty the overnight cases: my clothes and toiletries, Nick's dirties, and the contents of the bags the children took to Daisy's. Smiling, I stroke Tom's fluffy comfort blanket. I used to worry that he hadn't grown out of it, but there's plenty of time. You don't hear of a teenager carrying one.

Once the washing machine is thrumming away, I carry cup and MacBook to my studio in the back garden. Nick wouldn't allow the profusion of shrubs and flowers that lend romantic charm to Daisy's plot, but we do have an apple tree in the centre of our close-snipped lawn. Lacy white blossom is beginning to appear. Its sweet scent catches my nostrils as I pass.

The studio, a wooden cabin with a picture window overlooking the house, smells of pine. I sit at the simple table, sip my drink, and set to work on Daisy's designs. Absorbed in mood boards and furniture layouts, I hardly notice my phone ringing.

Tamara. She must be following up on my debit card problem. A twinge of guilt unsettles my stomach. She asked me to phone her back.

I swipe up to take the call.

"Hello, Tamara. It turned out Nick had made a transfer from our bank account. I'm sorry, it slipped my mind to tell you. Did you get to talk to him?"

"I did, but not about the bank." Tamara's voice is strained, the accent that Nick calls 'Mockney' more audible than usual.

"So how can I help? What has he left behind this time?" I didn't spot anything odd in our suitcase. Whatever it is, he must have mislaid it at the hotel.

"Stop." Tamara pauses. I hear her inhale sharply. "Gail, Nick is leaving you—"

"I beg your pardon?"

Her words make no sense.

"He's leaving you," Tamara repeats. "Making a fresh start. I'm pregnant with his child—"

No. This can't be happening. Nick's reliable PA has gone raving mad.

Even if I could formulate words, they'd stick in my constricted throat. Meanwhile, Tamara's crazy lies just keep coming.

"We're beginning a new life together here, in London. He won't be going to Bristol again."

She must have mental health issues to spout a fantasy like that. I'll have to tell Nick. It's a shame, especially with the stress he's under. He's had so much trouble finding a competent PA, and he seemed thrilled with Tamara.

At last, I manage to gasp my thoughts out. "You're delusional. Look, if you need help, I'm sure Nick would pay for counselling…"

He might, if I catch him on a good day. I can't imagine he'll let her keep her job, though. Which means even more stress for him, as he begins the recruitment process. More risk of a meltdown. More tiptoeing around him this weekend.

"Gail, you'll have to face up to it—"

Blood pounds in my ears. If I don't cut the call, I'll scream at her. "Got to go," I say, my voice unnaturally high.

No sooner have I hit the red button than I bellow. It's a frightening sound: lowing, like a cow.

The rage doesn't last. My jaw slackens, dizziness pressing me back into my chair as despair takes hold. I sob, head in hands, until my hot eyes have no more tears to give.

She's lying. Tamara is a hyper-efficient PA and Nick delegates a lot to her, but getting her pregnant? Why, she's so fat and ugly, she'd have to blind him before he was attracted to her. As for dumping me to live with her, he's far too strategic for that. It wouldn't play out well with his City friends.

Yet doubts worm their way under my skin. I only have Nick's word on Tamara's appearance. Suppose she's so hot that he's not thinking with his brain? Anyway, he took ten grand from our joint bank account. And he didn't answer his phone.

I steel myself to ring him again.

# CHAPTER 9 GAIL

## Day 1 - Monday

"Mum, can we sew buttons?" Mary has just learned needlework and can't wait to practise. If I wasn't so distracted, I might be more surprised that she's roped in Daisy's eldest son to help.

I usually take pleasure in joining in with the children's activities. But Nick hasn't returned my calls, and my fears are spiralling into overdrive.

Nick is a diabetic. He manages his blood sugar levels by balancing his carbohydrate intake with the insulin he injects every day. He could use an automatic pump, but he won't. Nick prefers to be in control.

But sometimes he gets it wrong. Exercise, or stress, can give him a hypo. That's when his blood sugar goes too low. Suppose the strain of launching his new product has tipped him over the edge? He might have fallen unconscious.

Or suppose Tamara was telling the truth?

I don't know which is worse.

"Mum." Mary tugs at my sleeve. Sam's wide brown eyes stare up at me.

"Okay. Tom has a couple of school shirts with missing buttons, so you can take one each. Let's go upstairs and I'll find them."

"No." Mary wags a finger. She entered a bossy stage when her brother was born, only a phase according to the health visitor, but she has yet to grow out of it.

"We want to decorate your apron." Sam giggles. The little boy has a cheeky chuckle like his grandmother. He has Matilda's black curls and amber skin too. They've clearly skipped a generation, as you wouldn't notice that Daisy has mixed-race heritage.

Sam's laughter is infectious. Despite my woes, I smile. "Go right ahead. Why don't you watch TV for a minute, while I get my sewing box?"

It's in the studio, where I keep craft supplies as well as fabric samples and design books. Returning with it, I bump into the two younger children carrying an old ice-cream tub into the garden. I don't even remember buying a family-size container like that. Each holds an end as they bear it in front of them, like a church offering.

"What have you got there, Tom?"

"It's a secret from olden times." My son smirks. "Granny said I couldn't tell you."

"Granny? When—"

"It's treasure, and we're going to bury it," little Sebby announces. In contrast to his brother, he's the spitting image of Gordon: pale, with spiked-up sandy hair.

"Well, don't make a mess," I warn. "Daddy won't like it if you dig up the middle of the lawn. Put it next to the apple tree."

"Aye, aye, me hearty." Tom rolls his 'r'. "Guess what, Mummy? We're pirates!"

"Pieces of eight," Sebby adds.

Tom sticks his tongue out. "That's what a parrot says."

"I'm a pirate's parrot," Sebby replies. "Squawk."

I leave them to it, barely noticing them as they drop their haul and scoot back inside to find Tom's yellow beach spade. They can't do much damage to the lawn with the tiny plastic implement. I'll inspect their work to see if I should fix it before Nick comes back.

If he's coming back.

Watching the boys from the kitchen window, I try my husband's number again. As before, it goes to voicemail. This time, I leave a message. "Nick. Please, please, call me now."

I can't be too strident. That's asking for punishment. At best, he'll simply ignore me.

"Tamara says…" I pause, hearing feet scamper in the hall beyond the kitchen.

"Mum. Where are the buttons?" Mary, eyes twinkling, leads her wingman towards me.

Sam jumps up and down. "We're ready," he shouts.

"Never mind. Please ring me," I beg, finishing there. Placing the sewing box on the kitchen table, I turn to Mary. "You know where everything is, don't you? If you take buttons that are in a set, ask me first. And make sure to tidy up afterwards."

It's an old-fashioned wooden cantilever box, with three trays either side. Buttons are at the bottom, a mix of singles and groups carded together. The compartments above hold needles, thread, zips and other items. Mary has used it before, and I trust her not to muddle up the contents. I'll keep an eye on Sam, though.

Sam snatches my slate grey linen apron from the alcove where it hangs. "This one," he says, unnecessarily, as I don't possess another.

The garment matches the kitchen's colour scheme. As with the pirates, whatever this duo do, I can amend it later if it's a disaster. Obviously, an apron doesn't need buttons. I watch as Mary scoops up handfuls and arranges them on the table. Heads together, the pair inspect their haul and whisper to each other. Presumably, they've learned about pearly kings and are aiming for a similar decorative effect.

That reminds me of London… where Tamara lives.

Tiptoeing upstairs, I shut myself in the master bedroom. I fling myself in the comfortable rocking chair arranged just so in the corner. Then I ring Nick again.

Voicemail.

He's busy at work, of course. Isn't he? After all, he's told me often enough that he hates interruptions. And Tamara must be lying, or on hallucinogens. Maybe she stole his cocaine. Drugs have never appealed to me, but I've had to accept Nick takes them. In the early days of our marriage, he explained it was normal for the City of London. Charlie, uppers, downers, whatever the latest big thing was — in the heady world of high finance, popping pills and powders eased Nick through his long days. He had no intention of stopping, of kissing goodbye to success, just because I disapproved.

I leave a longer message, my voice breaking into sobs. "Please… call me, Nick. Tamara said some very strange things… about being pregnant with your baby. We need to talk. Please, as soon as you can…"

I'm sniffing so much that it's impossible to say more. Anyway, I shouldn't leave the children alone any longer. Ending the call, I wipe a tissue over my face, and return to the kitchen.

I think enviously of Daisy, floating on a cloud of white wine. As I whip up a three-bean chilli to eat with the kids, I decide to stick a bottle in the fridge. Nick buys Chablis by the case from a local wine merchant. It will slip down nicely, and I'm not driving anywhere else today.

I've just taken my first sip when Mary tugs at my sleeve.

"Look, Mum." She points to their handiwork, her smile slipping. "Oops, we used two sets. Sorry."

"It's okay, sweetheart."

But it isn't. When I see what they've done, tears rise. I splutter into my wineglass.

“Oops,” I sniff. “Mummy has a nasty cough.”

The apron is laid out on the table. A heart is outlined in red buttons, the words ‘mum’ and ‘dad’ picked out inside it in black.

Is it a fantasy that’s about to fall apart?

# CHAPTER 10 NICK

## Day 1 - Monday

Nick can scarcely believe it. You think you know someone. You haven't just explored each delicious, intimate corner of their body, but you've spent time understanding their mind. In Tamara's case, the latter didn't take long. She's wired to be a worker ant: insignificant, efficient, existing to serve.

At least, he thought so. But it transpires Tamara has even fewer brain cells than that.

He puts down his phone, replaying Gail's voicemail in his mind. The message was clear enough. So was his last instruction to Tamara, the instruction she's chosen to defy. She will pay for that.

He gazes out of his window at the old oak tree, a rare specimen in the City, thus justifying a higher rent than the other side of the building. There's a payment due next week. He doesn't have the funds.

If only he hadn't followed his father into the family business.

It's too late now. The old man's jibes echo within his head. 'Not a great start, is it? I was crazy to listen to your mother. Still, who else would give you a job?'

Bile fills Nick's throat. He takes a deep breath, summons Tamara on the landline. "Can you come on through, please?"

Civility stops the moment she struts through the door. He's sure now, watching that triumphant smile play on her lips. He's going to wipe it off, and enjoy doing it. Oh yes. He may not know Tamara as well as he thought, but she doesn't know him at all. You don't call Nick Masterson's bluff and survive unscathed.

He starts harmlessly enough. "I believe you've made a mistake, Tamara."

"I don't think so."

Is she playing the innocent, or toughing it out? He doesn't care. Rage bubbles inside him. Nick feels his cheeks flame, but his voice is icy. "You told my wife about us."

Tamara shrugs. "So? She'd find out some day."

"If I chose to let her know. You have no right to worry her. And there's no way I'm leaving Gail, so how dare you make her think so."

"She might be leaving you. Have you considered that?" Tamara's defiant tone and bold gaze suggest an inflated ego.

Nick doesn't just want to prick it, but shred it into little pieces.

"Gail will walk out over my dead body," he says. He pictures Tamara as a corpse instead, a pleasing image. But she's standing before him, hands on hips, very much alive and well. Pregnant. No way has she had an abortion.

Nick is breathing heavily now. She's breaking through his cool exterior, and that's not good. He has to finish this quickly.

"Give me the keys to your flat," he demands.

"But you've got—"

He sees realisation dawn on her face. Tamara was about to say he already has a key. Her studio flat — for which his company pays a handsome rent, now overdue — is three floors down from his penthouse. He's a frequent visitor. When he's in London, it's a rare night that he doesn't pop in.

He moves out from behind his desk, advances towards her. "You're sacked, Tamara. I want you out of my life for good. Out of that flat. Give me your keys."

She flinches. It's almost comical, the fear in her eyes.

"No," she whimpers. "We can make it work. Please Nick, give me a second chance."

"There wasn't even a first chance."

Adrenaline pumps him up. He's right in front of her, but he holds back. Tenderly, he runs a finger around her fine features.

That gentleness, the calm before the storm, fools her. Tamara stupidly interprets it as softness. Weakness. She pouts. "You wouldn't throw me out of my home."

"Oh, I would." What must he do to convince her? What would his father do? Nick instinctively knows. He makes a fist. Swings it backwards. Smashes it forward, hard.

The blow to her abdomen sends her flying. She's skin and bone, plus the collection of cells requiring a helping hand out of this world. He hopes he's delivered that.

Tamara staggers to her feet, clutching her stomach.

"Keys in your handbag?" He stalks past her, gratified to note the green tinge on her porcelain skin. She's still winded from his walloping, unable to utter more than a moan.

He reaches her anteroom in a few strides. It's tidy, almost devoid of personal possessions. Within seconds, he's found and upended Tamara's Chanel tote bag. The butter-soft cream number cost him five thousand euros. She's blown it, the silly girl. Even if she books the clinic this afternoon, if she literally licks his boots, he won't take her back. He doesn't need the aggro. Nor does he want her speaking to his wife ever again.

He easily locates the keys, one for the apartment block, another for the flat itself, and a lanyard for office access. Placing them in his pocket, he calls through to the front desk.

He summons security staff, returning to his office to see Tamara lurch unsteadily towards his keyboard.

"Don't even think about it," he sneers, a thrill running through him as she shrinks back. He settles in his office chair, legs stretched out, handmade shoes on the desk in front of him.

"I'll tell the police," she threatens, pointing to her belly.

He yawns. "Your word against mine, babe."

Tamara's shoulders slump, her face and body seeming to collapse in on themselves. A tear catches in her eye.

Nick smiles. Finally, she realises who's boss. He'll have no more trouble from her.

# CHAPTER 11 GAIL

## Day 1 - Monday

Mary and Tom are tucked up in bed. They've had no bath tonight, because Gordon waited until nearly eight before collecting his boys. He claimed Daisy hadn't told him she'd be out; a likely story. I bet he forgot and worked late.

By then, I'd fed everyone with three bean chilli — only a small bowl for me, as I'd downed two glasses of wine. It helped me cope with the kids' homework, thirty minutes of hell on the promise of a tub of Ben & Jerry's. The two eldest had maths, not my strong point. For once, I found myself longing to give my children the freedom I enjoyed at their age. Where did that land me, though? I struggled just to get onto a fabric design course. They'll have to suffer the rigid structures of their schooling to glide into Oxbridge like their dad.

Why hasn't Nick been in touch?

Flushing, I pour another glass of Chablis. Forget the calories. I need this. I drain it in one gulp before scrolling through my phone's texts, WhatsApp messages and emails.

There's nothing from him. An email catches my eye, though, with its header: 'Help, Gail. My wife is dying.'

It must be spam. But my breath catches, because whoever it is, they know my name. This email hasn't hurtled through cyberspace to hundreds of thousands of addresses; it's been created specially for me. And who can ignore a plea to support a dying woman? I tap to open it.

'Dear Gail,' the missive reads. 'My wife has a terminal cancer diagnosis. We've exhausted our treatment options, and now all we can do is make her as comfortable as possible. Our new flat is soulless, and I know you are the woman who can turn it from a house to a home for the last few weeks of her life.'

Expecting a request for funding, or at least free services, I'm surprised by the postscript. 'PS time is of the essence. Money no object.'

It's signed 'J Smyth', and comes from a generic Gmail account: 'jsmyth' followed by a string of numbers. There's no clue as to who he, or possibly she, is. I can't assume they're a straight couple; they might be lesbians.

I don't recognise the name, but J Smyth has clearly heard of me. Unlike my best friend, this client isn't quibbling about cash. And if Nick leaves me, I'll need every penny I can lay my hands on.

# CHAPTER 12 JONATHAN

## Day 2 - Tuesday

Tilly believes houses have vibes. Not ghosts, but an imprint of the souls who have lived there. It's why she insisted on moving from Coombe Dingle, where she and Martin raised their family on the edge of woodland. Echoes of Martin's life remained in the property, a detached pile surrounded by nearly an acre of land. He'd loved gardening, apparently.

Tilly doesn't. She could have paid for hired help, Jonathan supposes, but she preferred to make a fresh start with him. When her children shunned her and denied access to the grandkids, she found a silver lining in the cloud. They didn't need dead space infused with memories, she told Jonathan, so she sold up and moved.

Their new harbourside apartment in Bristol city centre couldn't be more different from the suburbs. He wouldn't have considered living there. Tilly fell for the view, though. She talked him round.

Jonathan concedes there aren't many downsides. They have to keep headphones to drown the noise of drunken revellers, and a water pistol to defend the balcony from gulls. But they love hanging out together in the bars, art galleries and avant garde cinemas nearby.

Except Tilly can't. Not anymore. She shivers endlessly, precious energy ebbing despite his efforts to conserve it. He carries her from room to room, takes her out in a wheelchair. The gym habit he developed as a student has served him well, building his muscles and stamina. It's a long time since he was the weedy kid who couldn't fight back.

He's never told Tilly what Mike Gill did to him, or that it prompted him to seek her out. Those memories bring too much shame. He hates them even more than thoughts about his future, and the icy void that she'll leave behind.

Until then, he wants their flat to bring her comfort. Everything she sees must be pleasing to her eye. Sometimes he admits to himself that he has a secondary motive. When she's gone, he'll be reminded of her. Each room will be a shrine to Tilly, her flame keeping him warm and bright.

Still, he thought long and hard about contacting the Honourable Gail Masterson. As a centre for the creative industries, Bristol must be awash with interior designers. Surely another professional could divine Tilly's style? But that would take time he doesn't have. Gail knows Tilly's tastes and, according to Stan, likes her. He's encouraged that she agreed to an off-site meeting. It avoids disruption to Tilly's routine; an initial consultation at their flat would be too much for her. No, he will show Gail a short video of the apartment. Afterwards, she can visit briefly to fine-tune the details.

As he drives to his appointment with Gail, he reflects on Tilly's belief that properties take on the personality of their residents. If she's right, Nick Masterson's lair ought to be a house of horrors. Jonathan won't be going inside, though. There is a garden studio where Gail does her work.

When he arrives, Jonathan notices nothing exceptional about the detached Victorian villa. It's similar to the others in this peaceful road in Clifton. They're three storey cubes built from sandstone: not the elegant, creamy type seen in Bath, but locally hewn lumps of autumn-coloured rock. Each has a lawn out front, this one edged with lavender to protect it from the gravel drive. An oak in the corner, bright with new growth, casts a semi-circle of shade onto the pavement.

Twin Teslas, a roadster and an SUV, stand behind a glossy black gate. They alone hint at the owner's identity. It figures that Nick, psychopath extraordinaire, would covet a car made by Elon Musk. And have two of them.

Jonathan is expected at 10am. The studio must be around the back. He spies a wrought-iron gate spanning the gap between the house and a stone boundary wall. Beyond, a flagged alleyway leads to greenery.

The gate is locked. Jonathan checks the house number. Reassured it's correct, he climbs steps to the front door and presses the ceramic bell.

This is the point of no return. Jonathan's shoulders tense. Either Nick will answer — what fun that will be, after their recent conversation — or Gail, who slapped him when they last met. If he'd planned this better, he'd have grown a moustache and had his hair cut. But he didn't. He'd better hope she's forgotten or forgiven him.

There is no evidence of a camera in the porch. Gail's surprise is evident when she opens the door. Without hesitation, she slams it in his face. Well, she recognised him all right.

"Wait," Jonathan calls. "I'm sorry for any misunderstanding…"

There is silence. He is acutely aware of a thrush singing, a lawn mower nearby and the distant hum of traffic.

"…I really want to work with you," he yells.

Still nothing.

He shouts louder. "I'll pay whatever it takes."

The door remains closed. He presses an ear to it and hears no sound.

Jonathan's body sags. He slumps against the door, unable to believe he can't even do this one small thing for his wife. When he added the postscript to his email, he meant every word. For once in his life, he has money. He would spend it all to bring Tilly happiness. But he can't.

He scans the deserted street, two parallel lines of luxury houses. This isn't the kind of district where they sign on at the Jobcentre or labour in a factory. The inhabitants will be toiling away at desks. Despite the roadster on the drive, there's no sign of Nick, who is doubtless larging it in the City of London. That is Nick's turf, where he does deals and feels important. Other residents will be at home, though. The keyboard warriors, pensioners and yummy mummies, all quietly going about their business.

He'll give them something to listen to.

Jonathan begins swearing at the top of his voice.

A rattling sound tells him that a chain is being pulled across the door. It opens a crack. He glimpses a brown eye fringed with dark lashes.

"Go away, or I'll call the police," Gail hisses.

"Good luck with that," Jonathan says. He was right about Nick being away. "Why not discuss my design brief instead?"

"Because I'm not interested."

"What would it take to make you interested?"

"Stop pestering me. I don't know how you got my email—"

"Publicly available information," he says, "but actually, I have it because my company was a client of yours."

She sucks in air. "You're lying," she says, her tone dripping acid. "I've never done a commission for you, and I never will."

"You had a chunky assignment at—"

He wishes to explain that he and Tilly run Gill Spices together now, that Tilly doesn't have long left. He plans to plead.

Gail doesn't give him the chance.

"Go away," she repeats. Again, she closes the door with some force.

"She's dying!" Jonathan screams.

Once more, he shouts curses. Gail might well call the police, but it's a risk he's prepared to take. It's unlikely they'll come out. He isn't stealing her property or threatening violence. Disorderly conduct is the worst offence they could pin on him, and in Bristol, they have plenty more serious crimes to worry about.

After a minute or two, a grey-bearded man emerges from the house next door.

"Is there a problem?" he asks, his patrician voice reminiscent of a housemaster at Markham's.

"No, just a lover's tiff," Jonathan shouts, knowing Gail will hear.

The man blanches, and coughs. "I see. Well, I'm going to have to ask you to keep the noise down…"

The door opens fully this time. Gail steps outside. Despite her wild eyes and flushed skin, she remains heart-stoppingly beautiful. Nick Masterson doesn't deserve her.

"How dare you," she flames. Her harsh tone softens as she turns to her neighbour. "Peregrine, this man is lying."

Peregrine winces. He stares at his polished shoes, which have suddenly become objects of fascination. "It's none of my business," he mumbles. "I wanted to check you were all right, that's all."

"Can you call the police for me?" Gail demands.

"Er, is that wise?"

"You know how to stop this. We agreed on ten o'clock." Jonathan speaks at a more normal level. He matches Peregrine's public school accent, ignoring the temptation to say 'darling'. That would really give Peregrine pause for thought. Besides, he senses that Gail's certainty is wobbling. She's taken a step back and is fiddling with her hair.

"Give me thirty minutes," Gail says, tucking a lock behind her ear. "I'll meet you at the Avon Gorge Hotel." She glances at Peregrine, and adds, no doubt for his benefit, "They do great coffee."

"Very good," Jonathan says. "I'll see you there."

# CHAPTER 13 GAIL

## Day 2 - Tuesday

Talk about being placed in an impossible position. If I'd known 'J Smyth' was Nick's boorish schoolfriend, Jonno, I'd have blocked his email. Now I've been railroaded into a meeting. And Peregrine Jukes has not only been told that Jonno is my lover, but has heard me suggest an upscale hotel.

I must meet Jonno in a public space, though, and I need buckets of caffeine. Last night, I dozed fitfully, chewing over the message I finally received from Nick at midnight: 'Tamara full of s**t. I love you, darling. Explain later. xoxo'.

It left too many questions unanswered. I'm sure the resulting lack of sleep didn't help me to handle Jonno, not that he behaved well himself.

If he forgets his manners again, I plan a quick getaway, for which the Avon Gorge is perfect. Other Clifton coffee shops are cramped, but the hotel boasts a spacious terrace and café bar. Half of Bristol piles in during the annual balloon festival. I make a mental note to explain to Peregrine later.

As I park the Tesla Model X by the hotel, I yawn, wishing I'd just gone back to bed. However, if I don't show, Jonno will come back and cause a fuss again. Sure, it's stalking and harassment, but I doubt the police will care unless it escalates. Then rumours will fly, Nick will get to hear about it, and life will become seriously unpleasant.

I have no choice.

Having arrived early, I scope out the joint, a vast space with a faux-industrial look. Along one wall, a bar serves coffee. Stronger drinks are on offer, but I don't see anyone indulging at this hour. Daisy probably would; luckily, she's not here, and nor is anyone else I recognise.

Customers sit at wooden tables and benches, intense young men with curled moustaches and preppy clothes huddling over laptops in one corner, while ladies of a certain age have bagged another. I pick a table near the bar, sitting at one end of a bench. If necessary, I can call the bartender for help, or run out of the nearby door.

Ordering a black Americano, I power up my MacBook. I've also brought a few style magazines, which I flick through before spreading them out on the table.

Jonno's email claims his wife is dying. Surely he wouldn't lie about that? I set aside my contempt for the man, visualising her needs instead. She may require specialised furniture. I connect to Wi-Fi and bookmark a few websites selling hospital beds, mobility aids and the like. Then, leaving the magazine pages open to display relevant images, I search for more.

The task is so engrossing that I don't notice Jonno has perched himself next to me.

"Boo."

"Do you mind not sitting so close?" I edge away.

Jonno ignores my comment. He sips his drink and studies the pictures arrayed on the table.

"I thought we should start by discussing your wife's requirements," I say. "Can you tell me a bit about her illness, and any practical implications following on from it?"

Jonno swivels round, fixing me with a hard stare. "My wife has pancreatic cancer."

It sounds like bad news. Nick has diabetes because his pancreas is defective, but at least it's not killing him.

"I'm sorry to hear that," I say.

Jonno glowers. "Not as sorry as we were."

He's obviously not the easiest client. Again, I remind myself that this design brief is for a dying woman's benefit. And I need the money. After highlighting his lack of charm, Jonno is on the hook for triple my usual rate, and then some.

The glare vanishes from his brown eyes. "It's a disease that can strike randomly, and of course, we weren't expecting it. Tilly doesn't have any of the risk factors. She first experienced fatigue a couple of months ago, and we supposed it was a midlife issue."

"Midlife?" I wonder if I've misheard him.

"Yes. I believe it can be a peri-menopausal symptom." Jonno pauses. "My wife is older than me."

Politeness stops me asking how much older. Perhaps it's just a few years, and she's been cursed with an early menopause.

"Anyway, you asked about practicalities. The cancer has metastasised to Tilly's lungs and liver. A growth is pressing on her spine. She not only has to live with the knowledge that she won't be with us for long, but she's in agony. Morphine can only do so much. She's trying to stay on a low dose rather than fly away with the fairies."

"How mobile is she?"

"She can stagger a few steps in our flat. The décor bores her to tears, but in other respects, the place is perfect. All on one level, for example, and spacious. There's a wheelchair. We have nurses with her during the day, and they'll take her out when the weather is fine. She sits on our balcony too, watching the boats go by. Did I mention that we live on the Harbourside?"

"No. I'm sure the view will do her good. The soothing effect of water."

"Not when the booze cruises go past, or the seagulls screech." He shudders. "Features of harbour life they omit from estate agent's brochures. Anyway, the flat is new, or new to us. Magnolia walls, grey carpet. Did I see you flinch?"

"It's a common neutral scheme," I say, feeling I should tread carefully. He hasn't disclosed what he thinks of it personally. "Forgive me for asking, but hasn't your wife got enough on her plate? Painting, laying carpet, moving furniture — it's an upheaval. As she's there all the time, it would be happening around her."

Jonno purses his lips. "Don't think we haven't discussed that. She's adamant."

It crosses my mind that, whatever he says, she might already be spaced out on morphine. "Are you sure?" I press. "Wouldn't she be better off focusing on family and friends?"

Jonno freezes. "No. Absolutely not."

For a moment, we stare at each other. He clearly hates being contradicted. Eventually, he adds, "I've got a business to run. In fact, when we're done, I'll be dashing back for a meeting. Do you think I'd be looking at pretty pictures if it wasn't important to my wife? When we moved in three months ago, we decided to take our time in fitting out the flat. But now, time is not on our side."

"So," I ask, as there's no deflecting him, "you'd want it redecorated quickly?"

Jonno snaps his fingers. "Starting today. Up for the challenge?"

"Nothing I'd like more," I lie. "I'll visit this afternoon, then tomorrow, the trades—"

Jonno interrupts. "Make sure to keep it short when you come round. I'll show you a video of the apartment now. We've got half an hour. I'll email it to you as well. That should really be enough for you, shouldn't it? I was told you were good."

"You heard right," I say, with confidence I don't feel. On the plus side, it seems my contact with Jonno will be strictly limited. I give silent thanks to the universe for that.

"Great. Did you say the tradesmen can start tomorrow?"

"Provided you pay premium rates. And it will be a woman."

The likes of Daisy, beating suppliers down on price, always go to the back of the queue. For the right money, my favourite female decorator will juggle her workload. She'll tiptoe sensitively around Tilly. Not that she's a doormat. If Jonno tries any nonsense with her, she'll slap his face harder than I did.

Feeling more positive, I straighten up and stretch. "Can I see the video?"

He takes out his phone. "Here. I shot it earlier, while Tilly was still asleep, so there's no footage of the master bedroom. But it's as sterile as the rest. Take my word."

He's not wrong. The two-minute clip reveals luxury, but no soul.

"Let's discuss practicalities. I don't recommend changing furniture and carpets, although it's up to you. We can still transform the look of your flat with rugs, curtains, art and a splash of paint. Uplifting colours, feel-good textures. How does that sound?"

Jonno nods. "Can we get on with it?"

"Sure thing. I generally kick off by discovering the ambiance you're seeking — that feeling when you walk into a room."

Jonno holds up his hands. "Let's be clear. I'm expecting you to do all that fluffy stuff. I don't care what a home looks like, so long as it's dry and there's food in the fridge."

"You're not the first man to say that," I tell him, "but beer usually wins over food. If you did have a style, what would you say it was?"

Surprisingly, he answers without hesitation. "I'd be guided by the colours of clouds, sky and water. Ripples and random shapes, bringing the outside in. Nature and adventure. But ignore me. This is for Tilly."

He inspects the magazines for what seems like hours. It's probably only five minutes, during which I fidget, feet busy as if they yearn to run away. Jonno still makes me uneasy.

Finally, his finger points to a collage of pink, red and gold. Feature rugs offset jewel-bright Chesterfields. On a burgundy wall, baroque picture frames showcase blowsy roses. "I think you've really got her there," he says.

"Which elements say 'Tilly' to you?"

"All of them," he announces. "But of course, you'd know that, having worked for her before."

"Are you sure? I'm afraid the name doesn't ring a bell."

Dismayed, I blink at him, convinced he's contacted me by mistake.

I wouldn't have forgotten. It's not as if I'm overwhelmed with clients. But now it seems the dreadful scene outside my home, this awkward meeting, and my research have been a waste of time.

Alternatively, he's carrying out an elaborate charade to get me into bed. Well, that's not happening.

"Gill Spices?" Jonno prompts. "You must remember."

"Yes." As bile rises to my throat, I remember too well. Matilda Gill. Daisy's mum, the elegant CEO, bravely taking charge of the company after her husband died in an air crash. She was graceful, witty, fun: a dream to work with. And lonely. Easy meat for a predatory slimeball like Jonno.

This excuse for a man made a pass at me, seduced my friend and prised her mother away from a loving family. I can't bear to breathe the same air as him.

Jonno raises an eyebrow. "Are you all right? You've turned green."

I shake my head, mouth closed. Leaving MacBook, case and magazines behind, I run to the ladies' toilet.

Luckily, no-one else is in the powder room, and my breakfast was light: a small serving of strawberries. I've relieved myself of it within seconds of entering the cubicle. Dabbing at my face with a tissue, I consider running past Jonno and out of the door. But all my things are on the table beside him. I'll have to face the music instead. Tell him I've changed my mind.

Despite digging deep for a plausible explanation, I can't find one. Too bad. If he probes, I'll reveal exactly what I think of him.

Muscles clenched, I approach the table.

"I'm sorry, Jonno—" I begin.

Jonno waves a hand. "Don't worry. These things happen. And call me Jonathan, please. I left 'Jonno' behind at school."

"Well, Jonathan—"

"That's better." He beams at me. "You appear over that bug already. You know, I can't thank you enough for this. I just phoned Tilly, and she is beyond excited. It made her day."

My stomach lurches. I gawp at him.

"You can call it wishful thinking," Jonno says, "but your makeover might even prolong her life."

How can I refuse to do it? Rather than the loathsome Jonathan, it's Matilda who would get hurt. And she's already suffering enough.

I sigh. "Okay. Let's get moving."

# CHAPTER 14 TAMARA

## Day 3 - Wednesday

Tamara doesn't do friends. But acquaintances like Ruby are useful. While a couch in a Streatham shared house is a far cry from a waterside studio, it's only twenty pounds a night. And Tamara won't be there long, anyway.

"It's just until I get my own place," she told Ruby last night. "In the morning, I'll see the agency about another job."

They've both temped for the same agency in the past, sharing after-work drinks and stories of nightmare placements. Perhaps alcohol loosened Tamara's tongue too much. Yesterday evening, Ruby dropped her in it. As they twirled forkfuls of vegan pasta cooked by one of the housemates, Ruby sighed. She announced to an attentive dinner table that it wasn't the first time, and shouldn't Tamara stop chasing married men?

After her side order of humiliation, the chef had collared Tamara in the hall. He could get her a job at his workplace, he whispered. The eco-home developer was only down the road.

Tamara found him creepy. He stared too long at her chest, not an uncommon event, but she's choosier with men than Ruby thinks. Streatham is a dump too. She made polite but discouraging noises. But she reconsidered when she Googled the firm. The guy in charge looks seriously hot. It's an option if she can't find a better gig.

It's 10am now, and she's wallowing in a hot bath. Ruby gave strict instructions about the water being metered and only five minutes in the shower. However, with all the housemates out at work, what they don't know won't hurt them. And Tamara has had a busy morning already. At 4am, she was off to the City on the night bus, streets mercifully free of traffic. Nick took away her pass, but the night security man needed no persuading to let her into the office. She'd hazarded that nobody would tell him she'd been fired. The gamble paid off. He believed her tale of finishing a presentation before Nick arrived.

"Magic roundabout, huh?" he said. "Out late, in early." He'd always been a sympathetic sort, a fellow wage slave in the machine.

Tamara yawns. If she wasn't a woman on a mission, she'd have gone back to bed when she returned to Streatham. Instead, she must refresh herself for the task ahead. Choosing the most luxurious soap from the selection in Ruby's bathroom, she lathers up, enjoying the lavender scent. She sluices herself down. Dried with the softest towel on offer, she dons yesterday's clothes. They're all she has. Then she types the house Wi-Fi code into her laptop. She allows herself a chuckle because Nick won't notice the machine is missing. Even if he does, he's unlikely to suspect her. Having ensured she took nothing from the office when he threw her out, he won't expect her to have it now.

Google is her friend again, producing email addresses for the City of London Police and the Financial Conduct Authority. Tamara sends them documents. A lot of documents. She applies perfume and makeup, and walks to the bus stop.

Traffic is considerably heavier during the day, although the passengers on the Number 133 are less scary. The red bus creaks and groans its way to the Square Mile. Tamara parts company with it at the Monument. She teeters up Bishopsgate in her stilettos. These are taxi shoes, but she must be careful with money until she can retrieve the contents of her flat. She hopes the police will help. Quite apart from samples of Nick's DNA, there are valuables she will sell: gifts from Nick of jewellery and designer clothes. She'll be damned if she lets him throw them out or pass them on to his next lover. Placing a protective hand on her belly, she smirks. If she has her way, there won't be another lover.

Opposite Liverpool Street, the presence of a blue and yellow chequered car signals Bishopsgate police station. Sandwiched between fast food joints, it's a squat white cube with a forbidding granite entrance. Tamara intends to march in but, feet throbbing, it's more of a stumble. The lobby smells of disinfectant and polish. She wishes she'd used more perfume.

Tamara has never visited a police station before. She suspects others aren't as imposing, and their staff don't dress in a shirt and tie like low grade clerical workers. To her annoyance, a woman is already engaging with the sole policeman at the front desk. This is a polished granite and wood counter, with the City's coat of arms prominent on the wall behind. The shield bears a cross of St George to which a red sword has been added; Tamara isn't sure why. The Latin inscription, DOMINE DIRIGE NOS, strikes her as a waste of space. She didn't have the chance to learn Latin at school, and she can't see why anyone would bother. The ancient Romans have been dead for hundreds of years. Latin exists purely so rich men like Nick can show off.

The woman turns to leave, and Tamara steps forward to speak to the desk sergeant. She treats him to a dazzling smile.

"I'm reporting a crime," she says. "My boyfriend has stolen all of my belongings. Also, I emailed earlier, and I've brought a laptop as evidence. He runs an investment fund, but the returns he promises aren't real. He has to take in more and more money from new investors to pay the old ones. I think it's a fraud."

She knows it is for sure, but it doesn't pay to seem too clever.

The officer's face brightens. He's clearly interested. "Sounds like a Ponzi scheme. Thanks for coming in. Let me see who's dealing with it..."

# CHAPTER 15 GAIL

## Day 3 - Wednesday

I yawn, despite my concentration on my work. After another wakeful night, I took the kids to school on autopilot. Now I'm pulling together a list of soft furnishings for Jonathan, an easy task because we already agreed on the colour scheme. Annie, my decorator, will visit his flat this afternoon to measure up for paint. Jonathan made an advance payment yesterday.

That's the good news. I've heard nothing more from Nick, despite leaving messages. He didn't answer his phone. I couldn't sleep, constantly checking my mobile to see if he'd been in touch.

It's not unusual for him to forget about me when he's wrapped up in work, and of course, he's been stressed out recently. That may be why he hasn't transferred funds into our bank account either. The balance remains in the red, in spite of a welcome boost from Jonathan's deposit.

My stomach twitches with anxiety. What if Tamara's right, and he's planning to dump me? The warning signs are there.

I really need someone to talk to.

Daisy is the obvious choice. But can I trust her? She likes a drink, and she fancies Nick. And Nick's friend, Mike, is her younger brother. He's a lawyer, the first person Nick would consult if he wanted a divorce. Yet Daisy was frank about her relationship issues yesterday. She expects me to keep her secrets. Surely she'd be discreet too?

Sick with anxiety, I hover on the brink of indecision before tapping her number.

"Hey, Gail. What's up? Got a design report for me already?"

"Still working on it. It's quite complex."

In truth, Jonathan's project is ahead in the queue. As Nick would say, though, you never hint that another client is more important.

Daisy laughs. "Tell me about it."

"Look, I need advice on something. It's a bit personal." I try to keep my tone bright. She has her own problems; she doesn't need me falling to pieces in front of her.

"Ooh, intriguing. Come round for lunch, and we'll have a proper natter. Twelve?"

"That would be lovely, and I'll bring nibbles. See you then."

I check the time. If I leave now, I can walk, which will lift my mood and burn off a few calories. Jonathan's project can wait a couple of hours. He can't change their soft furnishings until Annie's painted at least one room.

Slinging celery, low-fat hummus and a bottle of kombucha into a bag, I set off. The day is cold, but clear and bright. Blackbirds warble in the newly greened trees. Beech, oak and horse chestnuts line my route.

It's only as I turn into her road that I decide healthy tea is a step too far for Daisy. She would undoubtedly prefer something stronger. Luckily, there's a small shop on the corner, one of those convenience stores that sell everything from shirt buttons to balloons to frozen chocolate cake. A flashing rainbow-coloured LED display announces 'DRINKS'.

Daisy drank Soave on Monday. Scanning the booze displayed at eye level on the wall behind the counter, I fail to see any. I'm not sure what to choose instead. Nick is the wine expert in our household. Then I spy a pretty, pressed-glass bottle of prosecco, which would at least fit with Daisy's aesthetic. I ask the sullen youth at the till to fetch it down and wrap it.

A bell signals that another customer has entered. A familiar voice says, "Thank the Lord I spotted you."

I spin round.

Is Jonathan stalking me? A chill sweeps through me, and I edge backwards until I'm nudging the counter. Only then do I notice that he looks terrible. If I thought my eyes needed propping open with matchsticks, that's nothing by comparison with his. They're bloodshot and puffy. His skin is grey.

"She's dead." Jonathan's voice is a hoarse whisper. "My wife died this morning."

"How terribly sad. You must be devastated." I look away, ashamed that I imagined he was following me. Of course he wanted to pass on the news.

He winces. It doesn't hide the tic niggling at a corner of his mouth. "We expected it… Still, I hoped she had longer. Wishful thinking."

"I'll cancel the decorator. You needn't worry about that."

"Thanks. Yes, stop all work. And I don't want the deposit back."

He appears about to say more, but the youth interrupts by asking me to pay. I turn back and wave my credit card at the machine. My palms sweat when, in a disturbing moment of déjà vu, the card is rejected.

"Here, let me." Jonathan steps forward and waves his own plastic at the contactless machine.

"No, don't." I place a hand on his arm. "I'd better not buy it after all. It was going to be a present for… for a friend. In the circumstances, I don't think she'll want it."

"Should I cancel the transaction?" The youth's tone is truculent.

I nod. No doubt Daisy will wish to drown her sorrows, but celebratory fizz won't be top of her list. Far better to leave her to select a bottle from her fridge.

"You're not on your way to see Daisy, by any chance?" Jonathan asks, a spark flickering briefly in his dull eyes.

"I can't say."

"Yes, then. Look, could I come too? It's just, well, I need to tell her. The number in Tilly's phone doesn't work. And Daisy lives on this road, doesn't she? I mean, that's what Tilly had heard, and here you are. I was going to ask in the shop if they knew which house…"

It seems my friend moved without giving her mother a forwarding address.

"…but would you mind?"

The shop's warm air stills and wraps itself around me. I choke, suffocating on the aroma of spices and disinfectant.

Once again, he's put me in a difficult position. I hate to refuse when he's just lost his wife, but Daisy won't thank me for bringing him along. There's nothing to stop Jonathan following me when I leave the shop, though. Even if I could rustle up a cloak and dagger stunt to throw him off the scent — walking to the park and doubling back? — he could get the address from the youth on the till.

Maybe not, though. When I risk a glance at the teenager, he's flicking through a lad's mag and ignoring the conversation.

"Jonathan, how about if I tell Daisy?"

His lips almost make it into a smile. "Would you do that?"

"You have my word."

Nick uses the phrase a lot. Who knows if he means it? But I do.

"Can you give her my contact details? There will be a funeral, and much else besides. I'd like her input."

"Okay." Poor Daisy. She'll naturally want to attend her mother's funeral, and so will Gordon and the kids. How awful for her, to have the stress of Jonathan's company as well as her grief.

She could use moral support. I'll ask her if she'd like me to come too.

"You will be kind to her, won't you? To Daisy," I add.

Jonathan rewards me with a searching glance. "You have my word," he echoes, scarcely quelling my fears.

Following him out of the premises, I wait until I can be sure he's out of sight. Without saying more, he gets into a car parked on double yellows, and drives off. He owns a Porsche with a personalised plate. Of course he does.

I shiver.

The tension within me releases itself and then builds again. I'm about to break bad news to my best friend. And explain that I've been dealing with the devil.

# CHAPTER 16 JONATHAN

## Day 3 - Wednesday

Jonathan's world is devoid of joy and colour.

He thought the tsunami of grief would hit him right away. Not so. From the moment he was woken by the night nurse, he has felt himself in a dream. He watched as this other Jonathan kissed Tilly's lifeless lips, hoped in vain that breath would bloom in them again. Thanked the doctor. Called the funeral directors his wife had chosen. Held her cold hand one last time until she was taken away.

The doppelgänger stood up. Stretched. Sighed. Walked to the registry office on Corn Street, past the sailing boats, rushing commuters, Big Issue sellers, all full of life they don't even value. Phoned his PA. Left a message for Mike Gill, whose work number is easy to find, even if he's too important to answer it himself. Asked Gail to tell Daisy. Rang Tilly's best friends and accepted condolences.

Now, Jonathan stares out of the picture window where his wife watched boats go by. Seagulls squawk, rowers shout, engines hum.

He doesn't see them. He cannot hear them. His body is an empty husk.

Unable to form a coherent thought, drained of energy, he slumps to the floor. He lies in a foetal position on the carpet, hugging his knees. His keening has no impact on his oblivious ears.

A whisper nags him from his subconscious: that she was always going to die first. It's the bargain you make with fate when you marry someone much older. But still… not now. Not yet.

Jonathan's gaze lights on the medication packets stacked neatly on a shelf. The nurse hasn't taken away Tilly's morphine tablets. Nor has the doctor. It is not their job. He could swallow a few and follow his wife. They will be together for good.

Except he doesn't believe in God and an afterlife, whatever they said in school assembly. Suppose all that comes after death is nothingness, a void stretching into the future forever?

But that's exactly how his life feels now.

Ending it has attractions.

Slowly, his limbs leaden, he stretches out a hand.

But he can't reach. Jonathan drags himself up onto his knees before collapsing to the ground again. He quivers and moans. Coaxes unwilling muscles to lift his torso from the floor. Crouches, staring at the boxes. So much power lies inside those small cubes of cardboard. They are the fulcrum between life and death.

While yet undecided, he can't ignore their lure. He crawls towards them.

His phone rings with the opening chords of 'Another Day To Die'.

At first, he doesn't notice. After a few seconds, maybe longer, the noise needles into his skull. It annoys him. That is its purpose. He deliberately downloaded an irritating ringtone because he couldn't disregard it.

Snarling, he stands up and grabs the phone. The caller is a Bristol number he doesn't recognise. What the heck. It might be the celebrant from the funeral directors. Jonathan jolts back to life as if from an electric shock. He owes it to Tilly to honour her with the dignified ceremony they planned together. What a pathetic fool he's been, putting himself first.

He shrugs off his self-pity like an unwanted coat, swiping the phone. "It's Jonathan."

"I know." A woman's voice hisses with spite and anger.

"Who is this?"

"Who do you think? It's Daisy."

"Daisy. I'm so sorry—"

"Cut the crap, Jonathan. Listen up. If you think you'll run off with my mama's money and my father's business, you're wrong. My brother's a lawyer, remember? The best there is. And he and I will sue your sorry arse."

# CHAPTER 17 GAIL

## Day 4 - Thursday

Just for once, I've managed to sleep. I'm well under, waking bleary-eyed when the doorbell rings long and loud.

By the time my brain realises what the noise was, the world is silent again. I take a moment to listen, then try to drift off. But the thud of heavy blows on wood jolts my eyes open. I notice bright blue light pulsating at the edge of the curtains.

This doesn't make sense. Leaping out of bed, I open the window, a chill draught dispelling my hope that it's a dream.

"What's going on?" I shout, teeth chattering.

"Police. Open up."

My eyes hurt as the strobe-like glare hits them. I struggle to focus on the two black-clad men and their vehicle.

"But…why? Is my husband all right?"

"Just open the door, please."

Thank goodness, Nick must be okay. But if it isn't about him, why are they here?

"Can you come back later?" I ask. "My children are asleep."

"No, sorry. Let us in, or we'll have to use force."

"Hold on," I plead, blinking at Peregrine and Maggie's house. A yellow glow has just spilled out from the top storey. Great. I have an audience.

Racing downstairs, I almost trip over the gym kit and book bags laid out for the school run. My hair is a haystack and my IQ depressed by a sleep deficit, but at least I don't need to throw on clothes. As usual, I'm wearing the silk Olivia von Halle pyjamas that Nick presented to me at Christmas so I'd 'look more feminine'. Not that he intended me to show off my nightwear to the cops, any more than I'd expect them to be experts on designer brands.

When I open the door, I notice a third officer present: a woman. It's she who waves ID in front of me.

"Gail Masterson?"

I nod.

"I'm Police Sergeant Ruth Cluff. We have a warrant to search your house."

What do they say about knowing you're old when police officers look young? I'm just nudging thirty, but I must have a good five years on Ruth Cluff. With long blonde hair tied back in a ponytail, she's fresh-faced yet severe. She is also wide awake, a hundred times more brisk and energetic than I feel.

She tilts her head to one side, making eye contact. Evidently, she expects me to say something.

"Erm," I stammer, "Come in. But please don't wake the children. They've got school later, and they need their sleep."

What they don't need is the shock of being woken by a police search.

"We'll try to minimise disruption for them. "Her stern expression softens, gaze sweeping over my flowery silk ensemble. "Olivia von Halle?"

"Yes."

She recognises her brands after all.

"Sorry we came so early. It helps us make sure there's someone home."

"You've missed my husband. He's in London."

"So I understand."

I gawp at her, about to ask how, when I notice one of her companions carrying a red metal battering ram back to their car. They were fully prepared to break down the door, then. I'm relieved they didn't.

Her colleagues troop inside.

I try to frame a question to find out why they have a warrant, but Tom's voice pipes up, "Mum! There's a police car."

I turn, looking at the top of the stairs. He stands haloed by the landing light.

"That's right, darling," I say brightly. "They want to look round our house. Isn't it exciting?"

He stares at the trio nervously, clutching the fleecy blanket he's used for comfort since he was a baby. It calms him when Nick starts hectoring the children. Of course, Tom shouldn't really need it still, and for an awful moment, I'm afraid I'll be judged on my parenting abilities. My panic eases when I remind myself the sergeant is here with a search warrant; she won't be interested in Tom.

Still, if he's anxious, it's disconcerting. Their school has taught my children that the police are people who help us. Hopefully, they'll continue to believe it after Ruth Cluff and her team have been through their toyboxes.

"He should go back to bed," I tell the sergeant. "But presumably you'll need access to the kids' rooms?"

"That's right," she says. "How many children are here?"

"My son, who is six. And my eight-year-old daughter."

"If you can keep him occupied, we'll focus on your boy's room first, then yours. We'll save the little girl's until last, unless she wakes up." She waves an arm in a large arc. "There's plenty to do. You have a large home, don't you? Before we start, I should say that you're welcome to watch us as we work. Many people choose not to, and it's up to you."

It isn't really, with Tom awake and curious. I'll concentrate on distracting him rather than shadowing the cops.

Ruth Cluff hasn't finished. "Also, is there anywhere you'd prefer me to look rather than my male colleagues?"

"Our bedrooms, please. And my husband's study." I decide to watch her after all. While I don't know what she's searching for, I bet it's Nick's drugs. There's a fifty-fifty chance she'll discover cocaine in his desk drawer. He may have a few pills too, for personal use. And I'll have to point the finger at him, because if I take the blame, I could lose the children.

Given a choice between Nick and the kids, it's no contest. They win.

Nick might be leaving me, anyway. I've heard nothing from him since that text on Monday night.

Finally, the light bulb moment arrives. It's been a long time coming: the effect of my sleep deficit. I shiver, and not with the cold. My skin crawls.

I ask the obvious question.

"Is Nick in trouble?"

# CHAPTER 18 NICK

## Day 4 - Thursday

Booking a chauffeur wasn't as easy as Nick expected. He had no PA to do it for him. No money. No phone. But the duty solicitor lent him a mobile to make a call once bail was arranged. Nick ordered the limo on his company's account. The news obviously hadn't made it to the executive car service yet. They're in for a shock when they try to get their invoice paid.

Nick's bank accounts are frozen, or at least, the ones that the authorities know about. They haven't yet identified his Liechtenstein funds, inherited from his father along with the Krugerrands. Nick's first priority is to lay his hands on the assets. Then he'll head for the sun. Somewhere discreet and private, where he can disappear. Thailand, perhaps, or Panama.

The Liechtenstein trust won't stay hidden for long. In his father's era, Liechtenstein's banking secrecy laws were ironclad. That's all changed. HMRC know about the cash. He doubts that taxpayer confidentiality will stop them telling the FCA. Meanwhile, they've sent him a huge tax bill which he doesn't intend to pay. Mike Gill's been wrangling with them for years on Nick's behalf.

He won't pay Mike Gill's fees either, especially since their telephone call yesterday. When you ring your best mate, your hotshot lawyer, from Bishopsgate police station, you expect help and sympathy. Mike provided neither. In clipped tones, he'd asked Nick to confirm his pension fund was safe — as if! — and then said he was unable to act. Conflicted out, apparently.

Nick ended up with the duty solicitor, a perfectly pleasant old chap who said he'd come across Ponzi schemes before.

"But it's not a Ponzi scheme," Nick had protested.

"What else is it, then?"

And, of course, there was no answer to that.

The tragedy is that he'd inherited a legitimate business. His tyrant father ruled the empire absolutely and successfully. It was clean as a whistle, reputable as a saint, and that's no doubt why the authorities applied a light touch for all these years.

But the house of cards has folded. The old man was right: Nick's a loser. If his father's ghost rises up and beats him black and blue, just like the old days, it'd be no more than he deserves.

Yet, if he can keep a clear head, Nick can salvage a bright future from the wreckage. Beaches, bars and bitches. And he's rarely enjoyed such mental clarity. Since the excrement hit the proverbial, he need no longer hustle for investors. Freed from those shackles, he's focusing on himself.

His plans don't include Gail and the children. He doesn't need them anymore. But he must return to the house in Clifton, if only to pick up the Krugerrands. It sticks in his craw, but he owes thanks to his father's foresight. Not only did the old man buy a hundred of the South African coins, but he told Nick how to protect them from the taxman. That stash, worth a quarter of a million today, will take him to Liechtenstein and beyond. They weigh an ounce each; he can easily carry them in a backpack.

He pictures the little cellar, accessed via a trapdoor under a rug in the downstairs loo. The gleam of gorgeous, shiny gold. His second passport is secreted there too. Taking advantage of an obscure rule for business travellers, he holds two. He's surrendered one to get bail, and he mustn't forget to collect the other. His insulin is essential too. There's so much to remember, mundane details that he used to leave for Gail or Tamara. Now, he's on his own.

Damn Tamara. Although the police wouldn't say how they acquired their information, he knows. Just wait until he's safe in his foreign hideaway. He'll take out a contract, engaging a hitman to inflict a slow and painful death on her. Nick smiles, then yawns. The thin mattress in his police cell wasn't conducive to sleep. He lounges back in the limousine's padded leather seat, and sinks into slumber.

# CHAPTER 19 JONATHAN

## Day 4 - Thursday

Jonathan took morphine in the end.

Not enough to kill him. After Googling it, he measured out just enough to get to sleep, to give him a good night's rest.

It's made all the difference. Tilly's loss still hurts, like a raw, gaping wound torn out of his side. But he can move forward.

He'll forget about women, of course. Casual affairs are a thing of the past. He won't seek another relationship either. No-one could replace the goddess who taught him how to love. Who showed him how to respect and cherish others.

He'll concentrate on his work. Jonathan is quietly proud that he's taking Gill Spices to the next level, building on Tilly's legacy. They've signed a new contract with the biggest food manufacturer in Europe. Their sales will double. His plans don't stop there, either. He's going to make the company truly global. Stan Voyze won't know what's hit him.

Is Stan up to the task? Jonathan wouldn't have queried the CFO's abilities before, but lately, Stan has seemed distant. Not quite as confident as usual. He's undoubtedly been distracted by Tilly's illness, as have they all. Even so, it would be best to visit the office today. Jonathan can share condolences with Stan and the others. He can warn Stan about the upcoming battle with Daisy and Mike. It should be a private matter, but Stan has known Tilly's children all their lives, and Jonathan suspects the pair will try to involve him. He needs to head that off at the pass. Then it wouldn't hurt to check progress on the factory extension with the site manager. Half the car park has been screened off with metal fencing. Tarmac has been removed and foundations dug. Builders should be beavering away, because he can't fit the new production line into the old factory's footprint.

Jonathan heads to the edge of the city in his Porsche, which he's owned since he was single. Classic FM plays in the background to soothe him. 'Spring' from Vivaldi's Four Seasons begins. It's an uplifting piece which would usually cheer Jonathan up, but it was Tilly's favourite. He switches the radio off.

Parking is now at a premium at Gill Spices, except for the directors. Jonathan has a reserved space near the office entrance, an unassuming revolving glass door. A glance at the construction work reassures him that it's on target. Good.

He braces himself for sympathy from his team. Not so good.

It isn't as soul-crushing as he fears. The receptionist asks him how he is and doesn't pry when he trots out the platitude that he's as well as can be expected. His PA hugs him and offers him tea with sugar. She's done neither of these things before — Jonathan drinks coffee and always makes his own. There's a lump in his throat as he thanks her. He accepts the tea and asks her to call Stan into his office.

Stan is late.

Jonathan catches up on correspondence, reading it in far more detail than usual. Anything to push Tilly's absence from his mind. He blanks out the feminine touches in his office, the memories embedded within them. Taking a swig of tea, he finds it has cooled to the chilly side of tepid.

Where is the CFO? Jonathan is about to ask his PA to chase Stan, when the man himself arrives. Jonathan stands up and gestures to the seat opposite.

Stan looks pale, although walking tall as usual. He doesn't sit straight away. Instead, he marches around the desk to Jonathan and claps him on the shoulder. "I'm sorry for your loss," he says.

"My condolences to you too. I know you and Tilly went back a long way."

"Twenty-five years," Stan says. "Martin and Tilly recruited me to resolve the millennium bug for them. I finished the project and never left."

"We should have had a party for your quarter century."

"Don't worry about it." Stan takes his seat.

Jonathan does likewise. "I have a delicate matter to discuss," he says, mouth dry with apprehension. Suppose Stan sides with Tilly's children?

Stan's lips twitch. "Me too. You go first."

Jonathan explains about Daisy's threat. He assures Stan that he will fight to retain control of the company, and it won't affect the expansion plans.

"Something else might," Stan says.

"Oh?" Jonathan isn't unduly concerned. No doubt there's some red tape to address. But the new contract is watertight, and so is the planning permission.

"You'll have heard that the Masterson Group has collapsed."

"What?"

No, he hadn't heard, having been rather preoccupied. It's the best news he's had all week. Karma has embraced Nick Masterson at last.

"Well, I moved all our money market funds there," Stan says.

"Did I hear you right?" Jonathan can't believe he did. "You placed our short-term cash in an investment fund?"

"Yes," Stan says miserably.

"But that's crazy. A fund like that is illiquid. Even I know that. We were only going to hang onto the money for a week, having drawn down the term loans early…" And mortgaged his home. Jonathan winces.

"Nick Masterson phoned me himself. He said he had a new product, suited to our needs. I'd always found him very reasonable, a clubbable chap. And of course, he's a friend of yours—"

"He's no friend!" Jonathan blurts out.

"Now you tell me." Stan drums his fingers on the desk separating the two men. His crouching stance suggests he's ready to run. In an injured tone, he adds, "The Masterson Group has been around for ages. And they offered the best rates."

Jonathan is struck dumb. He stares at his CFO, unable to blink, unable even to move.

"You signed the papers," Stan accuses.

What's that supposed to mean? Jonathan signs whatever Stan asks him to.

"Their website's down," Stan says. "I can't withdraw anything. There's an FCA investigation, and Nick Masterson has been arrested."

Jonathan has stopped listening. His company's cash has vanished. So has everything they borrowed, including mortgages on the factory and his flat.

If they can't make the stage payment to the builders tomorrow, the expansion will stop. But they're tied into the new sales contract with penalty clauses he never expected to see invoked. Their business partner will sue the pants off him.

He remembers Daisy's threat of litigation. "Join the queue," he mutters to himself.

# CHAPTER 20 GAIL

## Day 4 - Thursday

There's a shadow at the sitting room window. At least, I think there is. When I stare through the glass, I can't be sure what's real anymore.

Nick has been charged with fraud. Although Tamara's claim had me reeling in disbelief, this is even harder to imagine. His father set up the Masterson Group in the 1980s, before I was born. It's rock solid. I wish I knew how to help, but I can't even speak to him. When I asked Ruth Cluff, she was cagey. He was in custody, she said, and she was sure he'd get in touch.

It explains why he didn't ring back. They're only allowed one phone call, aren't they?

I hope he used it to contact Mike Gill. Nick needs bigger brains than mine on his side, and Mike is bound to step forward in his defence. Just in case, I've used our landline to leave a message with his office. Poor Mike. This is such a mess, and he's contending with his mother's death as well.

Daisy was beyond upset yesterday. With no idea her mum was ill, she was shocked that Matilda and Jonathan hadn't made the effort to tell her. As Daisy said to me, she'd blocked them on her phone, but how about snail mail? Even without her address, Jonathan could have contacted her by writing to Gordon at his company. She totally blamed him, muttering darkly about predatory marriages and Jonathan killing Matilda. I wouldn't rule it out. Jonathan's apparent distress could have been a cynical act, his payment for design services nothing but a smokescreen.

I didn't dare admit to Daisy that I'd been working for him.

She wasn't at the school this morning. Gordon dropped their children off. Not that I spoke to him. I was late, having waited for the police to wrap up before dashing out with the kids.

"They didn't find my treasure, did they?" Tom said.

I ruffled his hair, playing along. "You pirates buried it too well."

Mary said she wanted to be a police lady when she grew up. I guess she wasn't traumatised, which is a blessing.

The experience could have been much worse, but its effects linger on. Ruth Cluff's search focused on speed rather than tidiness. Every room was left in disarray. Also, she took my MacBook, iPad, iPhone and the

PC that the kids use for homework. She'll drop them back later when her colleagues have downloaded data from each device. It means I can't move forward with Daisy's project, even if my overwhelmed, foggy brain could function.

Over-tired and too wired to doze off, I tackle the chaos on the top floor first, thankful no drugs were found in the end. Moving downstairs to the kitchen, I make black coffee to boost my faded energy. I can't face food. Still, exhaustion catches up with me. I stagger to the sitting room and slump on one of our matching Linley sofas. Nick ordered them as soon as Daisy's brother bought a pair.

My husband demands our house is kept perfect. The furniture could be fresh from a showroom. Our kids know better than to leave sticky finger-marks. Yet the police have emptied our cabinets and shelves, and while I can't predict when Nick will return, I must clear the muddle.

A short break can't do any harm, though. My eyelids twitch at the edges, consciousness gradually shutting down. It's not sleep, just a fugue-like state where nothing matters anymore.

Nick's voice drags me out of my trance.

"Christ. The house is a tip."

He stands in front of me, lip curling. His office clothes are rumpled. Even though he's clean-shaven, there's a hint of body odour. Custody can't have been pleasant.

"Nick? Are you all right?"

"As well as can be expected." His eyes, hard as flint, flick around the room. "Police raid, huh?"

"Yes, I've been clearing up…" I falter as his brow furrows.

"Did they find anything?"

"No. They took phones, computers and some documents."

"My passport?" His voice is strained.

My memory remains stubbornly blank. "I didn't see it… Wait, they gave me a list."

It was a handwritten note. I fish it from the pocket of my jeans. "No mention of a passport."

"Good." He exhales. "Get me a drink, will you, and I'll see if it's still there."

"Anyway—"

He cuts short my attempt to quiz him about the police investigation, and what happened, and whether Mike Gill is on the case.

"No time for questions," Nick snaps. His gaze alights on a bottle, one of a collection the police have left in a corner of the room. "Make it a whisky. Lagavulin."

Niceties like please and thank you, the manners I try so hard to instil in the children, are absent. I'm used to it. It's typical of Nick when's he's under stress. But more disturbingly, it could be an early warning of a hypo, when his blood sugar goes too low. It happens when Nick has injected insulin, and then doesn't eat enough carbs – or when he gets stressed. And guess what? His stress must be off the scale right now.

If it's a hypo, he must urgently raise his sugar levels. Ignoring the signals could be fatal. He'll fall unconscious, and if he isn't brought round quickly enough, he might die.

Of course, Nick knows all this. But during a hypo, he's irrational. Angry. Violent.

Which is, as I've learned, normal for Nick when he's stressed too.

So, what do I do?

I can't risk saying nothing.

Shrinking away from him, I shuffle backwards towards the kitchen door. It's an escape route if he lashes out.

"When did you last eat, Nick? Wouldn't a glass of orange juice be—"

"Just get the whisky," he snarls.

Booze will send his sugar lower. It's the last thing he needs, but I won't win this battle. I'll have to try the subtle approach. When I fix his drink, I grab a banana in the kitchen as well as slipping ice into his lead crystal tumbler. Wordlessly, I hand him both.

Nick ignores the fruit, letting it fall to the floor. He grabs the glass. Within seconds, he's downed half the contents.

"Nick, about your blood sugar—"

"I'm starving," he announces, not exactly giving in gracefully, but he picks up the banana and munches it. "Mmm. How about coffee? And a toasted sandwich."

My stomach unknots itself. "You're on. Bread and water at the cop shop?"

"It wasn't that good. Anyhow, it's way past lunchtime."

He laughs, and although the sound is thin and metallic, I take it as an encouraging sign. Maybe when he's eaten more, I can find out what's going on. I hurry into the kitchen to prepare his food.

Nick is particular about his grilled cheese sandwiches. Only Waitrose mild cheddar will do. The sourdough must be exactly one centimetre thick, the cheese half that, the tomatoes thinly sliced. Not too much butter. While he doesn't whip out a tape measure, he's quick to criticise if he feels I've made a mistake. I assumed it was a hangover from boarding school, but when I grumbled to Daisy, she snorted with mirth. Meals were so disgusting at Markham's, she told me, that Mike was perpetually hungry. He begged his parents for food parcels. As soon as he returned home, he ate anything that wasn't nailed down.

I place the toastie on a tray with a bowl of jelly beans, holding my breath. The smell of molten cheese turns my stomach. Carrying the food to the sitting room, I come to a halt at the threshold.

My husband isn't there.

"Nick?" My shrill yell echoes in the empty space.

"What is wrong with you?" Nick's harsh voice matches his reddened, rage-filled face. He emerges from the lobby waving a little black book.

I set the snacks down on a coffee table. Just in case.

As he nears, I see it's not a book. His passport.

"Is this some kind of joke?" Nick fumes. He opens the document to the photograph page. Spectacles and a moustache, doodled in black ink, decorate the images.

"I don't know," I stammer. Can I make it to the kitchen before he kicks off? Upping his blood sugar will have to wait.

I inch away from him. "The children might have been having fun," I add lamely.

"Fun?" His nostrils flare. "You call this fun?"

"No…"

Nick spots my attempt to flee. With his rugby player's athleticism, he darts forward to block me.

Pain shoots through my right arm as he grips it.

"Don't blame the children," he screams, his eyeballs nearly touching mine, his spittle spraying my lips. "You did it, didn't you?"

"No. I told you, I had no idea where it was." Tears wet my cheeks. I'm hyperventilating, heart pounding as it tries to break free from my ribcage. He's going to kill me. Then he'll die too, because he's too unbalanced to eat, and no-one will be around when he falls unconscious. My children will be orphans because I was too slow in the kitchen. What an epitaph.

"Eat the jelly beans," I plead. "Or take a glucose tablet. Look, they're in our ensuite… I'll fetch them."

Nick's eyes flash. He slaps my face, hard, so there's an immediate sting and an echoing ache in my cheekbone. This will bruise. If I make it out alive, I'll be plastering on makeup for weeks.

No-one will guess why. Or if they do, they won't say anything. It will be like the time before. And the time before that.

"You think I was born yesterday?" Nick spits.

Freeing my wrist with a bitter laugh, he places his hands around my neck. "It's crystal clear. You almost had me convinced it was Tamara…"

Goggling at him, I gasp for breath. I'd forgotten all about her in my desperation to manage Nick's blood sugar.

"… but she doesn't have the brains. It was you. You tipped off the FCA. You took the Krugerrands. You're planning a nice life with your lover while I rot in jail, aren't you?"

"No," I splutter, hardly able to speak. "It isn't like that. I don't have a lover, and what's a Kr—"

His hands tighten. "Who is he?" Nick yells.

I'm choking. When I try to protest my innocence, only a cough emerges. My arms thrash out at him.

He increases the pressure.

With my final reserves of energy, I bring up a knee to his groin.

He lets go. I breathe at last, huge gulps bringing waves of pain to my chest. The relief is indescribable though. Golden.

Nick has fallen to the floor, clutching himself. Instinctively, I reach for a cushion and lob it at his face. It won't hurt him, but hopefully it will disorientate him. Half staggering, half running, I dash into the hall.

I must run. Hide, until he calms down.

Our doorbell rings.

# CHAPTER 21 JONATHAN

## Day 4 - Thursday

Jonathan knows who to blame. Sure, Stan should have had more sense. If a deal seems too good to be true, it always is. No doubt Stan received inducements: perhaps that's how he ended up in that strip club. But Jonathan can deal with the CFO later. Right now, he plans to get up close and personal with Nick Masterson.

A quick online search turns up plenty of news. Nick has been granted bail and told to stay away from the City of London. No prizes for guessing where he's gone. Soon, Jonathan is driving to that substantial stone house in Clifton, the property Nick shares with The Honourable Gail.

It would fetch a fancy price, but Jonathan isn't kidding himself. No doubt it's owned by a funky trust in the Isle of Man. Jonathan won't be the only person Nick has ripped off, either. When a company goes bust, nobody gets any money back. Especially once the lawyers have had their fees. Mike Gill and his ilk, dipping their snouts in the trough.

Whatever happens, Tilly is going to have the wake she dreamed about. He'll pay for it even if he's declared bankrupt afterwards. Even if he's thrown out on the streets, which is a real possibility with Gill Spices about to go bump, and a mortgage he can't now afford. Jonathan has been poor before. He doesn't enjoy it, but on past performance, he'll survive. A rich kid like Nick? Not so much.

Except Nick, with his trusts and tax dodges, won't end up poor. Jonathan can almost guarantee it. And he's going to make it his life's mission to uncover the loopholes Nick's using, and watch him until he makes a misstep. Payback.

He'll make sure Nick knows. Let Nick worry constantly whether he's said or done something wrong, to lose sleep while he guesses at the punishments about to be visited on him.

Give Nick a taste of his own medicine.

Jonathan parks in front of Nick's property. He opens the black iron gate and marches past the gleaming cars. He presses the old-fashioned ceramic bell.

The door swings open straight away. He doesn't even have time to step forward before Gail barrels into him.

"Whoa." He forms an impression of warmth and fruity perfume, but above all, momentum. Gail may be slightly built, but she's raced from the house like a bat out of hell. Jonathan nearly loses his balance, especially when she trips and throws her full weight against him. He puts his arms around her. Steadying her might just keep them both vertical.

Gail screams.

"Sorry." Jonathan mutters the apology without stopping to consider if it's warranted. He feels Gail wriggle from his grasp, realises she's righted herself, and shuffles back to give her space. Then he sees her reddened eyes. The imprint of a hand on her cheek.

School bullies don't stop. They find new targets.

"He did this to you, didn't he?" Jonathan says. "Nick?"

"Yes." Her voice emerges as a racking sob.

"And he's in there?" Jonathan points.

She draws a long, shuddering breath, and glances over her shoulder. It tells him everything.

"Run," he commands. "I'll call the police."

"No. Please—"

Whatever she was going to say, it's too late. Like a bomb on the point of exploding, Nick bursts outside, rage evident in his flushed face.

Gail yelps. Finally, she takes Jonathan's advice. There's a rush of air to his side as she bolts past him. He hears the squeak of the gate.

Nick tries to follow. But Jonathan is ready for his old nemesis. Every way that Nick turns, Jonathan blocks his path.

"Jonno! I should have known." Nick takes a swing.

Jonathan ducks it easily. They're evenly matched, or at any rate, more so than at Markham's. Jonathan works out. He's built up muscle. And he suspects Nick's fitness has wavered since he captained the school rugby team. Office life can do that to a man. Nick won't have tried to counteract it; he's too lazy.

Nick tries for another punch. This time, he aims at Jonathan's stomach. "I knew it. She's sleeping with you," he spits.

Jonathan sidesteps him.

Nick teeters forward. He's still ranting. "How long have you been screwing my wife?"

"How long have you been beating her up?" Jonathan asks. He notices Peregrine appear in the front garden next door. "Why don't you tell your neighbours all about it? Be my guest."

Nick’s eyes bulge with hate. Sweat coats his forehead. He glances around, spots Peregrine and jolts backward. “Get off my property,” he hisses. “Go follow your slut.”

“You’ve got it all wrong,” Jonathan says. He adds, loud enough for Peregrine to hear, “You’ve taken my money. And I want it back.”

The neighbour clears his throat.

Nick’s demeanour changes as if a switch has been flicked. “A misunderstanding, I’m sure,” he says, his voice oily. “Come in, and we’ll discuss it over a whisky.”

# CHAPTER 22 TAMARA

## Day 4 - Thursday

She's made a mistake, and she's furious with herself. But Tamara is nothing if not resourceful. So she's made her way to Bristol, a pocket-sized city compared with London, and an adventure into the unknown.

Her temporary housemates would barely recognise her. Nor would Nick. The sexy stilettos have been replaced by sneakers, jet-black like her jogging set and bumbag. Her face is free of makeup, her flaxen hair scraped back in a low bun, practical rather than flattering. She carries a ski mask, although she hasn't worn it yet. It would have looked out of place on the cheap National Express coach, which — imagine that! — dropped her a mere twenty-minute walk from Nick's house.

How much is it worth?

This is the best district of Bristol; she's heard Nick say so often enough. A huge stone house like this would be ten million in Hampstead. And the rest. That was the life she'd imagined: a bougie home with a Tesla in the driveway, and a brace of perfectly behaved children. Not that she's the maternal sort. Kids are a means to an end.

This one is going to be a goldmine.

She has let herself into the garden, soundlessly, through the wrought-iron gate across the drive. She has resisted the temptation to scratch Nick's Tesla. Now, she crouches in a dark corner, where two walls meet and an oak tree casts a shadow upon her. She is checking out the front of the house, but she is also thinking. Biding her time.

Raised voices can be heard from the property: Nick's, and a woman's. Tamara tenses up. She hadn't expected him to return to Bristol so soon.

It's no surprise that he's arguing with Gail, though. They don't get on. His father pushed him into marrying her. Nick needed a suitable wife as a social asset, apparently. Just Nick's luck that his father died months later, and Gail turned out to be no asset. She refused to move to London, where she could have helped Nick schmooze the capital's power couples.

He should have dumped her and chosen Tamara. Too late now.

The scent of lavender tickles her nostrils, and she stifles a sneeze. She scrutinises the property, trying to figure out how she can enter without anyone noticing. Perhaps she should wait until it's dark, pick a lock and creep inside.

A car pulls up to the kerb. Tamara's eyes widen as she notes a Porsche with a personalised plate. A man gets out, smart in a sharp suit. Tamara has seen enough of Savile Row to recognise its hallmarks. The jacket is cut to accommodate strong biceps. She approves of the stranger's athletic figure. A tingle of pleasure makes her smile. It's odd that she's drawn to him; he's not conventionally attractive like Nick. The sports car adds to his allure, she decides. Tamara imagines the two of them driving along a deserted beach, wind in her hair as she lounges beside him.

He might not be much fun, though. That worried frown suggests problems. He's probably Nick's lawyer. Boy, is he right to be concerned.

The man rings the doorbell.

A woman stumbles out, and into his arms.

Tamara peeks out from her hiding place. She can't see the woman too well, but she hears everything. Clocks the signs of abuse as Gail runs past, giving her a better view. Notices, with a flush of anger, that Nick's wife is pretty.

Then Nick arrives on the scene. An old fellow springs up in the neighbouring garden. Tamara shrinks back. It's getting too crowded. If they spot her…

It turns out that the visitor isn't a lawyer, but an aggrieved investor. Nick must have plans for him. He wouldn't turn on the charm otherwise.

The two men go inside, slamming the door behind them. The neighbour's gaze slides onto Tamara. His eyes widen.

A tight knot forms in her stomach. She'll have to bluff it out. "I'm a tree surgeon," Tamara says.

He nods as if he believes her, before pottering back inside his home.

She's alone again.

Tamara snaps on gloves. She scurries across the drive and investigates the side of the property. Finding a promising sash window, she jiggles the lower bars. A gap appears at the bottom. She winces at the creaking sound.

Crouching down and cupping a hand to her ear, she hears nothing. Tamara applies herself to the task again. Gently does it.

The opening widens.

She's got this.

# CHAPTER 23 JONATHAN

## Day 4 - Thursday

"Come into my sh… shtudy."

Nick's grin doesn't reach his eyes. He's slurring words. Jonathan remembers him doing so at school, having a diabetic episode after playing rugby. There was a rush to give him glucose tablets. But diabetes might not be responsible this time. A whiff of alcohol hovers around Nick. Whatever chemicals are driving his behaviour, though, he's unlikely to be stable.

Jonathan keeps his distance.

For now, they stay polite to each other, Jonathan saying nothing about the evidence of violence on Gail's face. She's got away, hasn't she? He's revolted by Nick, but he needs to focus on the money.

Nick steers his visitor into a ground floor study. This is dominated by a 'Wall Street' movie poster, signed by the actors and framed. Beside it, Nick's sporting trophies line the top shelf of a bookcase, although all the books are piled on the floor. The room also contains a desk, two office chairs and a mini fridge. Four Mars Bars are laid out on top of the latter. Nick stares at them, a confused expression on his face. Eventually, he grabs one, unwraps it and wolfs it down in three bites.

"Make yourshelf… yourself… comfy," Nick says. "I'll get the whishky. Lagavulin all right?"

"I'll have a beer," Jonathan says. He won't touch whisky anymore.

"In the fridge. Help yourself." Nick wanders out of the room.

Jonathan inspects the fridge, finding an opener attached to it with a magnet. Inside, pre-prepared insulin pens sit on the single shelf, with a handful of beer bottles below. He settles on a trendy IPA. The chilled bottle is cool in his hand, moist with condensation. He takes a swig. It tastes better than expected.

Nick returns with both a crystal tumbler and a sandwich, which he places on the desk. He takes the larger of the two chairs. "I told you to sit down."

"It was an order?" But Jonathan obeys, breathing deeply and necking more of the beer. He waits silently as Nick gobbles the sandwich and throws back all his whisky. Maybe Nick is up to a sensible, rational conversation. His speech is clearer, so it's possible he just needed food.

Still, apprehension tickles Jonathan's spine. He decides to test the ground. "Now, about the money," he says.

"I wasn't aware I had your money." Nick enunciates the words as if speaking to an imbecile. He stretches and yawns. "You declined my special offer, I recall."

"Stop playing games." Jonathan's irritation shows in his inflection. He chides himself. Nick responds better to flattery than fire. In a softer manner, he says, "I run Gill Spices. We placed a deposit with you."

Nick laughs derisively. "How forgetful of me. And I may also have overlooked the inconvenient fact that all my bank accounts are frozen. But you're not so perfect yourself, are you? You've forgotten you're banging my wife."

Jonathan is suddenly aware of the heartbeat pulsing through his temples, speeding up. He stares at Nick. "You're obsessed with that crazy idea. I'm only—"

He'd subconsciously prepared himself for a fight, but even so, Jonathan is caught unawares when Nick springs out of his seat. A swift left hook leaves Jonathan reeling. Nick, unbalanced by his own momentum, falls forward. Jonathan is shoved back into his chair and pinned down. He can't move his limbs. All his bodybuilding, the muscled biceps and triceps, are useless with Nick's weight upon them.

The reflection that it was always going to happen flashes through Jonathan's mind.

Bloodlust flames in Nick's eyes, a predatory gaze that Jonathan recollects too well. Then Nick's head dips, his skull smashing down on Jonathan's nose.

Pain explodes.

Spots of light dance in front of Jonathan's eyes. He forces out a hoarse scream. Because this could be his last day on earth, and finally, he's sure of one thing.

He doesn't want to die.

# CHAPTER 24 GAIL

## Day 4 - Thursday

Jonathan told me to go to the police, but I can't. Nick is in enough trouble. While he's trying to prove his innocence, the last thing he needs is more crimes added to the list. And when my children are old enough to understand, how would they feel if I'd betrayed their father?

Shivering despite the unseasonably warm weather, I check my pockets. Nothing. I'm standing around the corner with no keys, phone, watch, bag or coat. It would be madness to go back for them, even if Nick would let me in the house. But what's going to happen to him? He's definitely low on blood sugar. I hope he has the presence of mind to grab more sweets, or some glucose tablets.

Maybe Jonathan will help. Why did he turn up? Our business relationship was over. Perhaps Nick was partly right. While I have no feelings for Jonathan, suppose he's obsessed with me? The thought churns my stomach.

I stare into the distance, chewing over my worries. Then I remember that I have to pick the children up from school. I must look a mess. My cheek is still throbbing. I pinch the other one in an effort to redden it too, fluffing up my hair and encouraging the locks to fall forward. There's no way I can drive without my keys, and in my current mental state, I wouldn't be safe behind the wheel anyway. I begin walking, self-consciously avoiding eye contact with other pedestrians.

A BMW pulls up beside me. Daisy's husband, Gordon, winds down the window.

"Hey, want a lift?"

"No thanks. I need the exercise."

"Well, it's about to rain."

As if to prove his words, a large drop lands on my forehead. Dismayed, I spot the grey cloud looming above.

"Come on. Hop in."

Warily, I take a seat beside him, angling my face away. But it's no good. Gordon moves in for an air kiss.

I flinch. He's not usually so demonstrative, but then, I hardly know him. We've mostly met at parents' evenings, when he trails reluctantly after his wife.

"Mwah!" he exclaims in a theatrical manner.

"No Daisy? I suppose she's…" I falter as I spot his gaze fixed on the injured cheek.

"What happened to you?" he demands.

"I walked into a door."

Gordon scowls. "Are you sure? Listen, if you ever need someone to talk to, I'm here. And Daisy would help you too, okay? Take this." He reaches for his wallet, thumbs through it, and hands me a business card.

Hastily, I stuff it into a pocket. Thank goodness I'm wearing jeans.

Tight-lipped, he starts driving again. I say nothing, telling myself that I shouldn't disturb his concentration. Yet the journey feels like it's over in seconds. When Gordon parks a short distance from the school, I note that we're fifteen minutes early.

"You asked about Daisy," Gordon says. "She went for a walk on the Downs. Being surrounded by nature helps her recover when she's upset, which she is, as you'd imagine. I've taken the week off to give her space."

He glances at my cheek again. "The kids and I are off to the cinema after school. Want to come?"

It's tempting, but I can't pay my way. Also, however badly he's behaved, Nick needs my help. It's time to be brave, return home, and make sure his hypo doesn't spiral downwards.

I gulp. "Sorry. Nick is around—"

"So I see," Gordon says icily.

"Well." I avert my gaze. "Look, the rain's stopped. We'd better get our children, hadn't we?"

It's awkward, the walk of shame to the school. We tread the pavement in step, but we're both silent, not looking at each other. As he punches numbers into the keypad at the gate, Gordon whispers, "Call me if you need to, okay?"

The gate clangs shut behind us.

Gordon makes a beeline for another dad waiting in the playground for the bell.

Wishing I could turn invisible, I find a corner in which to skulk alone, peering at the dusty ground. If anyone asks, I'll claim I've lost a contact lens. Nobody knows I have 20:20 vision.

A buzzer sounds. School's out.

Hanging back, I see Gordon heading towards Miss Beazley's classroom. That settles it for me, and I collect Tom from Mrs Shah first.

"Mummy, your face is red. Were you crying?" my son says.

Mrs Shah stiffens, eyes narrowing as they sweep over me.

"Mummy has hay fever," I lie.

Mrs Shah visibly relaxes.

"I'll tell you about it later, Tommy," I say, keeping my tone breezy. "Let's see where your sister's got to."

She'll be with Miss Beazley, as usual, and it should be a Gordon-free zone by now. I clutch Tom's hand, enjoying the warmth, trust, and love wrapped up in that small palm. Touch wood, all will be peaceful when we return home. I will remind Nick that Tom wet the bed the last time his father shouted at him. It doesn't matter that Nick went through much worse as a child. He should understand the impact of parental cruelty: be self-aware enough to stop subjecting his children to it.

I find Miss Beazley talking to another mum, but the teacher immediately breaks off.

"Mrs Masterson, I was hoping to see you. Mary tells me—"

I hold up a hand. If I have one more conversation, one more pair of searching eyes on my face, one more expression of support, I'm going to burst into tears. Because it won't lead anywhere good.

"Can we talk tomorrow, please?" I ask. "We're due at the dentist in ten minutes."

Tom stares at me in horror.

"Of course," Miss Beazley says. "See you tomorrow."

I guide my kids out of the school grounds. A lump fills my throat. I'm in the company of the two people I love most in all the world, and I'm removing them from a place where they're safe. If only I'd asked Gordon to take them to the cinema with his sons. My head's in such a spin, I didn't think of it.

What awaits us back home?

# CHAPTER 25 GAIL

## Day 4 - Thursday

Nobody answers the door.

I press the bell for the fifth time. Again, nothing happens.

Tom's lip trembles. "I'm hungreee, Mummy."

"Can we have ice cream for tea?" Mary asks.

"Yes, but not yet. Silly Mummy forgot her keys," I say. "We'll have to ask Mr Jukes for help."

"Did someone call?" Peregrine waves over the garden wall, a sheaf of clippings in each thickly gloved hand.

When we moved in, Peregrine mentioned the neighbours kept keys for each other. We agreed to carry on with the arrangement, despite Nick's irritation. He grumbled that we'd be called out at odd hours to let forgetful old duffers into their homes. In fact, he was wrong. Peregrine has never prevailed on us. The only question now is whether he can remember where he keeps our spares.

He can.

"They're in the kitchen," he says. "Would you like to come in—"

"I really need to see if Nick is okay."

"—and have a chocolate digestive while I fetch it?"

"A biscuit! Mummy, please?" Tom wheedles, blue eyes appealing. He reminds me of my husband, back when we first met and Nick was trying to impress.

I bow to the inevitable. "Yes, but Mr Jukes is a busy man, so don't take long over it." Chance would be a fine thing. Tom can make a biscuit disappear simply by looking at it.

We troop after Peregrine as he shuffles past over-stuffed bookcases to his kitchen. Although his house is similar to ours in its layout, its styling is completely different. Maggie's crocheted throws cover the furniture, while photographs of grandchildren dominate the walls. The boy and girl smile out from images of various stages in their lives. They're babies, then toddlers, and finally towering over Peregrine with a Disney castle in the background.

Peregrine catches me glancing at them. "Growing up fast."

"Still happy to go on holiday with you at Christmas, I see."

His eyes grow misty. “They humour me and Maggie. We were allowed to meet Mickey Mouse as long as we took them to Universal Studios too. They keep us young, I always say.”

“Noah and Kate, isn’t it? How old are they now?”

“Seventeen and eighteen. He’s just passed his driving test, and she’s off to college in September.”

“You must be proud of them.”

“I am, particularly as Kate’s autistic. Maggie and I paid for her to go to a special school. We hope she can continue for the last term.”

His voice is suddenly strained, and I change the subject by asking where Maggie is.

“She’s at her flower arranging class,” Peregrine scrutinises my cheek. “You should talk to her. Want me to send her round?”

“No thanks,” I mutter.

The second we arrive in the kitchen, Tom homes in on the biscuit barrel, a large round tin decorated with a preening hen.

“Careful,” I warn him. “Let Mr Jukes open it.”

Peregrine obliges. “Why don’t you take two each, kiddos? Sit over there, where the crumbs won’t matter.”

They don’t need telling. As they munch their digestives, Peregrine beckons me with his forefinger. “You know what, Gail, I think Maggie moved the keys into our utility. Follow me.”

He isn’t lying. They’re on a shelf above his washing machine, each fob neatly labelled.

“Ah, this is yours, I think.” He hands a set over.

“Thanks.”

“I say, Gail, are you all right?”

“Never better,” I lie, fidgeting, my feet itching to run from his prying eyes. I thought Maggie was the nosy one.

My relationship with Nick isn’t perfect, I’ll admit that, but why does everyone else regard it as their business?

Peregrine won’t drop it. “I saw you earlier, with your love—”

“He’s not my lover,” I interrupt, a wave of heat burning my face. “Jonathan is my client. My design client.”

“With your lovely husband and your friend,” Peregrine says, “and you seemed terrified. Not to mention looking like you’d done a round with Mike Tyson.”

“Sorry?”

"Tyson Fury then," he clarifies.

Tom wanders into the utility room. "I've finished," he announces.

"Take another one," Peregrine offers. "If that's all right, Mum?"

"Yes, fine." I beam at Tom. "Mary can do the same."

"I don't think a sweet treat does any harm," Peregrine says. "Our Emily is like a policeman with her kids. No fizzy drinks. No sugar. No fun. They're only young once."

Tom and Mary's sugar rush is the least of my worries. On the other hand, if Nick doesn't balance his intake properly, he could die. "I'm sorry, Peregrine," I say, "thanks for your concern, but Nick isn't well."

"A nervous breakdown?" Peregrine suggests. "I've heard about the fraud investigation. You could have knocked me down with a feather when I heard Nick's name on Radio 4 this morning."

My jaw drops. Of course Peregrine has heard the news.

"It's a mistake," I falter, not sure I really believe it anymore.

"That's what I thought. Why, I invested funds with the Masterson Group only last week." Peregrine's eyes bore into mine.

He's worried about his money. And I'm going to have to get used to this. Peregrine won't be the only one among our friends, families and acquaintances. Nick is so persuasive, and lately I realise, so desperate. Who else is anxiously examining their finances, hoping against hope that they get repaid?

"It's nothing I can't afford," Peregrine says.

I suspect he's glossing over his fears. If Nick's company doesn't refund the money, it might affect Kate's chances of attending that school for one more term. Of getting the A levels she needs for college.

I can't look him in the eye.

"To be honest, I didn't expect Nick to be here," Peregrine says. "Thought he was in London, helping the police with their enquiries. He's taken out his stress on you, hasn't he?"

Peregrine is spot on. But I'm not admitting it. I fidget. "Listen, we have to go."

"You should go to the police. Leave the kids here for a couple of hours."

I flash him a tight smile. "They've got homework. I need to get them started on that. But thanks for the keys. And the biscuits."

"Any time."

He waves as we leave. Considering his money worries, he's been more than kind.

"Hello," I call, unlocking the front door.

There's no reply. Has Nick left? Or is he unconscious? My stomach flips and tightens.

"Mary, Tom, go to the playroom and switch on the TV," I command them. The chocolate biscuits will keep their energy levels up for a few minutes. That's enough time to investigate.

I check the kitchen and sitting room without success. By now, I'm almost convinced that I'll find Nick's study empty. But it isn't.

As soon as I open the door, I gag at the butcher's shop smell. But the sight before me is worse. Nick lies face down on the floor, completely still. Jonathan, covered in blood, is slumped in a chair. He's not moving either.

They're dead.

They've killed each other.

Bile fills my mouth. At least it stops me screaming.

# CHAPTER 26 NEIL

## Day 5 - Friday

"So, Operation Worthing."

Detective Inspector Sherry Duffy's cheeks dimple, and Detective Sergeant Neil Slater almost forgets he's cross about her promotion.

"It's a murder inquiry, but we haven't ruled out suicide yet," Sherry continues. She twirls a strand of golden hair around her finger. Neil has seen her do this hundreds of times: it's a subconscious tic, a sign of concentration. She's thinking about what to say next.

He knows Sherry nearly as well as his wife, although in a platonic way, of course. They've been friends and colleagues for six years.

He'd hoped to be a DI himself by now, though. It's more about the cash than the kudos. Gemma is talking about starting a family. And their cottage in Yatton is a money pit.

"Briefly, the facts are these."

He starts paying attention again.

"Nick Masterson's body was found by his wife, Gail, at their family home yesterday. She'd just brought the kids home from school. Masterson ran a hedge fund, but the City of London Police had launched an inquiry into his business. A Ponzi scheme was suspected. That investigation remains ongoing."

Sherry takes a sip of coffee. "Masterson wasn't alone in the house when Gail returned. His old schoolfriend, Jonathan Smyth, was visiting. He was discovered, unconscious, in the same room as Masterson. Smyth had received a severe beating. He was removed to Southmead Hospital and is not yet in a fit state to be interviewed."

Neil wonders why suicide was mentioned at all. It sounds like a burglary gone wrong, or a fight that went too far. Possibly both. "What does the wife say?" he interjects.

"Gail Masterson gave a brief statement to the uniforms who were despatched to the scene when the paramedics called it in. She claimed she left the house to fetch her children as Smyth was arriving. He interrupted a meal, she said. Masterson had only recently arrived home, having secured bail, and he was hungry. She'd made him a sandwich."

Dave Smeeth, a career sergeant, raises an eyebrow. "What's that got to do with the price of fish?"

Sherry smiles. “Good question, Dave. If I tell you that Nick Masterson was a Type 1 diabetic, it’ll make more sense. He was insulin dependent, apparently. Gail alleged that he was unable to manage his condition effectively while in police custody, and he was on the verge of a hypo when he came home. That put him at risk of unconsciousness and death. She suggested that’s what happened while she was out. But the evidence so far paints a different picture. I doubt that City need to worry about a lawsuit. We should be mindful of the possibility, of course.”

Sherry stops talking. The incident room’s stuffy air, fragrant with polish and coffee, is nearly silent. All Neil can hear is Sherry’s gel-tipped fingers clattering on her laptop.

Colour explodes across the whitewashed wall that serves as a projector screen. This is Bristol’s Bridewell police station, after all: every expense spared.

“Here we are,” Sherry says. “The property where the body was found.”

It’s a stunning detached stone house, probably of the same vintage as Neil’s cottage, but much grander.

“That’s Clifton,” Detective Constable Brittany Billinge giggles nervously. “I looked at a flat around the corner. Couldn’t afford it.”

“Not even when you worked in insurance, Britt?” Sherry teases.

“No, it was afterwards, when I’d joined the force.”

“You were right about the location,” Sherry says. “7, Harefield Road, Clifton. One of the best addresses in Bristol. Masterson and Smyth were located in the study. Watch the video.”

She clicks on an arrow. The camera pans across a handsomely appointed office, zooming in on a man slumped in a sinuous-shaped swivel chair.

“Jonathan Smyth,” Sherry says.

The view moves on to the body lying on the plush carpet.

“Nick Masterson.”

There is more footage taken later, once Smyth and Masterson have been removed from the scene and the CSIs have carried out an inspection. Sherry points out bloodstains and the position of a pair of empty insulin pens. Interestingly, the CSIs found them on the floor. They’re of the same type as others stocked, pre-filled, in a fridge nearby. The serial numbers aren’t sequential, but perhaps the pharmacy dispensed the drug from different batches.

Sherry emphasises that insulin will make a hypo worse. So much for Gail Masterson's assertion that police neglect was responsible. In any event, judging by the empty plate on the desk, her husband finished the meal she prepared for him.

They'll have to prove he ate the sandwich, of course. The autopsy will tell them, as well as confirming the cause of death. Although Sherry is still waiting for the results, the pathologist has flagged two round bruises on the deceased's right arm. They're the kind of marks an injection would make if you pressed a needle into the muscle. That delivers insulin faster than injecting fatty tissue, as diabetics usually would.

"Any prints on the pens?" Dave asks.

"Yes, but not Masterson's," Sherry says. "No suicide note either. It's possible he took his own life, as City are confident of a conviction, but murder is the most likely explanation. Especially as the pathologist also noted trauma to his kneecaps. As in, broken bones."

"More than simple fisticuffs," Dave says. "Did I spot some sporting memorabilia on the shelves? Those trinkets can be seriously heavy."

"Could be, but I'd keep an open mind. The CSIs are checking them over. Let's agree on our next steps. Dave, can you contact the GP and confirm he was a diabetic? Ask if he had brittle bones too. His wife says not, but there's no harm in asking."

"On it."

"Neil, I'd like you to interview Gail Masterson. She hasn't been advised of the extent of her husband's injuries, or that he appeared to have injected. Try to find out if she knows. See what she says about her husband's mood, the state of their marriage, his friendship with Smyth. His usual routine for injecting insulin. Does he jab his right arm, or somewhere else?"

Neil gives her the thumbs up.

"She might lie about that if she did it," Britt says. "Gave him the overdose, I mean."

"We should explore all avenues," Sherry agrees. "Neil, take Britt with you. Her first case, so you'll have to do all the talking."

"Are you sure?" From Neil's limited observation of Britt, you can't get her to shut up.

Sherry grins. "Tact is your watchword, no?"

# CHAPTER 27 GAIL

## Day 5 - Friday

"Would you like a cup of tea, dear?" Maggie appears, holding a tray laden with cups, teapot, milk jug, sugar bowl and a plate of buttered scones.

My mouth waters. Unusually, I haven't been oblivious to the baking smells drifting through the room for the last half hour. "Well…"

"I'll take that as a yes," Maggie says.

It's a mercy that I have good neighbours. As soon as the ambulance arrived yesterday, Peregrine was round, demanding to know how he could help. I allowed him to shepherd the kids back to his home right away. Maggie had returned by then, and I figured she'd care for them better than I could.

After the police had interviewed me, I followed. We stayed overnight. Our house is out of bounds: a crime scene, gates taped like a bizarre birthday gift, a PCSO stationed outside.

Maggie sets the tray down on a coffee table in front of the rocking chair where I'm sitting, a crocheted cushion at my back. She pours out three cups. Without asking, she adds milk and sugar to mine, and hands it to me on a saucer.

None of the crockery matches. It's odd what you notice when your mind drifts, searching for a haven to avoid jagged rocks. I stare at the spots, stripes and flowery swirls. The different shapes and pastel shades somehow harmonise with each other.

"I think you could use some sugar," she says, "to give you energy. I keep it for Perry — you know what a sweet tooth he has. Don't touch it myself, of course."

I blink, half-remembering. Has she mentioned that before? "You don't? Nick didn't either. Except when he was low..."

Tears well up.

Maggie passes me a tissue. "There, there, dear. I know. I'm diabetic too, though the other sort. Too many cakes, so here we are. Now, you must have a scone. The children made them."

"They've been so quiet. I ought to check—"

Maggie holds up her hand. "They're fine. Watching cartoons in our little TV nook in the kitchen. Laughter is the best medicine."

I sip the tea, drawing a grain of comfort from its warm sweetness. Putting it down, I pick up a scone. The first buttery bite is delicious. With a pang, I'm waylaid by a childhood memory of tucking into birthday cake. I used to enjoy food. But I've been afraid of it for so long.

I find myself sniffing.

Maggie is ready with more tissues, bless her. "Gail, dear. It will be all right, you'll see. Would you like some alone time?"

Dabbing at my eyes, I nod.

"Well, I'm in the kitchen if you want me. Take another scone. You've eaten nothing since you came through the door. Mary and Tom on the other hand… Well, they have big appetites."

"I'm sorry they gobbled all Peregrine's biscuits."

"Perry doesn't mind. They need spoiling, don't they? You were right to keep them off school."

She bustles off, a small, round woman in a hand-knitted crimson shawl. Mary called her Red Riding Hood's grandma this morning, and I can see why.

It was hard breaking the news to Tom and Mary. I waited until Maggie had given them supper, then told them that Daddy was with the angels. There had been a fight, and Daddy was very brave.

I didn't tell them Daddy lost the fight while his opponent survived. I hope Nick inflicted enough damage to make Jonathan's life hell from now on. Because that's what he deserves.

While I don't know exactly how Nick died, I can be sure Jonathan was responsible. No-one else was there, were they? My guess is that Jonathan attacked Nick, causing my husband to fight back. Using up every scrap of blood sugar. Falling unconscious. Dying.

How I wish I hadn't admitted to Jonathan that Nick hit me. But how could I predict my husband's friend would react so violently?

The kids sobbed their hearts out while I hugged them, guilty for bringing pain, wishing I could kiss their problems better. They didn't want to be left alone. I tucked them both into the double bed in Maggie's spare room. Then I climbed in with them. I stroked their silky hair, listened as their wails turned into the slow breath of night. Limbs entwined, somehow we all slept until morning. Then Maggie, already up and about, made them toast and jam for breakfast.

It's a novel experience to be looked after. My family are doers rather than carers; I was expected to make myself useful since the minute I could walk. My marriage followed the same pattern. Yet Maggie and Peregrine have shown unbelievable kindness.

I must have dropped off, because I'm suddenly woken by an awkward cough. Peregrine stands in front of the coffee table, one hand poised over the plate of scones.

"I'm sorry," he says, stretching back upright. "Maggie told me not to make a sound. Erm, she mentioned she'd been baking, and after all my gardening—"

Maggie returns, flashing him a warning look. "How are you, dear?" she asks me.

I grimace, speechless, because I can't wring out an answer. My overwhelming emotion is confusion.

I should miss Nick, but I don't. Not really. The need to please him was like a giant weight pressing on my mind. At first, I complied with his every wish because I loved him. But a darker impetus replaced my adoration.

Fear.

In an awful way, Jonathan's done me a favour. I could never bring myself to feel grateful, though. My kids have lost their father.

The doorbell rings, jolting me. It sounds exactly the same as my own.

"Who would that be?" Peregrine asks.

"Journalists." Maggie's tone resounds with disdain, as if talking about rats.

"I'll give them their marching orders," Peregrine offers. However, he returns accompanied by a young man and woman. Smartly dressed, he in a charcoal Harrington and chinos and she in a black trouser suit, they have a professional air about them.

"Perry, I thought—" Maggie says.

Peregrine puts a finger to his lips. "Detective Sergeant Neil Slater and Detective Constable Brittany Billinge," he says. "To see Gail."

Of course, detectives don't wear police uniform, do they? I can't help reaching for my cheek, subconsciously trying to cover the bruise. Then I recall that I piled on makeup earlier. Still, anxiety makes my legs wobble when I stand up to shake their hands.

Neil Slater stoops down to my level. His grip is firm. Dwarfing me even more than most men, his tall, broad physique reminds me of my husband when we first met. Despite his size, Nick came across as sweet and respectful.

I was an idiot to fall for the act.

"I'm sorry for your loss," Neil Slater says, and his grey eyes suggest he means it.

Petite Brittany Billinge seems altogether less engaged. She says nothing as she offers a limp handshake. Her face, framed by dark hair scraped back in a bun, is unreadable. I'm relieved when her colleague explains she's with him to take notes. He just has a few questions.

"I'll help in any way I can," I promise.

He catches Maggie's eye. "Is there somewhere that Gail can speak privately with us?"

"Stay put," Maggie commands. "Perry and I will make ourselves scarce. Shall I bring some refreshments? Scones?"

"Yes please," Neil Slater says. "That okay with you, Britt? Worth breaking your diet for."

A slight dip of her chin is the only response he gets. The junior officer sits on the sofa, placing a laptop on the coffee table as Maggie clears away crockery. When fresh tea and scones have been brought, Peregrine retreats to his garden and Maggie to the kitchen.

Neil Slater installs himself beside his colleague. "Now Britt's going to take notes, but we'll record the interview as well. Is that okay?"

"Absolutely." I'll do whatever I can to help them hold Jonathan accountable.

"Start by telling me what happened."

I give an edited version of events. Jonathan arrived as I left for the school run. At that point, my husband appeared in good health, apart from having low blood sugar. It was when I last saw him alive. I returned to find Nick dead, and his friend beaten up.

The police don't need to know that I fled from my husband in fear for my life, although I mention that Nick's behaviour was erratic. He was definitely on the edge of a hypo.

"If I understand right, Type 1 diabetes is a lifelong condition," Neil Slater says. "Can you describe what your husband did to manage it?"

"It's all about keeping blood sugar stable. He had to inject insulin. A hypo occurs if your blood glucose falls below a safe level. For instance, if you don't eat enough carbs afterwards, or over-exert yourself. Or get stressed. And Nick was very stressed, I'm afraid. He'd spent the night at a police station—"

"And can you also get a hypo if you inject too much insulin?"

"Yes, but Nick wouldn't…" My words dry up. I gawp at the detective. Nick was careful. He wouldn't have overdosed by accident. And I can't imagine him doing it on purpose. He was much too wrapped up in himself to take his own life. But surely that's what the detective is implying?

Things would have had to get very bad for Nick to commit suicide.

Maybe they had. Suppose the police were right about the fraud? And Tamara wasn't lying about the baby? My head swims with unwelcome questions.

There's no respite, either.

"Talk me through his usual routine with insulin," Neil Slater asks.

"He has pre-filled pens."

"Not a pump?" Brittany Billinge butts in.

"He doesn't… didn't like wearing one."

Pumps are convenient, because they constantly monitor blood sugar and deliver exactly the right dose of insulin. But you have to keep the pump hooked up to your torso all the time, and Nick wasn't keen on that. I'm beginning to suspect why, too. It would have cramped his style with the likes of Tamara.

Was she the only one? I shudder, already fathoming the answer.

"How would he use an insulin pen?" Neil Slater asks. "Go through the process."

"He'd click it to set the dose. Then he'd add a needle, and jab himself."

"Where?"

"Anywhere. If he's in Bristol with us … was in Bristol, then in the study."

From the detective's blank expression, I sense he expected a different answer. The penny drops. "In his thigh," I add. "Fatty tissue is best — it's the most effective way of getting insulin into the bloodstream. It doesn't hurt so much either."

"Where did he keep the pens, Gail?" Neil Slater asks.

"There's a fridge in his study here." I point in the direction of my home. "And others at his workplace and the flat in London."

"And did Nick inject from any of the pens just before you left for the school?"

I shake my head. "No. He needed sugar, not insulin. That's why I gave him a banana and some sweets…"

“I see,” Neil Slater says. “My colleagues found empty insulin pens near your husband’s body. Know anything about those?”

Open-mouthed and light-headed, I sink back into the chair. It doesn’t add up, unless Nick intended to end his life. But I don’t want to believe that.

Neil Slater waits.

The silence lengthens.

My mind has gone blank. Finally, I clutch at an alternative explanation.

“I didn’t see them,” I say, “but the police — your colleague, Ruth Cluff — did a search. I hadn’t finished tidying up. So maybe that’s why the pens were there.”

Neil Slater wrinkles his brow. “Okay, we’ll ask her. Now, can you tell me more about the other man who was present at the scene? You called him Jonathan. How do you know him?”

“He’s a friend of Nick’s. From school.”

“How often did they see each other?”

It’s a good question. “Rarely. Only at old boys’ events. I wondered myself why Jonathan visited yesterday. It wasn’t to see me—”

He raises an eyebrow.

“—because I’d done some design work for him, but that had finished.”

Jonathan’s arrival was a stroke of luck for me, though. It distracted Nick and enabled me to get away. I reiterate that Jonathan rang the doorbell just as I was going to the school, so I didn’t have time to quiz him.

What I really want to know is whether the police can bring charges against Jonathan for causing my husband’s death. It’s his fault that Nick’s blood sugar dived through the floor, and Jonathan would have been aware of his condition. They’d shared a bedroom at school. But Neil Slater brushes me off by muttering that they have a number of lines of enquiry. He changes the subject to my marriage.

Again, I edit the truth.

I tell him that Nick was six years older, and we were introduced by his cousin, my flatmate at college. We married shortly after I graduated and were blissfully happy.

Nick's controlling tendencies and Tamara's recent phone call aren't relevant to his death. And if I mention them, Neil Slater might suspect me of playing a part in it.

There's no point wasting his time like that.

The detective sergeant gets to his feet. "Well, thank you, Gail."

I hold in a sigh of relief.

"We'll be in touch when we have news," Neil Slater says. "And we'll send someone round to take your fingerprints."

My heart starts thumping.

"It's for elimination," he says. "The forensic team will have found prints all over the house, and many of them will be yours. And your children's. So they'll have to be fingerprinted too, I'm afraid. You can be with them when it's done, maybe make a bit of a game out of it."

I stare at him. Whatever he says, however smooth he is, Neil Slater must be wondering if I'm guilty. And the only person who can prove I'm not is the real culprit. Jonathan.

# CHAPTER 28 NEIL

## Day 5 - Friday

Neil notices that Gail has paled. Strange. Still, the poor woman has just lost her husband. He recalls Sherry's constant refrain when he was new to CID: 'Where's your empathy, Neil?'

"I really appreciate your help," he says to Gail. "And I'm sorry the forensic work is such an upheaval for you. There are a couple of reporters hanging around outside, too. Do you have anywhere else you can go for a while?"

Her lips tighten. "No. I can't afford a hotel."

He wonders why. This type of property speaks for itself: the residents can't be short of money. Then he recalls the ongoing fraud inquiry. Her husband's bank account would have been frozen, and probably hers too.

"We'll do our best to finish up, so you can go back home. Are your neighbours happy to put you up for another night?"

That raises a half-smile, and he's suddenly struck by her prettiness beneath the smudged make-up. Nick Masterson's trophy wife, no doubt. If they met when she was a student, the six-year age gap would have been more marked at the time.

"My neighbours are great," Gail says. "Luckily. Yes, I'm sure they'll let us stay. I think they love having the kids around. They even dug out old toys from the loft."

"Well, I'm glad you're sorted for now. I'll talk to my colleagues later and give you an update. Meanwhile, I'd like a word with your neighbour before I leave. Mr Jukes, isn't it? I believe he's in the front garden."

Gail's eyes widen. Her lips twitch. Is she afraid of what Peregrine Jukes will say?

Peregrine and his wife, Margaret, gave brief statements yesterday. Margaret claims she was out all afternoon. But her husband was around. He thinks Nick Masterson and Jonathan Smyth had a fight.

Neil is keen to discuss that with Peregrine. He shakes Gail's hand again, wishes her well and says he and Britt will see themselves out.

Peregrine is tying back a vigorous shrub that has spread along the wall between the properties and is trying to invade Gail's plot. Neil recognises the fragrant lilac blooms as wisteria, which climbs his cottage's porch. It flowered early this year, and is making a determined effort to reach the roof.

"Fast grower, isn't it?" he says, as Peregrine ties string to a gnarled branch.

Peregrine jumps. "I do beg your pardon, lad, you startled me. How's young Gail? A terrible thing to have happened."

Neil agrees that it is, in fact, terrible. "Is there somewhere we can speak without being overheard?" he asks.

Peregrine glances at the sitting room window. "Hmm. There's my shed," he suggests. "Plenty big enough for three."

Neil prepares his excuses in advance. He rarely fits into a shed all by himself. When he and Gemma bought a flatpack, they chose an extra-tall model.

Gesturing for the detectives to follow, Peregrine shuffles to the side of the house, where a narrow alley stretches beyond a high gate. He unlocks it.

"Come on through." He points to a structure at the foot of the back garden.

Neil can't make it out very well. The plot is lush with tall shrubs, some of which he can name and many he can't. A flagged path meanders through the greenery. He passes a pond, a line of rose bushes and a strawberry patch before they reach the shed. His doubts dissolve. This is not the kind he owns, a spider-infested cupboard for his lawnmower. It is a full-size room, boasting spotlessly clean picture windows and a green roof.

Within, no spiders are in sight. The space is dominated by a large rag rug overlooked by a squishy sofa. Tools have been banished to a corner screened off with trellis. To one side, a crate of beer bottles lies in the shade of a worktable.

Britt's eyes dart around. "This isn't a shed," she says. "It's a den."

"I like to think so," Peregrine agrees. "How about a craft beer? Take joy in this world where you can."

"Unfortunately, we can't drink on duty," Neil says, with a degree of regret.

"If it's all the same to you, I'm having one for medicinal purposes," Peregrine says, cracking open a bottle of Bath Gem. "I get these headaches, see, and painkillers don't touch the sides."

Britt nudges Neil and shows him her phone. Jonathan Smyth has regained consciousness and is asking to speak to police.

"We'll have to get over there," Neil tells her. He assures Peregrine that they won't keep him long. They just want to go over a few questions.

"Fire away." Peregrine perches on the worktable and points to the sofa. "Take a pew."

Neil warms him up with a couple of background queries. The Jukeses have lived in the house for forty years, having purchased it when Clifton was not trendy at all. They were teachers with a gift for DIY, which was just as well when they had a wreck to do up. Neil feels a burst of solidarity at this news.

The area has gentrified since, hence the arrival of the Masterson family when Nick was a schoolboy. They kept themselves to themselves. The father seemed ill-tempered, but he worked away and was easy to avoid. Nick and his younger sister were packed off to boarding school. Nick became a student before following his father to London, while the girl fled abroad to live on a kibbutz. Then Nick's father was killed in an air crash.

"Maggie always liked the mother, Trish, but she'd become forgetful. Two sandwiches short of a picnic," Peregrine says darkly. "We couldn't see how she'd cope. It was a relief when Gail moved in with her."

Gail became the older woman's carer until Trish went into a home. Peregrine doesn't have a bad word to say about Gail, but is less admiring of Nick. He hints that Gail is better off without her husband. Have the detectives noticed the bruise on Gail's face? The Jukeses think Nick hit her. Jonathan Smyth accused him of it yesterday.

Neil silently curses his lack of observation skills. All he saw was a beautiful woman wearing a lot of makeup. From the way Britt has shifted bolt upright, he suspects she didn't spot anything either.

"Talk me through Jonathan Smyth's arrival," Neil says.

"I was gardening," Peregrine begins. "Digging out the bindweed in the front. You can't get rid of it, no matter—"

"My wife says the same," Neil interrupts. "And when did you see Jonathan Smyth?"

"Around three o'clock," Peregrine says. "I think. Yes, because Maggie had been gone for about an hour. There was an altercation between my neighbours and Mr Smyth. They were all stood on the doorstep. I didn't know his name then, of course."

“What kind of altercation?”

“Oh dear, I can’t quite remember exactly what was said. But Mr Smyth was hugging Gail, and saying Nick must have hurt her. And Nick accused the pair of them of having an affair.”

A shiver passes through Neil’s body. He struggles to keep his expression neutral, glad Britt has managed it. This could be huge. It gives both Jonathan and Gail a motive for murder.

Peregrine leans forward, almost toppling off the table. He whispers, “I wouldn’t be surprised if it was true.”

“Why?” Neil asks.

“Because Mr Smyth told me they were lovers.”

# CHAPTER 29 JONATHAN

## Day 5 - Friday

The friendly older nurse bustles in. Jonathan recognises her manner, but not her face. It was blurry before. Now he can focus, he sees the bags under her kind eyes, the cornrows of bleached hair against her scalp.

She looks askance at his untouched sandwich. “Not hungry?”

He shakes his head, then wishes he hadn’t. Pain pulsates through his temples. His stomach gurgles, but he can’t face food. He feels sick, recognising it as an effect of concussion. It wasn’t the first time Nick knocked him out, and Jonathan doubts it will be the last.

The nurse tuts. “You want to be careful, young man. Here, can you manage a sip of water?” Picking up the jug left beside his bed, she fills a glass and holds it to his lips.

Jonathan takes the vessel with trembling hands. His throat is parched, and he swigs the liquid greedily. “Thanks, Sue,” he says, reading her name badge.

“You’re welcome. Anything you need, just ask. I shouldn’t say this, but that Nick Masterson was a piece of trash. My daughter’s lost her house deposit. I hope you hit him in the goolies.”

Jonathan doesn’t think so. He can’t remember.

“Listen, there’s a couple of police officers here to see you.” She gives him a piercing stare. “The ward sister said you asked for them. Is that correct?”

“Yes.” Jonathan now knows better than to nod.

“Hmm. Well, be careful. I’ll show them in.”

She marches out, returning with a man and a woman. They’re an odd couple; he appears to be twice her size.

“You’re police?” Jonathan asks, surprised they’re not in uniform.

“Detectives,” Sue says. “I’ve checked their warrant cards.”

“You can leave us to it, Sue,” the woman says.

“I’ll be back in fifteen minutes,” Sue warns her. “You’re not to wear him out.”

“We should introduce ourselves.” The man holds out his hand. “Detective Sergeant Neil Slater.”

“Detective Constable Brittany Billinge,” his colleague says. Her eyes sweep the room for what seems an inordinate length of time. There’s nothing remarkable about the plasticky furniture, plain cream paint, and lino reaching halfway up the walls. It's a standard institutional environment.

"Glad they found you somewhere private," she adds. "I was afraid you'd be on the ward, where they're packed in like sardines."

Jonathan supposes the hospital expected a police visit. He inches his body upwards, carefully, so he's sitting up straight. "Have you arrested him?" he demands.

"Who?" Slater asks.

Jonathan's headache returns. Are these people crazy? It's an open and shut case. What's stopping them? "Nick Masterson, of course," he says. "He attacked me."

The two detectives exchange glances. "No, we haven't arrested him," Slater says. "We're keen to get your account of events."

"Fair enough," Jonathan says, his irritation lessening. He guesses they have procedures to follow. It's not as if they don't know where Nick Masterson lives.

"I'll go through a few questions, and Britt will take notes," Slater says. He manoeuvres an easy chair to face Jonathan, and sits down. The seat's vinyl covering squeaks under his bulk.

The detective constable draws up a moulded plastic visitor's chair and balances a laptop on her knees. She smiles brightly at Jonathan.

He must look like an extra from a zombie movie. His crown is swathed in bandages, his face swollen and tender.

"Let's start at the beginning," Slater says. "When did you first meet Nick Masterson?"

"At Markham's, when we were both eleven. It's a boarding school. Unlike Nick, I wasn't rich. I got in on a scholarship." Jonathan feels the urge to explain he isn't from a monied background, even though the detectives show no sign of caring.

"And how did you get on with Nick Masterson at school?"

"I hated his guts."

A spark of interest lights in Slater's eyes. "Why was that?"

"Nick Masterson is a bully. He made my life a misery." Jonathan is determined to tell it like it is. He'll leave the detectives in no doubt about Nick's evil, selfish nature.

"His wife says you're friends," Slater says, "so what changed?"

The throbbing in his head threatens to overwhelm him. “Nothing changed,” Jonathan says. “She’s wrong.”

Slater leans forward. “Why did you visit Nick Masterson yesterday?”

Jonathan intends a hollow laugh, but it emerges as a rasping cough from his dry throat. “I run a company, and Nick has ripped us off,” he says. “I decided to have it out with him.”

“You were planning a fight?”

“No.” Jonathan makes no attempt to hide his outrage. “Of course not. I expected to be able to defend myself, though. He picked on me at school because I was small and weak. I’m fitter now. I work out. So, when he came charging out of his front door, my first thought was to dodge him. Which I did.”

“Talk me through what happened, from the moment you arrived at the premises.”

“Okay.” Jonathan takes a deep breath. “I parked on the road. Walked up to the house, Rang the doorbell. The next thing I knew, Gail had raced out and flung herself into my arms.”

He remembers her spicy perfume. The terror in her eyes. Bruises on her face. “He’d been beating her up. I challenged him. He accused me of sleeping with her.”

“He? That would be Nick Masterson?”

“Yes. He followed her out.”

“And then?”

“She ran away. I told her to call you.” Jonathan pauses. “She did, didn’t she?”

“We have no record of it,” Slater says. “But Mrs Masterson did call the emergency services later, when she discovered you unconscious.”

“Whoa. That was brave.” Jonathan instinctively jerks his head back, causing another surge of pain. Gail was a fool to return to Nick’s lair. Still, who knows what would have become of him otherwise?

Slater doesn’t react, except to ask how the debate between the two men played out once Gail had left.

“Nick tried to punch me. I sidestepped him, assured him I wasn’t involved with his wife.” Jonathan grimaces. “It was all about money, not love. He calmed down. Offered me a drink.”

“You accepted?”

Jonathan begins to nod, a twinge causing him to think better of it. "Yes," he says. "He'd got the wrong end of the stick, and he realised that. Or so I thought. He was civil. Pleasant, even."

He should have known it was that public school polish, shouldn't he? Jonathan closes his puffy eyes.

"But I made a big mistake. Nick waited until I was settled in a chair, then he attacked me again. He had the element of surprise. I was trapped. Pinned down. He kept hitting me. I thought I was going to die."

The atmosphere stills. Slater's sidekick, whose name Jonathan has forgotten, stops typing. She stares at Jonathan.

"How did you defend yourself?" Slater asks.

Jonathan clenches his jaw, recalling how quickly Nick overpowered him. "There was nothing I could do. I was helpless."

"You didn't reach for a weapon?"

"Can't you understand?" Jonathan yells in frustration. "I was at his mercy. Unable to move. Then I blacked out."

The door opens, and Nurse Sue appears, scowling. "You've had long enough."

Slater holds up two fingers. "Just a couple of minutes, please."

"It's okay," Jonathan tells her.

She glares at the detective sergeant, and slams the door behind her.

"Can you remember what you were drinking?" Slater asks.

"Why does it matter?" Jonathan says. But perhaps they think Nick roofied him. He may as well answer. "IPA, actually."

"Did you see where it came from?"

Jonathan is worried now. No wonder he lost consciousness. What did Nick Masterson do to him once he was under? Mouth dry, he helps himself to more water. Collecting his thoughts, he recalls Nick never went near the beer.

"I took it from his mini fridge," he says. "Nick couldn't have predicted I'd do that. He offered me whisky."

"The fridge in his office? What was in it?"

Jonathan pulls a face. Where are these questions going? "Beer. Insulin. Nick is a diabetic. He has to inject it."

"So I understand," Slater says. "Did you see him inject himself while you were there?"

"No."

"Did you inject him?" Slater peers at Jonathan.

"No. Why would I?" His tone reflects his increasing puzzlement; it's sharper than he intended.

"Was Nick Masterson right? Had you been sleeping with his wife?"

"No way." Jonathan bristles. "I'm… I was happily married. What day is this, again?"

"Friday."

"My wife died two days ago."

"I'm sorry to hear that," Slater says.

"I don't suppose he told you." Jonathan belatedly realises that Nick may not have known.

"I wasn't aware, no," Slater says.

Jonathan's head seethes with agony.. "Do we really need to carry on with this? Surely you know enough by now to charge Nick with assault?"

Slater folds his arms. "That will be difficult. Because Nick Masterson is dead."

# CHAPTER 30 GAIL

## Day 5 - Friday

The doorbell rings, and we both jump up to answer it. I trail after Maggie because I'm hoping that it will be Ruth Cluff with my phone. Even better, perhaps it's one of the forensics officers, suited up like the Ku Klux Klan. I can't wait for them to finish combing through my house.

I'm wrong on both counts. DS Neil Slater and DC Brittany Billinge stand on the step, sharing an umbrella against a sudden downpour.

"May we come in?" Neil Slater asks. "We have more information for Gail."

"You only left two hours ago," Maggie says. "What's changed?"

"We need to discuss it privately with Gail, if you don't mind."

Maggie directs me back to the sitting room with the detectives. Head swimming, I sit opposite them, the empty coffee table between us. "What did you want to tell me?"

"Jonathan Smyth has regained consciousness," Neil Slater replies. He pauses, as if waiting for a reply.

Dumbstruck, I stare at him. As far as I'm concerned, Jonathan Smyth could have remained in a vegetative state for the rest of his life.

Brittany Billinge eventually fills the silence. "We have more questions too," she says.

"I guessed. You've got your laptop out."

"Yes, same drill as before. I'll do the talking," Neil Slater says. "Ready to take notes, Britt?"

My gaze switches to the DC, catching her looking in my direction. It doesn't calm my tension. The duo remind me of two cats playing with a mouse.

Neil Slater squints at my cheek. "How did you get that bruise?"

I gawp at him. How come he's noticed? I've covered it up so carefully: primer, concealer, foundation, powder — the works. Although there's no need to defend Nick now he's gone, the standard lie trips off my tongue. "I walked into a door."

"Has this happened before?"

"Maybe?" My fingers tingle some more. Why am I gripped by guilt, when I'm the victim?

I bite my lip, standing on the brink of memories I can't bear to dive into. "You know, I don't think it has happened before," I say.

Neil Slater rewards me with a brief nod. "Can you tell us about your relationship with Jonathan Smyth?" he asks.

"My what?" I wonder if I've heard him correctly. "It's strictly business."

His shoulders visibly stiffen. "Meaning?"

"As I told you," I had mentioned it, hadn't I? "Jonathan paid me for an interior design project."

"Have you got proof you can show us? Invoices, et cetera?"

Without meaning to, I yawn. Their visit is both draining me and setting me on edge. "I'd help if I could, but your Ruth Cluff has my laptop. Why don't you ask her?"

"Thanks. We will. Now, I appreciate this is a sensitive subject, but have you ever had a closer relationship with Jonathan? A romance, or fling, even?"

My heart skips a beat. I start to tremble, and I can't even tell if it's caused by shock or anger. "Definitely not."

Has Peregrine repeated the ridiculous lie, or did Jonathan tell them himself? If Nick's schoolfriend stood before me now, I'd cheerfully kill him and spit on his grave. But I'd better not admit that to the police.

# CHAPTER 31 NEIL

## Day 8 - Monday

Neil takes a seat in the incident room and stretches out, yawning.

Sherry looks up from her laptop. "Hard weekend? Ah, don't answer. I know you were working."

"Gemma wasn't impressed. I did two night of gardening to win brownie points. Lucky the clocks have gone forward."

"Well, hopefully I can share some good news. Give the others five minutes to get here, and all will be revealed."

That sounds encouraging. Neil's spirits lift further when Britt sprints in with two takeaway coffee cups from his new favourite café. She's introduced him to it, an independent business near the hospital. They do a key worker discount. He and Britt are now in a daily round situation. She's shaping up well as a detective.

Pulling up one of the ubiquitous plastic chairs, Britt sits next to him. She hands him a cup. "There you go. The one with the third shot."

"I'm a good trainer, if I say so myself."

The others filter into the room: porky Dave Smeeth, stern-faced IT guru Lionel Balogun and forensic manager Amy Tarr. Young Ruth Cluff, a uniformed sergeant, has been volunteered as Family Liaison Officer. She built a rapport with Gail Masterson during the fraud investigation.

Sherry is junior for a Senior Investigating Officer, but you wouldn't know it from her confident stance. She starts the briefing by asking everyone to give updates. Dave is the sole exception: he's the briefing scribe, assigned to take notes and allocate actions and deadlines. His laptop is hooked up to the task manager in HOLMES, and he's already tapping away.

"All the deceased's devices have been checked for evidence of suicidal ideation," Lionel begins, his voice a monotonous drone. Neil reckons he's reading from a memorised script. "The City of London Police already have downloads, so that was an easy job. No evidence was found."

He pauses. Sherry seems about to speak, closing her mouth abruptly when he continues.

"Again, we had downloads of Gail Masterson's iPhone, iPad and MacBook already."

"You're welcome," Ruth murmurs.

"Er, thanks to Ruth," Lionel says. "No evidence of an inappropriate relationship was found. Gail Masterson has indeed been invoicing Jonathan Smyth for interior design work.

"However, what is interesting," his voice rises a notch or two, "is that Nick Masterson appears to have had an affair with an employee called Tamara Kaczmarek."

"We know—" Neil jumps in.

"Have you finished, Lionel?" Sherry interjects. "Yes? Okay, Neil."

"Tamara Kaczmarek was already in touch with City," Neil says. "She went to them to blow the whistle on Masterson's Ponzi scheme. They were happy to interview her for us. The notes should be in the system…"

"Are they, Dave?" Sherry asks.

He nods.

"Carry on, Neil."

"I'll let Britt have her moment. She puts it better than me."

Britt smirks. "She was his PA, and Masterson decided he wanted a very personal service. It was all hearts and flowers, him love-bombing her, until she told him she was pregnant. He fired her on the spot. She lost her home as well as her job…"

"A motive for murder?" Sherry asks.

"Arguably not," Britt says. "She claims she would have sued for child support, and Masterson's death complicates that. Anyway, she told City she'd never been to Bristol."

"She must have known he was a diabetic if they were that close," Sherry says. "What's her alibi for last Thursday?"

"She spent the day looking for another job."

"We could ask City to check that out. But let's hang fire for the moment. Dave, can you minute it?"

Dave sticks a thumb up.

"Anything else, Neil?" Sherry asks.

"Yes, Jonathan Smyth has been released from hospital. I asked him to let us know if he plans to travel outside the area. His answer isn't fit for your ears."

"Try me."

"The gist is that chance would be a fine thing."

"Still battered and bruised?"

"Yes. Also, his business is in trouble, and he blames Masterson."

"He's probably not wrong." Sherry sighs. "Ruth, what have you got for us?"

"Gail and her children are back home, and happy about it. Their devices have been returned. The kids are thrilled to get their computer games back."

"Nice to see satisfied customers," Sherry says. "Any more from Gail about her injury?"

"Still claims she walked into a door," Ruth replies.

Sherry purses her lips. "I see. Like Jonathan Smyth did?"

The room is silent.

"We'll move on," Sherry says. "Amy?"

The forensic manager smiles. "We identified a school rugby cup as the weapon that smashed Mr Masterson's kneecaps. As Dave said, those items can be heavy. This one had a solid metal base, and the fibres on that matched the deceased's trousers. We also paid particular attention to the empty insulin pens. Traces of fibres and soil were found. And a thumbprint, which we've now identified as Jonathan Smyth's."

"Hmm, only one print?" Sherry asks.

"Maybe he held the pen with a cloth, and it slipped?" Britt suggests.

Amy rewards her with a smile. "There are many possible reasons, but luckily, that particular print is very clear."

"I've also had word back from Flax Bourton on the post mortem," Sherry says. "Nick Masterson definitely died from an insulin overdose, and it was a big one. High insulin levels in the blood and no C-peptide, which proves it, I'm told. He'd have been rendered unconscious quickly. But not instantly. Had his knees been intact, he may have been able to get help."

She waits, no doubt to let the implications sink in. Sherry isn't above using dramatic licence.

"Neil, can you bring Jonathan in?" Sherry says.

# CHAPTER 32 JONATHAN

## Day 8 - Monday

Jonathan yawns. While exhaustion sent him soundly to sleep last night, his body is still recovering. The hospital advised him to rest. But that won't save his business.

"I'll get more coffee." Stan jumps up, collects both their mugs, and heads out of Jonathan's office.

They've been working all morning, poring over legal documents for their new supply contract and punching numbers into spreadsheets. Jonathan hasn't learned anything new. The outlook is bleak. If Gill Spices reneges on the deal, penalty clauses will wipe out the company. Yet they can't fulfil the requirements unless they expand the factory, and the money to do it isn't there. They can't raise more funds. The premises are mortgaged to the hilt, and so is Jonathan's flat, which is in the hands of Tilly's executors anyhow.

They're sunk.

Unless…

When Stan returns with strong caffeine, Jonathan says, "We have to squeeze more capacity from the existing kit."

Stan utters a short, barking laugh. "Can't be done," he says. "It's why we pressed ahead with the expansion."

"I get it." Jonathan tries to ignore the tension rising in his neck and jaw, the temptation to make a cheap jibe. He holds back because Stan is suffering too: no longer the urbane silver fox, his eyes sport the hunted air of a prey animal. Stan probably expected to be fired by now. Indeed, the CFO's presence winds Jonathan up. However, the company is more likely to survive with Stan on board. Stan understands the industry and has a grip on all the detail. He's not an operations man, though. They need the plant engineer.

Jonathan picks up his phone. "We'll brainstorm with Cam," he says.

"Do we have to?" Stan grumbles. He stares pointedly at his watch. "She won't be in yet."

"It's the twenty-first century. Flexible working is a thing."

Camilla Dyble does school hours only. She's been in since nine thirty. It turns out she's spent half her time hassling Jonathan's PA for a meeting.

“At last,” she exclaims, marching into the office in her uniform of Doc Martens and jeans. Her expression darkens once she spots Stan.

“Jonathan. Tell the bean counter to back off,” she demands, golden hair haloing her face like a lion’s mane.

“What’s up, Cam?” Jonathan asks.

“Nothing. That’s the point. The builders haven’t made it in this week, and when I asked why, they said he stood them down.” She points to Stan.

“Take a seat,” Jonathan says. “We’ll discuss it.” He has to tread carefully. When Camilla discovers they’re in trouble, she’ll be worried about her bonus. She might jump ship. If word gets out, others will follow.

When she’s drawn up a chair opposite him, Jonathan suggests Stan could make her coffee. It produces a scowl from Stan, but the CFO complies.

Once Stan is out of the way, Jonathan briefs her. Without naming Stan as the reason, he explains they’ve run short of cash because they’re caught up in the Masterson scandal.

Camilla is wide-eyed. “The guy who beat you up?” she asks, as Stan returns with the coffee.

So, she’s heard about that.

Jonathan clenches his fists. Everything’s difficult: his health, Tilly’s impending funeral, and the future of the business. For Tilly’s sake and the good of his employees, he must power through.

“It’s a mess,” he says. “Keep this confidential, as we don’t want to alarm our co-workers. Because I’m convinced we’ll turn it round with your help, Cam. We’ll bounce back bigger and stronger than before.”

It’s a convenient lie. He might believe it if he repeats it often enough.

“We need more space. More machines,” Camilla says.

“We all thought so,” Jonathan agrees. “I know you were a hundred per cent honest in your assessment and your business case. And in an ideal world, we’d expand as envisaged. But the money’s not there. Can we work our existing assets smarter? Shuffle our contracts?”

“I’m not sure,” Camilla says. “We’re running two shifts already.”

“Can you squeeze in a third? Plus weekends?”

“That gives no time for maintenance.”

“Any way of doing that quicker?”

"Yes, if you give me extra bodies. Hold on…" Her gaze drifts into the distance. "There are a couple of lads in the factory who are handy when the line goes down. We could give them formal responsibilities. A pay rise. Then there's the old kit we'd planned to scrap. You know, piled up near the loading bay? No space for it, but… let me think."

They spend so long thrashing out possibilities that Stan refills the coffee mugs. Finally, they have the bones of a plan. It's not guaranteed to work, but Jonathan is hopeful.

His PA knocks on the door. "Visitors, Jonathan."

"Who? There's nothing in the diary."

Her eyes dart from Jonathan to his colleagues. "A Neil Slater and a Brittany Billinge. They say it's urgent."

Jonathan frowns. What can they possibly want? He's already had enough of Slater's high-handedness, being threatened with the confiscation of his passport if he so much as books a city break. Not that he's going to.

"Fine. We've finished, anyway." He turns to Stan and Camilla. "That was very useful. Well done, both of you."

"Well done us," Camilla says. When they exit Jonathan's office, she makes small talk with Stan, the frost between them seemingly melted.

He barely has a moment to catch his breath before the detectives are standing in front of him. They're not smiling and he overheard them decline his PA's offer of coffee.

"Good to see you," he lies.

"Jonathan Smyth," Slater says, "I am arresting you on suspicion of the murder of Nicholas Masterson, and taking you into custody for further enquiries. You do not have to say anything—"

"Whoa, wait." Jonathan gawps at the officer, brain struggling to process Slater's words. His tongue feels too thick and heavy to speak.

Slater continues to give the caution. "—but it may harm your defence if you do not mention when questioned something which you later rely on in Court. Anything you do say may be given in evidence."

They cannot be serious. Jonathan's initial shock gives way to anger. Nick Masterson may be dead, but he continues to screw up Jonathan's life. Well, he's not going to let that happen.

"I'm not saying anything," he tells them. "Not without seeing a solicitor, and maybe not even then."

Leaping into the middle class has made him too soft. He'd forgotten the cardinal rule of the estate where he was raised: you face the police with silence. What was he thinking?

The gloves are off now.

# CHAPTER 33 EXTRACT FROM A PREPARED STATEMENT BY JONATHAN SMYTH

I went to school with Nick Masterson. He was a bully then and remained a bully as an adult. He is someone I would normally avoid, and I only visited him because I discovered he had defrauded my company of a substantial sum of money. I wished to discuss how we might recover the funds, unlikely though that prospect might be.

Arriving at his house, I saw his wife bore signs of a violent attack, which she admitted Nick Masterson had carried out. I urged her to call the police. Masterson then tried to hit me. I believed I had calmed him down, and agreed to a drink in his home office. There, he accused me of sleeping with his wife. He battered me senseless. I was hospitalised with concussion.

I have been asked if I hit Nick Masterson with a blunt instrument. I had no opportunity to fight back when he attacked me in his office, and I categorically deny doing so.

I categorically deny sleeping with Nick Masterson's wife.

I categorically deny killing him.

Obviously, I was aware that Nick Masterson was a diabetic. At school, I saw him inject insulin on many occasions. He had to stick a needle onto an insulin pen and measure out a dose. At no time have I assembled the medical equipment for an insulin injection. Nor have I ever given him or anyone else an insulin injection.

I have been informed that Nick Masterson died of an insulin overdose and that my fingerprint – a single one – has been found on one of his insulin pens. I cannot explain that, but nor can I understand the presence of just one print. Handling the pen to deliver an injection would require multiple touches, or so it seemed when I watched Nick do so at school.

If the case against me proceeds, I will be calling medical experts in my defence.

If I discover who has framed me for a crime I did not commit, I will be issuing court proceedings. I will also sue those responsible should I be forced to miss my wife's funeral.

# CHAPTER 34 NEIL

## Day 9 - Tuesday

"We had to let him go," Sherry announces to a collective groan from the team. "He claims he was framed, because there's only one clear print. It's arguable."

Amy, the forensics manager, holds up her hands. "Regrettably, sometimes one clear print is all we get. We also noted fibres, soil, and smudges that indicate further handling of the items, but we can't prove Jonathan Smyth left those traces."

"Any match for the fibres?" Sherry asks.

"Not his clothing. Possibly a jacket of Gail Masterson's, but she says she wasn't wearing it. We found it hanging in a wardrobe."

"It's always the wife," Britt says.

Lionel, the IT specialist, replies. "Statistics would support you if you said it's always the husband. It's far less common the other way round."

Neil feels obliged to be even-handed. "We could be looking at thousands of suspects. All Nick Masterson's investors, for a start."

Britt rolls her eyes. "They weren't lurking in his house, though. Anyone would think you'd been swayed by a pretty face. A bruised one."

"Domestic violence could be a motive," Neil agrees.

"If need be, we can widen our investigation," Sherry says. "But Britt's right. Gail had both motive and opportunity. For now, we should confirm what she was wearing on Thursday. We can ask the neighbours and the school. She doesn't have a Ring doorbell, but other houses on her route will. The school must have CCTV. Ready to allocate actions, Dave?"

He gives her a thumbs up.

# CHAPTER 35 JONATHAN

## Day 10 - Wednesday

Jonathan stumbles through the wood, dewy grass adding shine to his smart black shoes. This is where Tilly will be buried later. Where it will end.

Today is a celebration of Tilly's life. They will play Vivaldi and Mozart in the chapel, its white walls festooned with pink fairy lights. Her cousin, Laurette, is lined up to sing gospel and speak about Tilly's early years. The plans bear little resemblance to the handful of funerals Jonathan has attended before. There will be no priest spouting platitudes. No crematorium chimney belching out smoke.

He wears the Armani suit in which he got married, a sombre outfit except for his splashy magenta tie. The print matched his wife's dress. They had considered burying her in it, but she chose a crimson evening gown instead. It's made of vegetable-dyed silk, and will enrich the soil like Tilly's blood and bones. From her essence, a tree will grow. A birch, tall and slender, reaching for the sky.

He looks upward through the canopy of leaves, wishing he believed in God. How comforting to imagine angels welcoming Tilly into an afterlife. But despite the best efforts of Markham's and its rituals, he remains an atheist. His wife is lost to him forever.

Anyway, young as he was, he recognised that God's teachings took second place to Mammon at Markham's. The school endured on the fees paid by his tormentors' parents. Why would the upper echelons care if a scholarship boy got bullied? A pecking order existed, as on the estate, and he survived his childhood at the bottom of both.

While deception wasn't a natural instinct, he learned to hide his feelings. It must be at least twenty years since he cried. But now Jonathan sobs because he can. He is alone. No-one will hear him rail at the unfairness of finding happiness, long after he imagined it impossible, then seeing it snatched away. There is no risk of invoking the bullies' catcalls or the unwanted sympathy of friends.

Finally, Jonathan takes a deep breath. He arrived way too early, but the other mourners will join him in under half an hour. Wiping his eyes, he dons shades to hide the surrounding bruises. A hastily grown beard covers other marks. It is his role once again to mask up, to pretend to be what he is not. Tilly wanted laughter and music at her wake. For her sake, he will paste on a smile and charm the guests. He must be kind to Daisy and her odious brother.

Jonathan scowls.

Seducing Daisy was a mistake, but she'd probably hate him anyway. She thinks he has all Tilly's money.

Little does she know there isn't any now.

.

# CHAPTER 36 TAMARA

## Day 10 - Wednesday

Tamara has been smirking all the way on the coach to Bristol. The mystery man, Jonno, is no longer an enigma. Google has identified him as Jonathan Smyth, a Markham's old boy. While she couldn't find his address, she knows where he'll be today. At his wife's funeral.

Google refuses to tell her how to get there without a car. Tamara assumes information is flaky outside the capital, and she'll have more luck at Bristol bus station. But she's wrong. While the staff are helpful enough, it transpires that it's not Google that's unreliable, but public transport in the area. A Bristol postcode means nothing: they cover much of Gloucestershire and Somerset as well as the city. She must catch a bus to a small town she's never heard of, then walk for two miles.

That wipes the smile off her face.

Gloomily contemplating the cost of a taxi, Tamara has a lucky break. A Black family, mum, dad and two teenage daughters, have waited patiently behind her in the queue. The woman touches Tamara's arm.

"Hey, I think we're all going to the same place." She makes eye contact with the youth manning the information desk. "Do they have Ubers in Bristol?"

"Sure do."

"Okay, then." She addresses Tamara again. "Share with us. It won't cost us any more, so why not?"

"Thanks." Tamara modulates her voice, sounding classier than she has a right to. She recognises a south London accent when she hears one, and doesn't intend to share hers.

"That's agreed, then. Neville can book it, can't you darling?"

The man tips his hat to her, his expression impossible to read beneath a greying beard. He removes a smartphone from the pockets of his cream linen suit.

His wife, attired in a long magenta robe with matching turban, scans Tamara's black office jacket and trousers. "They didn't tell you the dress code?"

Heat spreads up Tamara's face. "No, I guess not." She'd planned to be unobtrusive, at least until she got what she wanted.

The woman tuts. “Bright and beautiful, darling. Dress to impress.” She reaches into a capacious bag adorned with a riot of appliqué flowers. Retrieving a long necklace of bold, fuchsia-coloured beads, she slips them over Tamara’s head. “That’s better. I was going to wear them, but Jalique and Belle said they were too much.”

The teenagers, presumably Jalique and Belle, giggle into their hands.

Neville looks up from his phone, his eyes dark pools in the shadow of a straw fedora. “It’s round the corner. By the Dental Hospital, wherever that is.”

“Ask your phone,” his wife commands.

He nods. “Follow me. We’re looking for a silver Honda.” His voice is slow and gravelly.

“Dad! There’s a million silver Hondas,” Jalique or Belle chides.

“It’ll be a people carrier. There’s five of us,” their mother says. Without waiting to be asked, she shakes Tamara’s hand. “I’m Laurette. Tilly’s cousin from London. We were on the same coach.”

Tamara congratulates herself on not springing back in surprise. She hadn’t expected Tilly or her family to be Black Londoners. When she spied on Jonathan in Nick’s garden, he came across as posh, the type who’d wed someone with a country estate.

Coughing to hide her embarrassment, she wriggles out of Laurette’s warm grip.

Laurette cocks her head to one side, suggesting a reply is required.

Tamara casts about for a lie. “I’m Tamara.” That much is true. Then she finishes with, “I’m one of Jonathan’s workmates. IT, you know? I do the job remotely from home, but I felt I ought to turn up—”

Laurette doesn’t give her a chance to draw breath. “Neville’s in IT, aren’t you, darling? Maybe you’ve come across each other before.”

“We might have done.” Neville scratches his cheek. His bass tones notch down further. “Did I meet you on a project in the City?”

“Yep, that was me.” Why had she hit on IT? To be fair, Neville is the most unlikely computer genius she can envisage. Tamara adds, “Bank of America.”

Luckily, Neville hasn’t worked for them, and as he tells her, one of the girls spots the Uber. By the time they’re seated, Tamara is pleading a convenient headache.

That doesn't stop Laurette from jabbering away, no doubt pleased to have a captive audience. The teenagers waste no time in inserting earbuds, while Neville is clearly not a talkative man.

"I feel so sorry for Jonathan," Laurette announces. She blinks a tear from her sweeping lashes, which Tamara has clocked as fake. "He's all on his own again."

"You like him?" Tamara asks.

"Like him? Darling, I love him," Laurette gushes. "He isn't up himself, the way my cousin's ungrateful kids are. Think they're better than us. It's because they pass as white, isn't it? Tilly paid for them to have the best education, and they decided she wasn't good enough for them."

"Oh? I hadn't heard that," Tamara says. "Jonathan never talks about his stepchildren."

"Well, he wouldn't wash his dirty linen in public," Laurette observes.

Neville nudges her. "Like you wouldn't, you old gossip?"

Laurette pretends to cuff his ears. "I'm forewarning her. She could put her foot in it."

Tamara has every intention of doing just that. The pit of her stomach roils, a seasick feeling gripping her as the Uber lurches over Bristol's potholes. It's not only the state of the city's roads that concerns her. She's all but certain that she'll have to make her own way back after the funeral. Her new best friends won't be so chummy soon.

She smiles weakly as Laurette explains how Daisy and Mike enjoyed a privileged upbringing 'thanks to Tilly's hard work,' but repeatedly showed disdain for their mother.

"Racism." Laurette shakes her head. "Michael never wanted his mother at his school speech days, because she was dark-skinned. The father, yes. He was mixed race like her, but he looked white, didn't he? Anglo-Indian. Watch us get the cold shoulder from Michael and Daisy later. You'll see. They'll turn up their noses, like they've smelled a fart in the lift."

"Daisy's husband is all right," Neville says. "Enjoys a drink."

"Under the thumb, though," Laurette opines.

Tamara tunes out, until Laurette says, "Of course, they hate Jonathan."

That grabs Tamara's attention again. She decides to get to know Daisy and Michael. "Really? Why don't they like him?" she asks Laurette.

“He’s swiped their inheritance from under their noses. Serves them right, if you ask me.”

“Is it a lot of money?”

Laurette chuckles. “Darling, she owned Gill Spices. He’s set for life.”

Tamara quails. Is she making a mistake?

She hadn’t appreciated Jonathan’s wealth. He’ll be in the market for a new partner too. She considers tweaking her plans for the day. They’ll undoubtedly upset him, and that’ll be her bridge burned. But wasn’t Gill Spices one of Nick’s investors? If she’s right, Jonathan’s riches are a mirage.

“So, Jonathan supports homeworking?” Laurette says. “I should ask him if he needs an IT apprentice. Jalique’s going to get straight A’s at A level, aren’t you, Jalique?”

Tamara still isn’t sure which daughter is Jalique. Focused on the competing beats of their earbuds, both girls ignore Laurette.

“The apple doesn’t fall far from the tree,” Laurette says, proceeding to extol her daughter’s virtues.

With the urban sprawl of Bristol behind them, the cab speeds past lush green fields. The countryside seems empty to Tamara, a vast space of nothingness. She prefers the buzz of cities. It’s a relief when the driver announces, “Here we are.” He turns off the main road, slowing fractionally to tackle a rutted country lane, and finally stopping in a car park.

Tamara staggers out of the cab, a light breeze licking her hair. She stretches, letting Laurette receive directions from a man in a black suit, obviously a member of staff. No-one has told him about dressing to impress.

Their destination is as unpromising as anywhere they’ve passed on the way, with converted farm buildings dotted around a formal garden. Laurette exclaims at birds singing in the trees nearby. Tamara nods, as if she either knows or cares about the fauna and flora. She stifles a yawn.

Laurette leads the group to a structure that was clearly once a barn. A young woman, her clothes not dissimilar to Tamara’s, welcomes them to a lounge inside and suggests they help themselves to coffee and cake. Tamara doesn’t need telling. It’s a long time since breakfast, and she’s eating for two. She sinks into an easy chair, placing her coffee cup and plate of brownies beside her.

The lounge, with its pastel colours and comfortable seating, reminds her of a hotel where she accompanied Nick on business trips. Her brow furrows as she spots Gail, her arm around the shoulder of a sobbing redhead. Tamara swallows. Gail doesn't know what she looks like, she reminds herself.

Laurette has made a beeline for a bearded man wearing shades. With a jolt, Tamara realises it's Jonathan. As she watches, Laurette points to her.

Tamara has no doubt they're discussing her fictional IT work. Cover blown, her only choice is to bring her plan into action. She berates herself for not asking Laurette to point out Daisy and Michael. Ideally, they would be part of her audience, but she no longer has the luxury of time to ensure they're here. The room is only half full, Laurette's family being the sole Black faces. Tamara remembers, though, that Laurette said her cousin's children passed as white.

Jonathan is scowling at her, and it's not hard to work out why. Tamara takes a couple of bites of brownie to boost her energy. She stands up and marches over to him.

He makes as if to speak, but Tamara doesn't give him the chance.

"Why did you murder my baby's father?" she demands.

Chatter stops. The old barn is silent as heads turn towards her.

"You're a murderer," she repeats. Now she can only hope Jonathan has enemies, and some of them are here.

# CHAPTER 37 JONATHAN

## Day 10 - Wednesday

Heat blazing through him, Jonathan glares at the crazy blonde. She's been lying to Tilly's cousins, and now she's disrupting this private and intensely personal occasion. How dare she?

"What are you talking about," he hisses, "and who are you?"

If he expected a sensible reply, he's disappointed.

"I'm Tamara," she says. Her hands make fists on her hips, what Tilly would call a power pose.

His frown deepens. "I don't care what you say your name is. I want to know what you're really doing here. You're a journalist, obviously. Which seedy rag sent you here?"

From the corner of his eye, he notices Gail staring in his direction, her face ashen. Mike and Daisy, who had positioned themselves as far from him and Laurette as possible, are edging closer.

His heart thumps. They've put her up to this.

"Get out," he says, voice thick with anger and pain.

"Jonathan," Daisy's loud whisper will be audible to half the room, as she doubtless intends, "This is my mama's funeral, not your personal soap opera. Keep it down."

Jonathan grits his teeth. He must not argue with Tilly's monstrous offspring. Not here. Not now. Wildly, he looks around for the greeter. "Do you have security?" he demands of her.

"It's okay, I'm going." The blonde locks eyes with Daisy. They must be in it together. But, without another word, the interloper turns on her stiletto heel and stalks out.

# CHAPTER 38 TAMARA

## Day 10 - Wednesday

Tamara trembles as adrenaline ebbs away. Meekly, she allows herself to be escorted to a car park by the young woman who welcomed her into the lounge. They say nothing to each other. That suits Tamara just fine. Putting on an act is exhausting.

Nevertheless, she has more drama up her sleeve. Strolling up to the nicest car she can see, a Porsche, Tamara fumbles in her handbag. "Oh no, I've dropped my keys. Would you mind terribly if I looked for them?" She simpers, using her best voice again.

"Not a problem," the girl replies, her clipped tone and downturned mouth suggesting that it is. "I'll ring the office. Which car is it?"

Tamara points to the Porsche. As she makes a pretence of scanning the gravelled path back to the lounge, her chaperone is on the phone.

Ahead, she sees the guests filing into the chapel, another old agricultural building. The sound of violins wafts on the breeze. She can't imagine anyone is enjoying themselves, but funerals aren't meant to be fun.

The girl puts a hand out to stop Tamara from joining the throng. It doesn't prevent her from winking at Daisy, identifiable from her outburst earlier. She also spots a man who is clearly Daisy's brother, Michael. They share the same curly red hair, although his is close-cropped, while hers tumbles over her shoulders. Laurette was right: you wouldn't know they were mixed race.

How can she attract his attention?

"Michael," Tamara hisses.

That does the trick. He turns away from the brunette hanging off his arm. His eyes meet Tamara's.

'Catch you later,' he mouths, before ostentatiously saying something to the brunette. Tamara assumes this is his wife, and the four small children following them belong to him. They are being marshalled by a pale, stick-thin teenager. She's probably the nanny.

Tamara stands taller. She has allies. Her greatest challenge is communicating with them. She must find a way to stay here until the mourners are ready to leave. Continuing her delaying tactics, she asks if she might look in the lounge.

Of course, the search is fruitless, but it’s an opportunity to fake a dizzy turn where she can fall down safely.

“Oh,” she gasps theatrically, collapsing into an armchair.

A first aider is fetched to her side. Tamara blinks, eyes wide, groaning as if groggy. She is given sweet tea, and told to sit quietly. Another brownie is brought for her. The young woman hurries away to attend to the next phase of hospitality. Lunch will apparently be served elsewhere in the building. Tamara's argument with Jonathan, and the need to find keys, have been forgotten.

She waits under the watchful eye of the first aider, a middle-aged man. Occasionally, she catches the strains of boring classical music and a slightly more entertaining burst of gospel singing. When a babble of conversation reaches her ears, she guesses the mourners have left the chapel.

Evidently, they aren’t returning to the old barn at once. The sound of their voices trails away. But then Michael pops his head around the door.

He is alone. As his eyes light on Tamara, Michael smiles. He strolls over to her. She catches a whiff of expensive Penhaligon aftershave, a blend Nick used to wear. He claimed it was made exclusively for him. Tamara’s stomach curdles.

"I haven't got long," Michael whispers. "Give me your number. Look, mine’s on my card."

She takes the fancy, gold-embossed square he proffers. It bears the logo and address of a top London law firm. She recognises his name as one of Nick's clients and so-called friends. Great. By now, he must hate Nick and won't think too kindly of her when he learns she worked for him. She’ll have to be careful.

"You want to meet in London?" she asks, keeping her voice down. The first aider has moved away to fill coffee cups, but he’s glancing over. She doesn’t want him to hear.

Michael taps his foot, peeking at his Rolex. “Look, text me so I’ve got your number,” he commands. Like Nick, he has the air of a man used to getting his own way. He removes a phone from his pocket, staring at it until he’s sure she’s complied.

“Good,” he says crisply. “We're staying in Bristol overnight, at the Marriott Royal. Could I see you in the lobby at four o'clock? Send a message if you need to rearrange.”

"I'll be there," she promises.

She's no fool. Naturally, he's curious about her claim. He'll want to know if she can prove it. How will he react when he discovers she can't?

She'll have to persuade him that, with friends on her side, she just might make the allegation stick.

# CHAPTER 39 GAIL

## Day 10 - Wednesday

The hotel's public spaces are grand, all velvet, marble and gilt. In contrast, its conference zone is bland and anonymous. I knock tentatively on a light wood door. Having seen how Jonathan handled Tamara at Matilda Gill's funeral, I'm even more sure that he's responsible for Nick's death. He'd have denied it otherwise. But what did he do instead? Had her thrown out.

He's a guilty man, all right.

Still, I'm amazed I agreed to Daisy's cloak and dagger act.

Daisy's brother opens the door, holding out a hand. "Welcome." He draws me into an air kiss with the handshake. Is he wearing the same aftershave as Nick? I wrinkle my nose. Nick always said that Mike Gill copied everything he did.

Mike waves me inside, and I do a double-take. It's not just Daisy seated at the square office table. Opposite the door, a blonde watches me intently. Tamara.

Mike notices my gasp. "For all our sakes, we have to collaborate," he says. "No-one said this would be easy."

Daisy, who invited me, shifts in her chair and looks down at her Louboutins. I can't believe she didn't know Tamara would be here.

Close up, it's obvious Tamara doesn't resemble the north face of a south-facing cow. Nick has lied about that, but what's new? I'm learning that he lied about everything.

"Sit down," Mike says, motioning to a padded chair at ninety degrees to my husband's mistress. "This is a council of war. Are you in, Gail?"

Am I? All I know is that my head is swimming, and the sooner I take a seat, the better. Slumping into it, I brush moisture from my eyes and try to concentrate.

The funeral was painful, but I'd promised Daisy I'd go to support her. I've been telling myself that I've come to this drab room for my friend too. Tamara's presence doesn't change that. Nor does it alter the fact that I owe it to my kids to bring their father's killer to justice.

I guess that I'm in after all.

Mike offers me Sauv Blanc. For the first time, I notice glasses in front of everybody, and an ice bucket on a stand by his side. The bottle empties completely when he pours my drink. Mike phones through to the bar for some more. I suspect Daisy has made a head start, while I note that Tamara isn't stinting herself either, pregnant or not. Yet who can blame any of them after a harrowing day?

"Thanks for coming, everyone," Mile says. "I've gathered us together because we all believe Jonathan Smyth had a hand in Nick's death—"

"For goodness sake, Mike," Daisy interrupts, "Get to the point. This isn't some boring lawyers' meeting that you're chairing. Jonathan killed Nick, and he killed Mama, and the police have let him get away with it."

"Precisely." Tamara uses her telephone voice. It's as if she's mimicking Daisy. "They arrested him. Quite right too. He was sitting there alone with Nick's body. No-one else could have done it except you, Gail."

She takes my breath away. It's bad enough seeing Tamara playing the victim — Tamara, who knew full well my husband was married — but I can't just sit back and let her aim poison darts at me. I have to get out.

But when I rise unsteadily to my feet, Mike places a hand on my arm.

"Wait, Gail." He flashes Tamara a filthy look. "Please stay. She was only making a rhetorical statement. Tamara knows Jonno did it. We all know."

"What can we do?" Daisy asks.

"Legally speaking, nothing," Mike says. "Out of all of us, only Gail was at the scene—"

Tamara glares at me, her gaze challenging.

"—and by the time you arrived, Nick was already dead, wasn't he?"

"That's right." I give a potted summary of my statements to the police. My voice breaks. "He died of an insulin overdose. Nick had his troubles, but he wouldn't make that kind of mistake. He'd been injecting for thirty years. And he wouldn't have killed himself, even with the stress of his business. Not even if he'd unexpectedly got a gold-digger pregnant."

I can do insults too.

Mike jumps in without giving Tamara a chance to speak. "It wasn't suicide. But as I said, there is no legal route to convince the police of Jonno's guilt. In time, we could mount a private prosecution. You may find that a beneficial course of action, Gail, but it's expensive."

I scan the faces in the room, realising I'll be on my own. Mike has virtually announced he won't be chipping in. Tamara's cheap suit broadcasts her lack of resources, while Gordon controls Daisy's purse strings.

"The cops obviously thought they had their man, but they didn't have enough proof," Mike says. "So, if we can give them more evidence—"

"You mean plant it?" I blurt, stiffening as I stare at him. "No way. That's a criminal act."

"I don't mean that at all." Mike switches from a commanding presence to an oily, smooth tone. "But if Jonathan can be persuaded to make his guilt more obvious, the police will have an easier job proving it."

Despite the wine, my chest tightens. I grimace. "Why would Jonathan do that?"

"Because we'll trick him," Daisy says, "and you're the woman who can do it."

# CHAPTER 40 LACEY

## Day 12 - Friday

Lacey wakes up grinning. Just for once, it's not because she played with her Rabbit last night. She hasn't found romance lately, and her toy is the next best thing. But she's leaping out of bed because she's about to earn twenty grand.

No-one has offered that sort of cash for a legit job before. When they learn she's a helicopter pilot, dodgy characters dangle easy money in front of her. She assumes it's all drug drops, and says no. But Michael Gill isn't the type to do anything illegal. He's a lawyer, high up in a leading London firm, and thoroughly respectable. She flew him from the London Heliport to a friend's farm after he'd pulled an all-nighter two days ago.

There are worse careers than ferrying rich businessmen around Britain. She's seen interesting places: exclusive private airport lounges, country manors, top hotels. Oil rigs too. The riggers are her favourite clients. Although they're rough and ready types, they work hard for their wages, stuck in a metal box out at sea. Lacey tries not to be jealous of wealthy people who book a helicopter as easily as a cab, but it's a battle she's losing. She's up to her eyeballs in debt. On top of the student loan, she borrowed to pay for her flight training. Her salary is swallowed by interest and rent. Then she's had to lease a car so she can drive to airports at odd hours.

Perhaps she should have stayed with her ex. Her finances nosedived when they split three years ago, Lacey's costs doubling overnight. But her pride is worth more than money. She'd been crazy about him and thought he loved her too, but he cheated with a skinny rich girl. And if he did it once, he'd do it again. A curvy girl from Cardiff can't compete with those posh stick insects.

She's on her own.

Michael has offered her a chance to get back on her feet, to repay the balance of her training loan. Most of her passengers treat her like a robot, part of the machinery taking them from A to B, but Michael is different. On Wednesday, he insisted on chatting. At first, Lacey replied in monosyllables, afraid he'd get sleazy. The memory of her recent flight with Nick Masterson was still raw. But no, Michael just wanted to talk.

He was on his way to his mother's funeral after working through the night to get a deal signed. His wife was already in Gloucestershire, and distinctly unimpressed with him.

It's clear who wears the trousers in that marriage.

He was good company, though, so much so that Lacey ended up confiding her money woes. She feared she'd be working forever with nothing to show for it. Michael was sympathetic. He was in the same boat, he told her. His pension had gone south in the Masterson Group collapse.

Lacey didn't mention that she'd met Nick Masterson twice. That she wouldn't have trusted him with a ten-pound note. She's not that tactless.

Anyway, Michael may have lost his pension fund, but he isn't short of readies. Before they'd landed, he'd suggested he help her out. He'd even supply the aircraft, which belongs to another of his chums.

Imagine having mates who just happen to have a spare helicopter lying around.

The fates have smiled on her. It was easy to rearrange her shifts and take the day off. Another Helicon pilot messaged in their team's WhatsApp group to request a swap. Win-win.

It's a stag weekend prank, Michael says. Like in the old days, when the guys would put their buddy on the milk train to Glasgow. They're just taking it a little further.

Humming a Beyoncé tune, Lacey jumps out of bed. It's time to get moving. The helicopter, a Squirrel, is waiting at Cotswold Airport. So is her first passenger. She mustn't be late.

# CHAPTER 41 GAIL

## Day 12 - Friday

I'm in so deep now, I'm not sure that I'll ever come up for air. Jonathan is snoring on the back seat of my Tesla, with Daisy sitting beside him to make sure he's still alive. Which he is, judging by the booming sound of his breath. Whatever I added to his coffee, it hasn't killed him. Yet.

A chill spreads across my shoulders, and I notice I'm drenched in sweat. How could I let myself be talked into this? Until today, I'd never so much as exceeded the speed limit. Now, I've kidnapped a man by slipping illegal drugs into his latte. At least, I'm guessing Daisy didn't get them at the local pharmacy.

It makes no difference that he's a creep and a murderer. I shouldn't have done it.

As I negotiate winding country lanes, my ears are alert to the slightest sound, my eyes flicking to the mirrors. I expect the police to arrive at any moment, sirens blaring and blue lights blazing. We can't get to the farm in Gloucestershire soon enough.

That's when my part will be over. Once I've dropped Jonathan off, it's down to Michael. He'll persuade Jonathan to confess. I've no idea how, but Michael is confident he can do it. All he needs is the chance to talk man to man.

'You saw how he avoided me at Mama's funeral?' Michael had said. I had to agree. Jonathan made no effort to speak to Matilda's children, which was yet another reason for me to stick close to Daisy. I wasn't in a hurry to spend time with him either.

This is an extreme way to force Jonathan to talk to Michael, though. And suppose it doesn't work? If Jonathan goes to the police, we're all in a mess. Yet Daisy is as cool as a glass of chilled Soave.

"Turn left at the next junction," she says. She's using her phone as a satnav. For some reason, she thinks it's more reliable than the Tesla's navigation system.

I take my foot off the accelerator and prepare to brake. Out here, sideroads appear suddenly: small gaps in the hedgerows. They usually involve a sharp turn. The approach to this lane is gentler, but a giant pothole looms ahead once I've swung round the corner. It's impossible to avoid, and I grit my teeth as the car rattles.

Jonathan groans.

"Is he all right?" I ask Daisy.

Glancing in the rearview mirror again, I notice she's slipping a balaclava over his head. Nick would call it a ski mask. My tension rises another notch. "What are you doing?"

She doesn't answer. Instead, I hear my own voice turning shrill as I ask, "What does Michael have in mind, Daisy? For pity's sake, tell me."

She sighs. "Michael? Nothing. He's made himself scarce. As per usual, when the going gets tough."

"Then what do you—"

"Get a grip, girl," she snaps. "We're here. See that gate? Stop the car, or you'll miss it."

I slow to a halt. "But it's a field."

"Exactly." She jumps out, leaving Jonathan's head lolling over his seatbelt. The silvery metal gate rasps in protest as she struggles to open it. Daisy curses. After a couple of minutes cajoling, it gives way with a screech.

She gestures to me to drive in and park just inside.

Obscured by a tall hawthorn hedge, my car is invisible from the road. I don't give it a second thought until Daisy closes the gate.

I wind the window down. "Hey."

"Countryside Code," she says.

"Yes, but we're in the middle of nowhere," I gasp. "This is a cornfield. You just told me there'd be no Michael, but there's nothing. No farmhouse. No people."

My hand sweeps round for emphasis. All I can see is fields and trees, unless I'm missing something. I pray that Daisy doesn't produce a gun. By now, I wouldn't put it past her.

Instead, she points to the sky.

# CHAPTER 42 TAMARA

## Day 12 - Friday

Tamara yawns, even though she's slept exceptionally well. Michael paid for a room in an ancient inn, centuries older than the nearby Cotswold Airport. Despite its age, the place was luxurious. Unlike the house share in Streatham, she had a bed. No trains rattled by. She was woken by birdsong before feasting on a full English breakfast. Nothing has caused her a problem except Lacey's conversation.

By rights, they shouldn't be able to hear each other. The chopper's racket is so loud, they're wearing noise-cancelling headphones. But the headsets come with connected microphones. Lacey says she doesn't often use them, because her business clients like to be left in peace. She's also mentioned that she lives alone. Lacey evidently doesn't have many opportunities for a chat, and she's making up for it now.

"So, this is a single-engined Squirrel," Lacey says. "Technically, this one is a Eurocopter AS 350, although they're made by Airbus these days. Last year, Airbus took our whole team out to France for a party."

Tamara tunes out.

"You should have seen how much champagne we drank."

That's more like it.

Tamara says "Yes" or "Uh-huh" from time to time, letting her mind wander. Michael is front and centre of her thoughts. He seems pleasant enough, and he's obviously still rich despite Nick's best efforts to rip him off. She considers taking a job in his law firm and cosying up to him. His wife holds too much sway over the man, though. She doesn't feel the alpha male vibe, the sweep of roving eyes, that she sensed with Nick.

"Michael's nice to work for, isn't he?" Lacey says.

The comment takes Tamara unawares. "I guess so. I don't work for him, we're friends," she says.

Lacey's gaze doesn't move from the controls, but an eyebrow quirks up. Tamara purses her lips. Does Lacey imagine she's an escort? Michael said he'd told Lacey this trip was part of a stag weekend. Now Tamara thinks about it, it may seem weird to Lacey that a woman is involved.

Tamara shrugs. Best not to be too precious. She'll never see Lacey again. And they're picking up the other girls too, bossy Daisy and meek Gail. Lacey can make of them what she will.

Gail. How ironic that they've ended up on the same side.

"Well, obviously, I'm doing this for money," Lacey says. "I'm sick of scrabbling for every last penny."

"Tell me about it," Tamara mutters.

"I haven't been able to afford a holiday since I split with my ex."

Tamara wishes she could afford to sleep in a bed more often, let alone go on holiday. She scrutinises Lacey's plump face and body. The pilot's lack of self-care would deter any man worth having. Tamara has more sense. She can take her pick. If she made a mistake with Nick, too bad. She's turning it around.

Lacey continues to whinge. "He's definitely the one who got away. I can't believe it sometimes. Jonathan was only a teacher when we lived together, but now he's in charge of a big company. You know Gill Spices?"

Tamara pricks up her ears. "Gill Spices, you say? And your ex is called Jonathan?"

"Yes. You've heard of them, then." Lacey's tone turns from impatience to bitterness. "Have you met him?"

"Not sure," Tamara says weakly, clasping her hands together until the knuckles whiten. She types a quick text to Daisy: 'Pilot knows J'.

Although she has no idea whether mobile phones work this far above the ground, she receives a reply straight away. 'I'll take care of it,' followed by, 'Get him to stay in cabin.'

'Him?' Tamara texts back.

'Pilot.'

It isn't just Lacey who makes assumptions about gender, then.

Butterflies fill Tamara's belly. But maybe that's because the ground is getting closer. It's as if she's strapped into a lift descending too fast. She gulps.

Lacey must have heard her. "Don't worry, I know what I'm doing," the pilot says.

# CHAPTER 43 GAIL

## Day 12 - Friday

The helicopter's clatter dispenses with my chance to quiz Daisy. We both gawp as the grey metal craft buzzes down, landing mere yards away. When the deafening noise finishes, we turn to each other.

"What—"

"We have to get him in the chopper," Daisy says. "The cabin has two seats in front and three behind. We can both sit in the back, either side of Jonathan."

"No." I cross my arms. "Absolutely not. I thought I was bringing Jonathan out here for a chat with your brother. I'm not flying away with him to some unknown destination—"

"It's not unknown," Daisy says, huffing. "Michael and I planned it all. We've agreed it with the pilot. Jonathan will be dropped on an island. It's off grid, so he'll be safe, but out of contact. When the police realise he's disappeared, they'll know he's guilty, won't they? So they'll actually put resources into proving it."

"You reckon?" Despite my sceptical words, I can see there's a chance their plan will work. But it's risky.

I shake my head. "Daisy," I adopt a wheedling manner, as I once would have done when Nick raised his hand. "If we carry on, we could get into trouble. It's kidnapping, a criminal offence. But if we stop now..."

Daisy's eyes narrow. "And what have you done already, drugging him and bundling him into your car? It's too late to back out."

"I don't know what you gave me for his coffee."

"That's not the point. You used it, Gail. Anyway, the police want to make an arrest for Nick's murder. Who's the prime suspect if it isn't Jonathan?"

"I didn't kill my husband."

"You would say that, wouldn't you?" Her voice is hard.

I doubt we'll stay friends after this.

"I'm taking him back home," I say. "Or to his office."

"Do that, and I'm dialling 999 now," she threatens, her pitch rising. "I'll tell the police you abducted him. And just you wait until Jonathan wakes up and confirms it."

"But you're involved too."

"Am I?" She laughs. "He doesn't know that. He was already asleep in your car when you picked me up, remember? You can't prove I was with you, Gail, and I'll deny everything. Look, just help me get him inside, then you can go."

Reluctantly, I glance at the helicopter, and give a brief nod. She's right. I'm too far down the road to turn back. But the scheme will fall apart if we can't coax Jonathan into the craft. And that won't be easy. Quite apart from Jonathan's drowsiness, it has no steps or ladders.

"How do you even get in?"

"See the skids?" Daisy says, "The ski-like runners that touch the ground? You climb up the struts."

I wince. "I could do it by myself, I guess…"

Alone, it's a straightforward task, but shifting Jonathan in there? It might be too much even for the pair of us. Daisy hasn't made the task smoother by putting on her favourite three-inch heels, the same Louboutins she chose for Matilda's funeral. At least she's swapped her usual floaty dresses for jeans, jumper and a flowery scarf.

"Would he clamber up himself if we wake him up?" I ask Daisy. "If we tell him he's going to bed?"

"I haven't got a better idea," she admits, her tone more amicable now I'm doing what she wants. "First, we have to move him out of the car. Take a shoulder each?"

She opens a rear door. "Out," she yells.

Jonathan snores. He's still under.

Daisy slaps a balaclavaed cheek.

"Ouch," he slurs. "Wassat for?"

"Stand up," she commands.

Jonathan's legs twitch.

We drag him out of the Tesla between us. Luckily, the combination of manhandling and fresh air breathes life into him. He staggers drunkenly to his feet, seemingly happy for Daisy and me to help him stay upright. Slowly, panting with the effort, we ease him towards the silent chopper.

The cabin door opens. Tamara, wearing sensible sneakers rather than sexy stilettos, steps down. When she spots me, her frown mirrors the way I feel about her.

"Help us get him in," Daisy says.

Tamara smirks, evidently finding the comment humorous. "You push, I'll pull." She calls back inside the cabin, "One of these guys is drunk. Sorry."

"Where's the pilot?" I ask. "What if he won't let Jonathan travel?"

Tamara's eyes turn flinty. "She doesn't know, does she?" she says to Daisy. "Listen up, Gail. The pilot will do what we say. That's what Michael is paying *her* for. But we don't want *her* to find out it's Jonathan, because *she's* his ex-girlfriend."

Daisy sucks in a breath. "What? Michael's fouled up, then. Just wait till I see him."

"Whatever." Tamara sounds bored. "Good that you put a ski mask on Jonathan. Keep him quiet, okay? I'll go back in the cabin and haul him in."

"We should gag him." Daisy removes her scarf and stuffs it in Jonathan's mouth.

My breath catches. I become aware of the booming of my heart. This could go badly wrong. If we end up killing Jonathan, we'll be charged with murder. There's a greater risk that Nick's death will be pinned on me.

"Suppose Jonathan chokes on vomit?" I protest.

"Well, you'd better keep an eye on him to make sure he doesn't," Daisy retorts.

"What?" I gape at her, dizzy, as if swimming on the edge of a whirlpool. "We already talked about this. No way am I going with you."

"Your call," Daisy sneers. "You seem so worried about precious Jonathan. Why would you care?"

I examine Daisy's face. She's serious. I doubt she'd shed a tear if Jonathan died. She'd simply tell the pilot to dump him in the sea.

Maybe that's her intention. It won't matter to her whether he's dead or alive.

What do I do?

The maelstrom spins faster, sucking me in.

Tears blur my vision. I swallow, scarcely capable of speech. "My kids… I've got to pick them up later, and—"

"Don't be such a drama queen," Daisy says. "We'll only be a couple of hours."

It seems I'm travelling to the island after all. Whether I want to or not.

# CHAPTER 44 TAMARA

## Day 12 - Friday

Tamara sits quietly beside Lacey, marvelling at the scenery below. Apart from the odd business trip with a randy boss, she's never flown anywhere. She takes no notice when Lacey explains her route. As long as they arrive at Farigg Island before nightfall, she doesn't care whether Lacey flies via the moon first.

"…so I'm taking the Manchester corridor," Lacey says. "That's controlled airspace, and I'll put a squawk on – probably code 7366. That means we shouldn't need to talk to ATC. Once we're away from the area, no-one need know where we are. Of course, we'll have to radio ahead to Kirkbride to get fuel…"

Tamara snaps to attention. "We have to stop for fuel? Don't you have enough?"

"No. Weren't you listening before? It's three hours to the island, and the tank only holds fuel for two and a half. But we can save time hot fuelling, if that's concerning you. We'll call ahead and pay upfront, then they'll refuel the kite with the rotor running. I won't need to get out."

"Definitely do that," Tamara commands.

Now Tamara begins to worry. What if the flight can be tracked? Perhaps all this technical detail that Lacey has been feeding her has a purpose after all. But no-one except she, Daisy and Gail know that Jonathan is onboard. Lacey hasn't even realised. She's panicking for nothing, isn't she?

Tamara needs the police to believe Jonathan is a killer. His disappearance will convince them that Nick's death was murder. If it's ruled a suicide, her life insurance claim fails. She's read the small print.

Tamara pats her belly. Her million pound baby has the smartest mummy ever. Taking out an insurance policy on the daddy was an inspired move.

You didn't need a crystal ball to see Nick was in for a challenging time. Once the Ponzi scheme came to light, he'd learn he had enemies. And prisons can be dangerous places.

"Can you give me your credit card?" Lacey asks.

Tamara scowls. "What for?"

There’s a sharp intake of breath from Lacey. “The fuel. You told me to call ahead.”

Tamara clenches her jaw. Michael should have taken care of that. He’s the moneybags behind this operation. Still, his sister is the next best thing.

“I’ll get Daisy to do it,” Tamara says. “Hook me up to her.”

The rear headphones are on a different circuit, but Lacey can connect the two. As soon as she does, Tamara hears Gail moaning about being late back for her school pickup. Why is Gail so hung up about her children? It won’t kill them to wait a couple of hours. Once Tamara has extracted a credit card from the reluctant Daisy, she asks Lacey to sever the two audio circuits again.

She reads out the credit card number when Lacey phones through to the airfield, taking care to memorise the details. They might come in useful one day. Then she switches off from Lacey's technobabble to daydream about her payout.

# CHAPTER 45 GAIL

## Day 12 - Friday

Surely there are uninhabited islands in the Bristol Channel, or off the Welsh coast? But no, Daisy finally admitted we were heading for Farigg in Scotland.

When I complained it would take too long, she said sniffily that Mike had arranged it and he knew what he was doing. She'd told Gordon to pick up her kids, and he could collect mine too.

I stared at her. Mary and Tom are both subdued these days, and I'd wondered if I should have kept them at home for longer. Socialising might be a step too far for them. Of course, abandoning them would be worse, so I told her I'd ring the school. Then I felt the absence of a bag on my shoulder. Patting my pockets just to be sure, I remembered I'd left all my belongings in the car. Thanks to the haste and confusion of manoeuvring Jonathan onboard, I had no phone.

"Can I borrow your mobile?" I asked.

"Do it once we're rid of him," Daisy said.

Jonathan rewarded her attention with a groan.

But after hours in the air, we must be getting close. We've been hugging the coast for a while, and if it weren't for my rocketing stress levels, I would enjoy the view. A clear blue sky is reflected in the rippling sea, foamy waves breaking on the sandy beaches that line the shore. Occasionally, a cluster of roofs denotes a farmstead or village. It's ages since we passed a large settlement. Perhaps that's why Mike chose this part of the country. It isn't as touristy as places nearer Bristol.

The pilot veers inland, flying over fields and the brown wiggly lines of rivers. Roads and buildings appear: a small town, with an airfield at its edge. The runway races towards us as the craft descends.

"Our refuelling stop," Daisy says, unnecessarily. "She's not even switching the engine off. We'll only be ten minutes."

Pulling a can of pinot grigio from her handbag, she takes a swig.

I squeeze my eyes shut, feeling the aircraft levitate as I relive the moment when Mary sidled into her classroom this morning. Minutes later, I'd set off for my 'coffee date' with a surprised Jonathan. What a stupid decision that was, falling in line with Mike's crazy plan.

If it was Mike's plan. In spite of his high-flying legal background, I noticed him deferring to Daisy at the hotel. Her bossy streak is becoming more and more apparent. Maybe he's been giving in to his elder sister all his life. Maybe she hates Jonathan because she can't manipulate him. Maybe Nick did too.

Maybe I got this all wrong.

I have no proof that Jonathan deliberately provoked Nick into a fight. On the other hand, I have plenty of evidence that Nick had a hair trigger temper, especially when his blood sugar was low. I finger my cheek.

If only I could turn back the clock.

"There it is," Daisy points out of the window. The empty can rattles at her feet.

Sandwiched between us, Jonathan stirs. He moans again and kicks out.

If he wakes up, we're in trouble.

# CHAPTER 46 LACEY

## Day 12 - Friday

Lacey breathes a sigh of relief when she sees Farigg Island ahead. It's unmistakable, a splodge of green and yellow dropped in the blue ocean like a missing jigsaw piece. She's found it hard work making small talk with Tamara. Hooking up the rear audio to hers, she announces that they'll arrive at their destination shortly.

Michael's friend groans. Exactly how drunk is he?

A twinge of unease prickles Lacey's scalp. This is a bleak place to leave anyone, let alone a man with a hangover. She brought a couple of ornithologists last October, and she thinks there's a basic shelter, which is why she suggested the island to Michael. But they haven't agreed a process for collecting his friend later. Michael didn't even suggest it. Strange.

It's weird that Michael sent three women with his buddy too. She always thought stag parties were men only. When she picked up Tamara this morning, Lacey assumed her first passenger was a sex worker. She still wonders, but then the others turned up. Surely they're too classy: this Daisy, who described herself as Michael's sister, and her skinny friend?

Lacey took an instant dislike to that woman. She bears a passing resemblance to Gail Masterson, although her face is gaunt and she hasn't piled on so much makeup. What an effort it took to be polite to Gail and Nick Masterson last week. They may not have remembered her, but she recognised them, all right. Jonathan's awful, boring reunion ball had been the worst night of her life.

Maybe her usual clients, the curt and dismissive businessmen, aren't so bad after all.

A flurry of seabirds fly up to meet the descending craft. They flap around, squawking. Curious or indignant? Lacey can't tell. She's hardly an expert, although she always keeps an eye on avian wildlife. The island seems alive with them. They must have been here last time, as she was carrying birdwatchers, but they didn't make an impression on her then. They couldn't have been so interested.

So far, they've been smart enough to keep some distance — not much, but enough to avoid a hit. Still, some of these babies are large. Even a single strike could affect the rotors.

"Shoo," she says, as if that will make a difference.

"What?" Tamara says.

"The birds. We've disturbed them. I'm going up again, try hovering until they disperse."

"They're nesting." That's Daisy's friend. The woman adds, "That makes them aggressive. And look, there's a great skua, over a metre across its wings. We can't leave him here. It's too dangerous."

"Landing is too dangerous," Lacey echoes.

"Hello? This was your idea," Daisy accuses. "Unless you always intended to waste our time and my brother's money, I suggest you get down there right now."

"It's not safe," Lacey protests.

"Then find a way to make it safe. Mike hasn't paid you yet, has he?"

"No," Lacey says, although she's received half upfront, which is what she'd agreed with him. She checked her banking app earlier.

Her muscles tighten and she feels sick. She knows what's coming next. It's not as if she exactly needs the other ten thousand pounds — she can rely on her monthly salary to eat — but she'd like to repay that loan. She feels she lives to work rather than working to live.

"Mike expects you to deliver," Daisy says, leaving Lacey in no doubt that it's what his sister expects.

The two siblings look alike, but how different they are. Under his stuffy suit, Mike is laid back, while Daisy's flowery exterior hides the charm of a crocodile.

Lacey should have known the easy money was too good to be true. And she's not prepared to risk her life, or anyone else's. If the rotors fail, they're all dead.

Still, maybe she can land without a hitch. She needs to stop letting the birds freak her out. Get away from them. "I'm going to gain height for a better view," she says, "and find a spot free of unwanted wildlife."

"If you insist," Not-Gail says. "Look, they mostly nest on crags and cliffs. The rocky bits. Search for a flat area with plenty of vegetation. Say, right there. You see the golden colour? That's gorse. There will be heather too, although it's not flowering yet. It should be safe to land."

Naturally, Lacey can't see where the woman is pointing, but she gets the gist.

"The bonxies — that's the great skuas — do like the moorland, though. But perhaps we'll get lucky," Not-Gail says.

“Who knew we’d have a nature lesson?” Tamara observes tartly.

Lacey makes a point of ignoring her. She manoeuvres upwards, viewing the vast, acid-yellow expanse of gorse. Warily, she scans the area as she heads for it. Nothing flies towards her.

It’s clear.

She begins the descent.

A huge, deep brown shape looms ahead. It’s too close, and Lacey’s instincts push her into evasive action.

“A bonxie!” Not-Gail exclaims.

Lacey has no time to comment she’d figured that one out. She swerves to the left to miss it, the craft juddering as she overcooks the turn in her haste.

“It’s flown away,” their self-appointed instructor says. “Typical scare tactic.”

“Shut up, Gail,” Daisy says. “Lacey, reassert control, will you?”

Gail? Lacey clocks the name, while realising she detests Daisy far more than her friend. What a patronising cow, stating the obvious. Lacey is well aware of her responsibilities. She concentrates on smoothing the Squirrel’s flight, allowing it to descend.

A sudden jolt rattles her teeth. Has the rotor been hit? The cabin shakes. But they are barely six feet above the ground now. Engine whining, she persuades the craft to land, runners gliding over bushes and tussocks.

As the rotors stop roaring, Lacey takes a deep breath. She made it. Yet she envisaged silence, and instead, the empty air has filled with screams. What are the women so upset about? She’s brought them to Farigg and made a safe landing. What more do they want?

Then Lacey hears the man swearing. A chill runs through her as she recognises his voice.

Jonathan.

# CHAPTER 47 JONATHAN

## Day 12 - Friday

"Where am I? Let me out," Jonathan shouts. His voice doesn't sound right. It's both slurred and muffled. There's something in his mouth, a wad of fabric that tastes of perfume. He claws at it, retching. Throws it to one side. Next, he tears off a set of headphones and a ski mask.

A buzzing clatter overwhelms his ears. He places his hands over them. Tries to stand, puzzled at the force pressing down on his torso. The ground rocks beneath him. He falls back into his seat.

Forcing his eyes to focus, he looks around. Daisy cowers in an adjacent chair. He should have known. Her presence is an evil omen. Wherever she pops up, bad news follows. But what is Gail doing here? She sits on the other side of him, brown eyes wide like a frightened fawn's.

The last thing he remembers is meeting her at a coffee shop, a roaster's pop-up on that trading estate near Gill Spices. They drank vanilla lattes. She was waiting for him with the syrupy drinks; she'd ordered two by mistake, apparently.

He recalls a bitter taste. Now he knows why. Not that his mind is working properly yet, but he can make the connection even with brain fog and a thumping headache.

Jonathan swears. The clamorous drone stutters and stops. So does the juddering movement of the floor. He unbuckles the seatbelt that restrains his body. Staggers to his feet.

He's in a helicopter. Surrounded by women. Every man's dream.

Except… these women are something else. Apart from Gail staring at him and Daisy screaming, the suicide blonde who accosted him at the funeral is grappling with the pilot in front.

"No, you can't do this," the pilot yells.

It's Lacey.

This must be a nightmare. Not real at all. If he just closes his eyes, it will all disappear. He begins to drift off.

Daisy shouts, "Do you want your money or not?"

For a blessed moment, silence reigns. Then he hears a click and a swooshing sound.

"Get out," Daisy orders him, tugging at his jacket.

Fine, he decides. Anything to get clear of this coven. Although maybe Lacey isn't a witch; she doesn't need a broomstick to fly, does she? A slurred chuckle emerges from his lips.

He moves his leaden limbs to do Daisy's bidding.

# CHAPTER 48 GAIL

## Day 12 - Friday

Sweat moistens my top lip. I'm responsible for this. In his right mind, Jonathan would be asking questions. Threatening us all. Stopping us from leaving him on this bleak rock teeming with angry wildlife. But whatever Daisy supplied me with, it's dulled his senses. He's staggering out of the cabin.

He might die.

He's a sleazy gold-digger for certain. Possibly a killer too. But he should face the force of the law. He doesn't deserve this.

And nor do I, or my family. Because if the police find out, they'll lock me up. What will happen to my children then?

My thoughts turn to my parents. My sisters. Their lives are spent passing through faraway places, always on the move. That lifestyle works for them, but it never suited me. My kids deserve a base. Stability. The certainty that they're important, not an afterthought, a hindrance to a world of thrilling adventures.

How could I lose sight of that? I've been such a fool.

Jonathan is outside already. By a miracle, he's upright; he made it down the skids without falling. And without thinking twice, I jump after him, the tussocky earth almost tripping me as I land.

A chilly breeze cuts into every inch of exposed skin. Clutching Jonathan's arm, I plead with him. "Come back."

"Get off me." He shoves me away. His glazed eyes seem distant and unfocused. Maybe he's not seeing what I can: the helicopter, and the wild landscape around us. Perhaps he imagines we're sitting cosily in a coffee bar.

"It's Gail. You can trust me," I say, although that's a lie, of course. Look where it's got him.

Wind rushes past the nape of my neck, strands of hair blowing in front of my eyes. I brush the locks from my face, just in time to glimpse a brown and white blur zip over Jonathan's shoulder.

Jonathan jerks backwards. "What the heck?" he says.

"A bonxie. Warning us off."

"A whattie?"

"It's a big bird, a great skua. There will be a nest—"

He screams.

"Gail, get back inside," Daisy shouts. "We're going."

The rotors whir and clatter.

"Jonathan!" I grab his hand, try to tug him towards the skids. But he's rooted to the spot, quivering.

"Leave him." Daisy's yell is faint above the roar of the engine. "He's not invited. Do you hear me, Gail?"

"We can't dump him and leave him to die," I retort.

The great skua squawks, swooping towards Jonathan's crown.

"Move," I bellow at him, pulling him towards me. He shifts just enough that the aggressive bird misses and glides upwards again.

I have no doubt it will return. Meanwhile, Jonathan's terror is palpable, his eyes wide and his lips flecked with spittle.

"Gail, stop playing games. Let go of him and come on up. We can't wait, can we, Lacey?"

I don't hear the reply. The craft levitates a foot or so, hovering for a few moments. I could reach it. Just. Yet there's no time to persuade Jonathan to follow, and I'm not strong enough to force him.

Daisy screeches, "Now, Gail. While he's distracting the bird."

Bile surges up my throat. "No. You can't use him as a decoy."

But that's exactly what they're doing. Our pilot must be afraid the bonxie will hit a rotor, and she knows it can't while it's occupied with Jonathan.

The loud drone picks up speed and volume. When Daisy opens her mouth again, I have to read her lips: 'It's too late, Gail. We're going.'

The chopper zooms upwards, as if pulled by an invisible string.

Gaping at it, I'm too late to save Jonathan from the bonxie's next dive. With a swish of air and thwack of its beak, it pecks the top of his skull.

He sways, collapsing forward onto me. We both crash to the ground, our fall fortuitously softened by springy heather. The bird, obviously pleased with itself, utters a triumphant squawk and flies away.

Pushing Jonathan off me, I sit up. The helicopter is a mere speck in the sky. It's not coming back.

Suppose it never will?

I gulp. Despite Jonathan's presence, I feel terribly alone.

They've left me. With the man who killed my husband.

But Jonathan can't hurt me right now. He lies slumped on the ground, groaning. Blood trickles from his head, staining the vegetation beneath.

At least he's semi-conscious. The great skua has done less damage than Nick. However, this time, there's no way of calling an ambulance.

Or is there?

"Jonathan," I say softly, "do you have your phone?"

He moans in reply.

He must have it, though. I didn't taken any of his possessions from him earlier. Whatever the consequences for me, I have to call the emergency services. This escapade has gone too far.

"Jonathan, I'm going to check your pockets. Just for your phone, so I can get help."

He poses no threat in this state, yet I shudder as I pat him down. There's a promising oblong object in a trouser pocket. Holding my breath, I pull the item out.

It's a Moleskine notebook.

Tears moisten my eyes. What an idiot I was, to imagine it would be that easy. Sniffing, I rifle through all his pockets. My search produces a wallet, pen and keys, but no phone.

Daisy must have removed it in the car. Anyway, without a phone mast in sight, who knows if we'd get a signal?

A herring gull glides down beside Jonathan, regarding him with a cold, alien gaze. I shiver. Has the blood attracted it?

"Go away," I shout.

It struts this way and that, keeping its distance, but close enough to spot the rings around one of its legs. It's wearing two: one made of silvery metal, and another that might be pink plastic. I gasp with relief. A human being must have tagged the bird. There could be other people on this island. But where?

"Jonathan, we need to explore."

He's silent.

Slapping his face, I scream at him. "Jonathan, wake up."

He grunts.

"Don't quit on me, Jonathan."

I scan the horizon, and at last, I see it. In the distance, sunlight glitters on a small granite hut. I make out a door and a window. It's perhaps a mile away. Yet, while I could easily walk to it, Jonathan can't. And I daren't leave him alone at the mercy of scavenging birds.

"Jonathan, please. Jonno!"

"I've told you before. Call me Jonathan."

He’s not only speaking, but he can also string two sentences together. I’m so relieved that I burst into tears.

# CHAPTER 49 LACEY

## Day 12 - Friday

Lacey switches off the intercom. She's not speaking to those bitches. When they refuel at Kirkbride again, she'll tell Tamara to sit in the back with Daisy. Then she'll let herself cry, where they can neither see nor hear her.

How could she betray Jonathan like that? Whatever Michael set up, it wasn't a stag weekend. She simmers with indignation, guilt gnawing at her stomach. She had to leave when she did, though. Those seabirds were going haywire. When she saw the opportunity to avoid them, she'd have been a fool to ignore it.

If she hadn't escaped Farigg then, there was a real possibility of a fatal crash.

It's not as if Jonathan faces a tangible threat to life and limb. Sure, he'll be scared, but it's about time he confronted his fears. However lively the birds may be, he's big enough to frighten them off. He isn't alone, either. Gail is with him.

Lacey clenches her teeth. What will the pair of them be doing together? Daisy was caught unawares when Gail jumped out with Jonathan, but Lacey suspects the widow planned it. Her husband's body is hardly cold, and already she's chasing a replacement.

When Lacey left him, Jonathan claimed he wasn't interested in Gail, and she wasn't into him. Suppose it was a lie? They might have been having an affair all along. Or perhaps Gail murdered her husband so she could pursue Jonathan.

Jonathan could be in danger. What if he isn't attracted to Gail after all? If he doesn't obey her whims?

Lacey could call the emergency services, but they wouldn't be thrilled to walk into a love nest. Instead, she'll ring Jonathan, just to make sure he's okay.

Her finger hovers, then she swipes and hits his number. It goes to voicemail. Her call evidently isn't important to him.

A flash of anger brings warmth to her face. She imagines the couple cosy in that little croft the ornithologists use. The bothy, they call it. Lacey dropped the party there when she came to Farigg before.

Spitefully, she prays that the hut is already full of scientists. That would ruin the moment.

Anyway, if he gets fed up, Jonathan can ring 999 himself.

She counts to ten and calms down. It occurs to her that a disgruntled Jonathan could cause trouble for them all. She must warn Michael.

And ask for danger money.

# CHAPTER 50 GAIL

## Day 12 - Friday

The birds no longer bother us, although Jonathan shudders at their cries in the distance. He hasn't said another word. Perhaps it's the effect of the drug, or his head injury, or he's simply exhausted. We have a tacit agreement to reach the hut, and it's heavy going. There is no path. Stumbling over uneven terrain, I'm soon panting with exertion. Fatigue sends me tripping into a spiky gorse bush. Jonathan hardly seems to notice, and certainly doesn't offer sympathy. Luckily, jeans save me from the worst of the thorns.

My stomach roils. The building provides cover, but will it be a trap? I focus on my hope of meeting the scientists who tagged the gull: allies to help Jonathan and to protect me from him.

Perspective is deceptive. At a guess, we end up walking for hours. By the time we arrive, the sun has moved from straight overhead to the long shadows of afternoon. I'm footsore and aching all over, hunger gnawing at me and throat dry. Jonathan looks to be in a worse state. His eyes are hollow. The blood from his wound has clotted, congealing on his hair, neck and clothes.

"We made it, Jonathan." The good news is that the shabby wooden door isn't locked. It creaks as I push it open, and flecks of paint fall off.

The bad news is that no-one else is here. We're greeted by a musty odour and a deserted, spartan space. The hut's walls, constructed from squarish lumps of rock, remind me of home. That's where the similarity ends. This is a single cuboid room with a stone floor and corrugated roof. Furniture is basic too. String hammocks lie neatly folded on a shelf, wooden chairs are stacked in a corner, and a table has been pushed against them. A couple of kitchen cupboards sit next to a Belfast sink without taps.

I guess it's no worse than some places I lived as a child.

"Home sweet home," I say, with a breeziness I don't feel.

Jonathan slams the door closed, a slow smile creeping over his face.

I edge away from him.

His brow furrows. "Birds," he says, as if that explains everything.

"Why don't you sit down, and I'll explore," I suggest.

Being busy helps to combat my unease, but it doesn't take long to go through every cranny in the tiny hut. I discover chipped crockery, cutlery, pans, cleaning supplies, matches, water purification tablets, a tin of porridge oats, a camping stove with an empty gas cylinder and a wind-up radio. Another tin contains candles. We'll be using one tonight, as there's no electricity supply.

My stomach flips over in disgust at the cereal, which smells stale. But we'll need food to keep our strength up, so overnight oats are on the menu.

First, I must find water.

"Just popping outside," I tell Jonathan.

He grunts. His face is pale, still bruised from the beating he received from Nick. Now he's added another injury. At least we have shelter, and he can rest.

It's a relief both to leave him and to come across a full water butt behind the hut. Sullen and silent, Jonathan slumps in a chair while I return for a bucket and fill it. I add half a dozen purification tablets, leaving the door open to mitigate the stench of chlorine.

"Shut it," Jonathan says.

I jump, startled by his voice.

He staggers to his feet. "What kind of sadist are you?" he grumbles, giving the door a shove.

"I wanted to clear the air. Stop the smell..."

My voice peters out as I recognise the signs of anger. A vein throbs on Jonathan's forehead. He glares at me.

"Keep the birds out, okay?" he rasps.

"All right," I soothe, fixing a smile on my face while my heart thumps. The last thing I need is an argument with him. Look what happened to Nick.

"Why did you bring me to this hellhole?" he demands. "I know — you either want to kill me, or drive me mad."

"It was a mistake."

Jonathan's eyes narrow. "I'm the one who made a mistake. Your actions were entirely deliberate. What did you put in my coffee?"

I gawp at him. The truth is, I don't know.

"Don't tell me, then, Gail. Who cares what it was? It did the job for you."

“I’m sorry,” I reply, because I am. I’m also terrified he’ll turn violent. Despite the drugs, his wound and the lack of food and drink, he’s regaining energy. Rage must be pumping him up.

“I’ve worked it out,” Jonathan says. “This is tied in with Nick’s murder. You already tried to fit me up, and it didn’t work. So you’re having a second go, with dear Daisy helping you. I presume she’ll report me missing?”

I squirm. He may be hazy on the fine details, but he’s broadly right.

“You did him in after all,” Jonathan says. “I don’t blame you.”

He makes a theatrical bow. “Well done, black widow.”

My legs feel as if they’re about to give way. Hastily, I sit on the chair he’s vacated. Jonathan is the last person I’d expect to accuse me. After all, he injected Nick with the fatal dose — or did he?

He could be bluffing, of course.

Jonathan paces the room. His lips tighten. “You wanted to throw the cops off the scent. But why did you come with me? Ah. That was your mistake, wasn’t it?”

“No,” I protest. “The whole thing—”

“—How dare you try to frame me, and drag Lacey into it too?”

“I’m sorry,” I repeat. My gaze falls on the window, the clouds into which the helicopter disappeared. I wish I was anywhere but here, listening as Jonathan lays out my guilt. Swallowing a sob, I try to focus on my breathing.

“And now you’ll poison me.” His tone is calmer as he sniffs the chlorinated water.

“I’m stopping you from poisoning yourself,” I point out, voice quivering even though I’m on safer ground. “It’s rainwater from a barrel outside, and not safe without purification. Don’t touch it for half an hour. The tablets need time to work.”

“In that case,” he stares meaningfully at the hammocks, “I’d like to sleep.”

“Can you wait? Let me clean your wound first.”

Jonathan flinches. “Stay away from me.”

“But it could get infected.”

He glowers.

I sniff, unable to stem my tears. “I’m sorry this happened. But please don’t refuse my help.”

Jonathan huffs. He fumbles with a hammock, strings it up and climbs in. Within minutes, his snores resound in the confined space. His burst of energy, if that's what it was, was short-lived.

I sit down and stare out of the window.

A storm has blown in. The birds quiet as rain beats against the glass, heavy drops drumming on the roof. Even inside, the temperature falls. I shiver, picturing my children eagerly waiting for me to collect them from school. Hot, sticky tears drape my cheeks.

Will I ever see them again? Or will Jonathan and I starve when the porridge runs out?

My parents would be in their element now, catching fish and roasting seagulls. They wouldn't let self-pity overwhelm them. What would they say?

My gaze flicks to the old-fashioned radio, similar to one they used to own. It's what's called a transceiver. As well as receiving a signal, it can transmit too — a continuous wave, which you switch on and off to create Morse code.

I could send an SOS signal. Three dots, three dashes, three dots.

Unfolding the handle, I begin to rotate it. A green light blinks on.

"We're cooking with gas," I tell the slumbering Jonathan.

# CHAPTER 51 NEIL

## Day 13 - Saturday

The day promises to be a bad one before it's even begun. While his wife enjoys a Saturday lie-in, Neil has to work a shift at Bridewell. And he's just discovered that Gail Masterson has gone AWOL.

"Told you it's always the wife," Britt observes, handing over a cup of admittedly excellent coffee.

"Subtlety is obviously your middle name," Neil says.

"Pot, meet kettle," she replies.

He curses himself for not teasing more information from Gail when he had the chance. Maybe Britt was right, and he was swayed by a pretty face. After six years in CID, he should be better than that.

Why would she go on the run, though? Despite Britt's opinion, Jonathan Smyth remains the prime suspect in Nick Masterson's murder. Ruth Cluff flagged foul play as a concern when the Masterson kids weren't collected from school last night. Sent to investigate, Ruth found no-one at the Harefield Road address. No reply to phone calls and messages. Yet Gail had previously presented to Ruth as a good mother, engaged and caring. Ruth is adamant that the disappearance is out of character.

They put out a media release earlier, with a photo, which Neil suspects Ruth obtained from the neighbours. It's taken in their garden, and features Gail with her children, their little faces blurred out. The pair are safe in an emergency foster placement. Meanwhile, Ruth is trying to trace relatives, albeit with some difficulty. Gail's immediate family live abroad, as does her husband's only sibling. His mother has Alzheimer's. Neighbours volunteered to take the youngsters in, but there's no protocol for that.

Emails are already arriving in the project mailbox. Neil sifts through them. A sighting in a coffee shop, with a man. That's unlikely, given the location is a trading estate on the edge of Bristol. Why would Gail patronise it when she can choose from a dozen cafés in Clifton Village? Still, he'll ask for CCTV footage. Then there's a Daisy Gainsborough who claims to have information. She also wishes to report a murder. When should she come in to make a statement?

Neil phones the number she has supplied. After confirming her name and address, he gets to the point.

"I understand you're reporting a murder. Why didn't you ring 999?"

He can practically hear her shrug at the other end of the line. "Because I only just put two and two together," she says.

"And you know where Gail Masterson is?"

"Not exactly. But I hope I can be of assistance to you."

She sounds young, keen and upper class. The sort of person who would move in Nick and Gail Masterson's circles. Neil asks her to come to Bridewell straight away, which she estimates will take twenty minutes, 'because parking is so, so dreadful in central Bristol.'

He doesn't time her, but he sends Britt out for more coffee, and they're another cup down when they receive a call from the front desk.

Britt collects Daisy from the waiting area, a row of plastic chairs bolted to the floor. Their meeting room is slightly more salubrious, in that the furniture can be moved.

Neil stands up to shake Daisy's hand when she's ushered in. She's not as young as he expected. Artful use of cosmetics makes it hard to tell, but she's possibly the other side of thirty. Is she planning to attend a garden party later? Everything she wears is decorated with flowers, from her long tunic to her patterned shoes and the silk rose in her red hair.

"Nice to meet you, Daisy," he says. "I would offer you a drink, but our machine produces the worst tea and coffee in the city."

"It can't be that bad. I have a machine at home," she says. Her words trail off. Clearly, she's realised that he's talking about a different kind of machine altogether.

Neil asks her to sit down, obtains her consent to tape and video, and they begin.

"You wish to report a murder?"

She nods.

"Would that be 'yes', Daisy?"

"Yes. My mother was murdered by her husband. For her money."

She begins to tell the sort of tale that is becoming depressingly familiar to the police. A younger man worms his way into a lonely widow's life. He declares his love. Soon, they're married. She changes her will. Her death follows with indecent haste.

And the man involved? Jonathan Smyth.

Interesting.

“We’ll check it out,” Neil promises.

“Thank you.” Daisy sniffs. “It’s terribly upsetting.”

“Of course,” Neil soothes. “You emailed about Gail Masterson?”

“Yes.” Daisy drops her voice to a conspiratorial whisper. “I wouldn’t be surprised if Jonathan killed Nick Masterson too. There’s no smoke without fire, is there?”

“Sometimes there is,” Britt says mildly.

Daisy rewards her with a filthy look. “Well, Jonathan Smyth and Gail Masterson are close friends. Very close. Maybe he knows where she is.”

Neil freezes. The description of the man in the coffee bar tallies with Jonathan Smyth, all right. Perhaps Daisy is on to something.

# CHAPTER 52 GAIL

## Day 13 - Saturday

I have a system now. Purify water. Wait. Wind up the radio. Send SOS repeatedly until battery fails. Wind it up again. Send SOS. Hold nose to blot out the taint of chlorine, then drink. Make sure Jonathan does too. Swab his wound. Soak oats. Transmit SOS signals again. Wind up radio. Eat mushy oats. Make sure Jonathan does too. Try not to throw up.

Rinse and repeat.

We don't talk more than necessary. Jonathan mostly dozes in his hammock. So, while my hands are busy, my mind has time to reflect. To focus on Mary and Tom. To wonder why I made decisions that could cost my life and their happiness.

Which means I'm crying.

"Giving in to self-pity?" Jonathan asks.

I guess sympathy is too much to hope for.

"My kids. I worry about them." Continuing to turn the radio's handle, I don't even look in his direction.

"You should have thought of that before."

"Thanks, Captain Obvious." I add sourly, "Yes, I should have gone with Daisy. Left you to the bonxie."

"That would have given Daisy a kick. Me and the birds." His laughter is hollow.

I frown. "What is it with you and birds, anyway?"

"Don't pretend you don't know," Jonathan sneers.

Silence stretches between us again, until he says, "Maybe you really have no idea. Well, your dear friend, Daisy, is close with her brother. I'm sure he told her what happened at Markham's. Let me fill you in."

# CHAPTER 53 JONATHAN

## Before

Jonathan sits with his roommates at breakfast, part of a crowd, yet still on his own. He only opens his mouth to shovel food in it, as speaking invites laughter and heavy-handed mimicry of his Bristol accent. The grub is an unexpected bonus of boarding school. While the other boys complain about the quality, he's delighted to receive three square meals a day. You can help yourself to as much as you want. After cereal and juice, there's bacon, mounds of scrambled egg, hash browns, mushrooms and beans, none of it raw or burnt. He chews on the crunchy, salty bacon, hoping that Nick won't slap his back with force. It happens a couple of times a week. While he could cope if he knew it was coming, the point is that he doesn't. Nor can he be sure when a tormentor will whisk his chair away as he's about to sit down.

But Nick is all smiles this morning. Jonathan suspects it's because he helped the other boy with his maths homework. Nick is good-looking, the sort of pupil who ends up on the front page of the admissions brochure. He charms all the teachers. On the rugby field, he's smashing it. But he's thick as the proverbial excrement. It won't hold him back in life, of course; Nick is clear about that. He's being groomed to take over the family business.

Nice work if you can get it.

"Hey, Jonno," Nick says.

Jonathan raises an eyebrow. He's smart enough to keep his mouth shut.

"It's Saturday. Exeat. Me, Hazard and Gilly are going to the beach. Want to come with us?"

"Isn't it out of bounds?"

"Who will know? Unless," Nick's eyes narrow, "you're planning to snitch on us?"

"No." Jonathan tries to still his breath. His heart is already racing. If anyone else tells the teachers, Nick will think it was him.

He'd planned a quiet day in the library, his favourite place. But it's too risky to turn down Nick's invitation.

"I'd like to go," he says.

"Great. See you in ten." Nick gets up, whacks Jonathan between the shoulder blades, and strolls out of the dining hall.

Harry sniggers. "Don't be late." He piles Nick's crockery, and his own, onto Jonathan's tray.

Winded, Jonathan cleans up the food he inadvertently spat out. Finishing his breakfast, he returns to the dorm for cash. He has a little squirrelled away, enough for his bus fare.

The journey to a faded seaside resort takes an hour. Nick's chumminess is gone; he joshes with his two buddies, making no attempt to include the awkward fourth member of their group. Jonathan doesn't mind. Although the school has a rural setting, he never has a chance to go sightseeing. The countryside is still a novelty to him. He enjoys staring out of the window at the flat green land, the black-splodged cows and lively lambs.

They arrive at the promenade. A breeze prickles Jonathan's skin and delivers salt to his nostrils. Competing smells of vinegar and candyfloss drift from stalls lining the seafront. It's already busy, the April day unseasonably warm, and trippers are picnicking on the beach.

Jonathan wants to stand there, drinking in the view, watching gulls glide and caw. But the other boys make a beeline for an amusement arcade. They proceed to lose money in the machines. Jonathan tags along, ignoring their jeers at his failure to participate. On balance, he'd rather suffer social death — after all, what's new? — than walk ten miles back to school.

Nick wins a cheap pack of cards from the teddy picker. He throws it on the floor in disgust. "How about ice cream, lads?"

"I can't afford—"

Nick grins wolfishly. "My treat, all right?"

"Er, thanks." He follows the trio to a pastel-coloured van parked nearby.

"Strawberry and vanilla cones?" Nick asks. He's buying for all of them.

A machine produces pink and white, sugar-scented swirls. Nick hands them first to Harry, then Mike. He keeps hold of the third. Then, at last, he bears the fourth, triumphant, like the Statue of Liberty.

"Come and get it, Jonno."

Jonathan reaches up, but not quickly enough. Nick smashes the fragile confection down on his head.

“Run!” Nick commands.

Jonathan stumbles around, trying to brush the cold, squidgy mess from his eyes. He can’t see. The top of his head aches with the sudden chill, as if it’s been dunked in a freezer. Then he feels the scratch of claws in his hair, a sharp tap, a gull’s screech.

He screams, thrashing about…

# CHAPTER 54 GAIL

## Day 13 - Saturday

“So, what happened?” My muscles tighten. That’s so like Nick. I can smell Jonathan’s fear. After a decade with his persecutor, the emotion is my familiar companion.

“There was a family standing behind us. The dad fought the bird off. Belted it with a brolly, one of those huge golf umbrellas.”

“I know the type. Nick bought hundreds to give away.” How proud I was to spot strangers using them, with their prominent Masterson Group logo. I didn’t have a clue.

“The family used theirs as a sunshade.” Jonathan frowns. “They were kind people. Sat me down, bought me another cornet. But I made a big mistake. I mentioned Markham’s School, and then it all kicked off.”

“Let me guess. They phoned the head.”

“His deputy. We were all grounded. And Nick knew who’d grassed him up,” Jonathan says gloomily. “Best days of your life. As if.”

“I’d have preferred an education with some structure,” I mutter.

“Really? You didn’t go to boarding school?”

“Home educated. We travelled around. My parents were digital nomads before the term was invented. Still, I’m settled in one place now. Assuming I get back.”

The battery is topped up, and I begin signalling.

Dot, dot, dot. Dash, dash, dash. Dot, dot, dot. Pause.

How long will I have to do this? I could be broadcasting into a void.

A beam creaks as Jonathan leaves his hammock. He stands beside me, focusing on my hands as I tap out the pattern. A whiff of body odour makes it through the dominant stink of chlorine.

I breathe slowly in and out, forcing myself to ignore him. He’d be mad to stop my transmission. However unlikely, it’s our only chance of escape.

“You come across as basically decent,” he observes. “Even if you kidnapped me and killed Nick Masterson. I can’t understand why you chose to marry a prick like him.”

“I didn’t kill him.”

Dot, dot, dot. Dash, dash, dash. Dot, dot, dot. Pause.

"Maybe I believe you," Jonathan says. "Maybe I don't. But I didn't murder your husband. Nick knocked me out before I had a chance to do him any damage."

Of course he'd deny it. But he could be telling the truth. If he is, how did Nick end up dead?

Dot, dot, dot. Dash, dash, dash. Dot, dot, dot. Pause.

"Anyway," he says, "you didn't answer my question."

"I didn't choose Nick," I admit. "He chose me. And he was so sweet then, in the beginning. But it wasn't just his looks and charm. I liked his solidity. His ordinariness, although he'd never agree he was ordinary."

Jonathan laughs bitterly. "Oh, he is. Was. Bullies all work off the same playbook."

"I wanted to stop running. But I ended up trapped." Shuddering, I scan the tiny, comfort-free room. This is a trap too, and Morse code is my only hope. I send the next SOS.

"I'm sure we'll be rescued soon," Jonathan says. He stretches out his legs. "We need to agree on our story."

"Story? We'll tell the truth." The weight of being brave is almost crushing me, though. My children might be lost to me forever. Blinking a tear away, I continue tapping.

"Listen," Jonathan says. "I'm not telling anyone you drugged me. You did, didn't you?" His eyebrows twitch up. "But you saved my life."

"After we landed here. Which we wouldn't have done if I hadn't—"

He interrupts. "Then there's Lacey. I don't know how she got dragged into this, but I want to keep her out of trouble."

"She's your ex, isn't she?"

"Right. And she deserves better."

A catch in his voice invokes my curiosity. I peer at him. "Why did you two break up?"

"Because I hit on you."

I purse my lips, wishing I could block out the memory. "Well. We all make mistakes."

"It wasn't a mistake."

I hold my breath. If he's planning a repeat because I'm the only woman in range, I need to put him straight. "Jonathan, I'm not interested."

He grimaces. "I know. But I mean it. I wanted to get back at Nick—"

"Because of the seagull incident?" I cut in, tension stiffening my jaw. "You waited a long time."

"No. Not that. Earlier in the evening, he'd groped my partner, Lacey. Told her she didn't need a loser boyfriend. But he could help, because he had an open marriage. So, he'd take another room at the hotel and show her what a real man could do for her…"

The wind howls outside. A chill freezes my blood. "Are you serious?" I demand.

Of course he is. He's talking about a man who robbed investors and impregnated his PA. What else did Nick do behind my back?

"My behaviour wasn't perfect, I admit," Jonathan says. "I was three sheets to the wind. And I decided to put his open marriage to the test. Epic fail."

"We didn't have an open marriage."

"Quite. You slapped my face." He sighs. "Lacey broke up with me too."

I allow myself a swift sideways glance. He looks pale and miserable. The women in his life have been far stronger than me, I realise. Matilda, running a business and flouting convention with a younger husband. Lacey, ditching him at the first sign of infidelity. Yet when I suspected Nick of cheating, my greatest fear was that he'd leave.

I wouldn't have thrown him out.

I couldn't have summoned the courage.

I'm weak. That's how I ended up here. And there's no guarantee I'll ever get away.

Dot, dot, dot. Dash, dash, dash. Dot, dot, dot. Pause.

"You couldn't explain to Lacey?" I ask. "Beg for forgiveness?"

"She's a one strike and you're out kind of girl," he says gloomily. "Also, she spotted me snogging Harry's wife three days later."

I feel sick. He'd almost persuaded me he wasn't a creep after all. But he's being extremely frank. Perhaps in a minute, he'll confess to murder.

I transmit another SOS signal before asking, "How did that happen?"

"We were in a country pub. I didn't know there was an airstrip down the road."

"But Harry's wife?"

"Believe it or not, after you slapped me, Sophia slipped me a note with her phone number. I nearly threw it away. But then I remembered how Nick, Harry and Mike had tormented me at Markham's. How they'd jeered when Lacey walked out. They'd ruined my life. And at last, I could get back at them."

Gulping back bile, I splutter, "By sleeping with their wives?"

"Harry's wife. Mike's sister…"

I put the radio down and turn away, so angry I'm trembling. He seduced Daisy in a sick quest for revenge. I can't look at him, because if I did, I'd slap his face again.

"Jonathan, I've got news for you. Women are people. Not objects. I'm not a man's possession…"

"You reckon your husband believed that?"

How dare he.

"No," I yell, "no, I don't. And you'd grasp, more than anyone, that I learned that lesson the hard way."

"I'm sorry."

Really?

He doesn't sound sorry. His tone is reasonable, as if we're chatting over a coffee. Like that will ever happen again.

The sympathy I felt five minutes ago has evaporated.

"I behaved badly," he says, "but you have to understand, Gail, that I've changed. For the better. Because when I met Tilly, I fell in love."

"And that erases the past?" My voice sounds alien, loud and harsh. I wouldn't have dared to speak to Nick like this. "Spare me the self-justification, Jonathan. It's small wonder that Daisy hates you. If you had an ounce of integrity, you'd turn over your inheritance to Daisy and Mike. Give them all the money."

His laughter is strained. "Thanks to Nick, there isn't any."

"Stop blaming him for your problems." My muscles quiver as I storm out of the hut, slamming the door behind me.

I have to forget about Nick and rebuild my life. Why can't Jonathan do the same?

# CHAPTER 55 GAIL

## Day 15 - Monday

We've run out of oats.

This is bad.

I have to find another food supply.

Jonathan won't be any use. We've hardly spoken since our row. And this morning, he didn't wake up.

He was groggier yesterday, complaining of a headache when I cleaned his wound. I spotted pus seeping out of it. Although I've purified the water and used plenty of soap, an infection must have set in. It's all the more reason to keep turning the handle and sending distress signals.

I have to get help for him. For me. For the sake of my children.

But first, I'm setting rabbit snares. I noticed a line of flattened vegetation near the water butt. Following it revealed a cluster of round black pellets. Although I feel sick at killing another living being, it's either them or me. And I'll only set a couple of traps, and stay outside to watch them, so I can make sure death is quick.

I cycle through childhood memories. You start with wire. There's none to be found, but string will do instead. I hack several lengths off a hammock. It beats fashioning a rope from plant stems. The local vegetation will come in useful later, though, as we'll need fuel for a fire. I'll keep an eye open for brushwood.

"I'm going out, Jonathan," I say softly.

He snores. His newly stubbled face has a waxy cast, white with flushed cheeks. Placing a hand on his forehead, I feel heat rising. I loosen his shirt buttons and dab exposed skin with a damp towel.

How much longer has he got?

A sea fret licks at the moorland outside, damp tendrils chilling me as I pass through. I set a pair of traps and skulk nearby, trying not to shiver. It's vital to stay still.

The mist burns away. Gulls screech overhead. Then a lower-pitched note rumbles in the background. Turning through 360 degrees, I spot it.

A helicopter.

The tiny dot grows larger.

Lacey's coming back.

I jump up and down, waving and hollering, even though common sense tells me she won't notice with the rotors deafening her. Soon, I can't hear anything either. The craft is almost overhead, a red and white-striped airborne whale floating above.

It's not Lacey after all. But it doesn't matter, as long as the pilot has seen me.

Have they, though?

# CHAPTER 56 GAIL

## Day 15 - Monday

Thanks to the paramedic on the helicopter, Jonathan and I have been whisked to the hospital in Paisley. The coastguards who found us say I'll just need a routine chat to the police, then I'm free to go. Jonathan is in a worse condition, however. Throughout our forty-minute flight, he remained asleep. He's been stretchered in for treatment. Meanwhile, the nurses found a small office where I can wait alone. They also rustled up a cheese sandwich and a glass of water.

This is literally the best food and drink I've ever tasted. Relishing each mouthful, I run a hand over my full belly when I'm done. But my spirits don't remain raised for long. Energy restored, my thoughts turn to Tom and Mary. How can I let them know I'm okay, or even travel back to them? My phone and money are stuck in a field in Gloucestershire, sitting in a handbag inside my car. So are various cards that may not work anyway.

Perhaps the police will help.

I tap my fingers on the desk, hitting a whitewashed wall with my elbow when I stretch. The room is no more than a cubbyhole, but I was informed I was lucky to have it. It belongs to a manager, nameplate on the door, whose unexpected sickness has given his colleagues a breakout area. Apart from a bank of locked filing cabinets and a window overlooking a blank wall, it boasts a laptop table and two armless typing chairs. The sparse furnishings are nevertheless a hundred times more comfortable than the hut on Farigg.

Someone knocks on the glass door.

"Come in," I shout.

I have an instant impression of black uniforms and a room that is suddenly overfull. Two young men, their caps and logoed stab vests identifying them as police officers, crowd into the space.

"Good afternoon." The first through the door has nabbed the spare chair. "I'm PC Drew Mackay of Police Scotland, and this is my colleague, PC Jamie Hill."

Jamie Hill scowls at him. He leans against the table.

"I understand that you were picked up from Farigg by a search and rescue team," PC Mackay says. "Is that correct?"

He has a pronounced lilt, rolling his ‘r’s.

I laugh nervously. “Yes, that’s right.”

“Well, we’ll need to ask you a few questions,” he says. “Standard practice, nothing to worry about. Are you ready to start?”

“Absolutely. And I’ve got questions too, mainly because I don’t have any money to get home.”

“Home is where?”

“Bristol.”

“That’s in the south of England, isn’t it?” PC Mackay fingers his chin. “Okay, we’ll deal with it when we’ve been through the facts. Can we begin with your name?”

“Mrs Gail Masterson.”

“Mind if I call you Gail?” PC Mackay asks.

“Please do.”

“Walk me through when and how you arrived on Farigg, Gail.”

My mouth is dry as I begin. This is where I must hope that Jonathan tells the same lie. That he twists the truth as we agreed, despite our differences.

Assuming he remembers by the time he wakes up.

“We hoped to do some birdwatching.”

An eyebrow arches upwards. “You can’t do that near Bristol?”

I cross my arms and legs, then hastily uncross them in case I look defensive. “Not the great skua,” I say.

“Ah, the infamous bonxie. Not to be messed with.”

“As we found out.” I paste a smile on my face. He’ll expect a helpless female. There’s no reason to disappoint him.

“Hmm.” He frowns. “Nesting season. The coastguards mentioned they had to be cautious. What measures did you take to protect yourselves and the birds?”

“Well…” I sigh, hoping I’m not overacting. “The pilot had taken ornithologists there before without any issue. She didn’t expect problems with the birds. And she landed some way from them anyhow, or so she thought.”

I pause, looking longingly at the empty water glass.

“Do you need a drink? Let me fetch you one,” the other man offers. “I spotted a tap outside.”

“We’ll suspend the interview until he’s back,” PC Mackay says. “It’s just routine. We’re trying to paint a picture of what happened.”

PC Hill reappears with a full glass. I take a sip, grateful for an excuse to be silent.

“A great skua flew towards us and repeatedly dived at the helicopter.”

PC Mackay jolts back. “Whoa. That’s dangerous. You could have crashed.”

“Yes, our pilot was worried. The rotors had slowed almost to a standstill because we were on the ground, but she was afraid for our safety if she lifted off.”

“Rightly so,” PC Mackay murmurs.

“So Jonathan — that’s Jonathan Smyth, who’s here in hospital — jumped out. As the only man in an otherwise female group, he believed it was his job to deal with the threat.”

The officer rolls his eyes.

“He shouted at it, so it attacked him. What did you say about the great skua?”

“You don’t mess with a bonxie,” PC Mackay repeats.

I sense the man’s gaze boring into me. Swallowing, I wonder how much longer I can maintain the lie. But I have to try.

“He collapsed and started bleeding. I climbed down to help. The bird wasn’t put off. It buzzed around us, and the pilot screamed that she’d have to take off again. She panicked, I think. Before they ascended, my best friend said she would call the emergency services. Get assistance.”

Jonathan and I had agreed that we’d present Lacey as blameless. One of the other women must take the rap. While it was a tough call, I decided Daisy deserved the biggest share of the grief. A true friend wouldn’t leave me in the lurch.

“I am sorry,” PC Mackay says, “but there is no record of a 999 call about Farigg, at least, not until a radio ham alerted emergency services this morning. A distress signal was broadcast, by Jonathan Smyth, I assume?”

“That was me, actually.” I reign in an impulse to be smug. “It was all I could do, when help didn’t come. By then, I wasn’t only concerned for Jonathan’s well-being, I was frantic with anxiety about my children. And still am.” That much is true, at any rate.

PC Mackay asks who else was in the helicopter. I give a brief description of the pilot, whose name I claim not to remember. Then there was my friend, Daisy, who organised the trip, and Tamara, my late husband’s trusted PA.

I dab at my eyes, hoping the police don't question the others. Presumably, it would involve a trip to England. Do they have a budget for that? But although the trio may give completely different accounts — less likely in Lacey's case, if Jonathan wakes up and manages to speak to her — I'm not sure it matters. The police won't be able to prove I deliberately left my children without a carer. I'll be reunited with Tom and Mary, and we'll fly into a bright future of sunshine and butterflies.

Or perhaps we will once we're over Nick's death. So much has happened since, but it was only last week. Despite suspecting the world is a better place without him, I need time to grieve.

"Well, thank you," PC Mackay says. "We'll do some paperwork to wrap up, then—"

PC Hill catches the other man's eye, and points to his phone.

PC Mackay purses his lips. "I'll just confer with my colleague and come right back," he says.

Fidgeting, I worry that they won't return. Perhaps they have a more important case to tackle than a search and rescue debrief. Still, if they won't help me travel back to Bristol, I'll call Daisy. There's a landline in this office. Surely I can get it to work? She may be surprised to receive a call asking her to pay my fare home, but it's the least she can do after dumping me on Farigg.

I peer through the glass door. The officers haven't left. PC Mackay is on his phone, gesturing with animation. PC Hill spots me, and mouths 'Wait'.

It feels like hours before PC Mackay pushes open the door again. He remains standing, his expression dour as he says, "Gail Masterson, as you know, I am PC Drew Mackay, and this is PC Jamie Hill, from Police Scotland. We are here on behalf of Avon and Somerset Police. You are being arrested on suspicion of the murder of Nick Masterson…"

I gawp at them, so dumbfounded that I offer no resistance when PC Hill snaps on handcuffs.

# CHAPTER 57 NEIL

## Day 17 - Wednesday

"For the benefit of the rest of the team, shall we watch Gail Masterson's interview?" Sherry asks.

"It would be useful," Dave Smeeth purrs.

Sherry taps her laptop keyboard, and the recording plays out on the incident room's whitewashed wall. Neil and Britt identify themselves and ask Gail to confirm her name.

She's wearing a standard issue custody grey tracksuit. Even in this poor quality video, you can see she is tired. Her hair straggles around her shoulders, and dark circles accentuate her eyes.

The discussion proceeds, with Gail interrupting Neil's first question by asking when she might see her children. Neil answers politely. He's non-committal. The pair are safe and well, but next steps depend on the outcome of the police investigation.

Sherry pauses the video. "Nice work, Neil," she says.

"Thanks. We haven't raised the possibility of neglect charges at this stage."

Sherry nods. "Good point. We took her into custody in Bristol at—"

"—7pm yesterday," Dave Smeeth says.

"Right, thank you, Dave. We're not in a position to charge her with murder yet, and we'll apply for a custody extension. But if there's enough evidence of child neglect, we should progress with that charge ASAP. It would buy us time."

Sherry presses play, and they see Gail once again denying that Jonathan is her lover. He is her interior design client, a friend of her husband's. Her voice falters on the word friend.

Seeing Sherry's fingers hover over the keyboard, Neil raises a hand. "I picked that up," he says.

The recording proves it. Pressed as to what kind of friend, Gail says they shared a room at boarding school. The two men weren't close afterwards, but met occasionally since. She goes on to repeat both the account of Nick's death that she gave Neil before, and the details she provided to Police Scotland.

"Well," Sherry says, "what do you think, Neil?"

Neil throws up his hands. "Somebody's lying. Gail's consistent. I'll give her that. But birdwatching with Daisy Gainsborough? Interesting, isn't it, that Gail denies she and Jonathan are lovers? Daisy says they are. Yet Daisy also claims to have no idea of Gail's whereabouts. If you believe Gail, Daisy dropped the pair of them on Farigg."

"Yes, interesting. Let's see whose story checks out." Sherry fiddles with a strand of golden hair, catches herself, and stops. "What about the rest of Daisy's statement? Dave, I'm aware that her allegation of murder has been the subject of a separate investigation. However, you're working on it, and it will help this team if you'd share findings."

Dave coughs. "Mrs Gainsborough claimed that Jonathan Smyth killed his wife, who was Mrs Gainsborough's mother. She's dead, all right, but the death certificate stated the cause as advanced pancreatic cancer. I spoke to the GP who attended, and he confirmed the diagnosis and said she'd been receiving palliative care for three months. In his words, it's a disease that can go wrong quickly.

"He put me in touch with the nurse who stayed at her bedside on the night she passed away. The nurse confirmed a natural death. While this took place in the deceased's home with Mr Smyth present, she said he went to bed at eleven. She didn't see him again until she woke him to advise him of his wife's passing. Without prompting, she said she'd swear an oath on it. Make of that what you will."

"What do you think, Dave?" Sherry asks.

Dave replies without hesitation. "Be wary of trusting anything Mrs Gainsborough says."

"We should interview her again," Sherry suggests. "Maybe it's overkill, but I'd like Dave, Neil and Brittany to do so together. First, Neil and Brittany can find out what Jonathan Smyth has to say for himself."

"Is he out of hospital then?" Neil asks.

"On his way to Bristol. The only problem is that Police Scotland tell us he's a man of few words. To be precise, 'No comment'. But I'm sure you can win him over."

# CHAPTER 58 EXTRACT FROM A PREPARED STATEMENT BY JONATHAN SMYTH

After the stress of my late wife's funeral, my stepdaughter, Daisy Gainsborough, invited me to go birdwatching with her. She thought that getting back to nature would help us both decompress. Daisy is a woman of substantial means and believes money is for spending. She chose a picturesque island location in Scotland and arranged a helicopter to take us. This was intended to be a daytrip. I expected we would have a picnic with champagne, snap a few photos for Daisy's Instagram, and fly back.

I thought it would be just the two of us, but Daisy had invited friends. Gail Masterson, who I knew from her interior design work for me, has recently also suffered a bereavement. The other guest was a woman called Tamara, a stranger to me except that she had gone uninvited to my wife's funeral, where she made a scene. I believe Daisy felt sorry for her. I was not looking forward to her company, but fortunately, she was seated in front next to the pilot. I sat in the rear with Daisy and Gail.

By coincidence, the pilot was an old friend, Lacey Lewis. I know her to be a helicopter pilot of several years' experience. Thus, I would expect her judgement of external conditions to be sound. She advised us that she had flown to Farigg before, had not encountered problems, and did not anticipate any on this occasion. She is not to blame for what happened.

When we landed, I left the aircraft first, followed by Gail. There was a particular type of bird we wished to see, a magnificent specimen called the great skua. One of these was wandering too close to the helicopter for comfort, and I wanted to scare it off. I waved my arms at it, and it flew away. I did not realise it would then return and attack me.

I must have been unconscious, as my next memory is of waking up outside on the island. My head was painful and bloody where the bird had made contact. Gail was with me. She told me the helicopter had left for safety reasons, and Daisy had promised to get help for us. I do not know why no help was forthcoming immediately.

Gail and I made it to a hut used by visitors to Farigg. We were the only occupants. There were basic supplies of food and water, and a short wave radio. We used this to send SOS signals. I recall little else, because my wound was infected. I became delirious. We were, however, rescued by an HM Coastguard SAR team after three days on Farigg. I was transferred to the Royal Alexandra Hospital in Paisley, where I remained until my arrest. I emphasise that I have not murdered anybody.

# CHAPTER 59 NEIL

## Day 18 – Thursday

It is recycling day at Daisy's prestigious address in Redland. Passing a cursory glance over the black box outside, Dave Smeeth winks at Neil. "They like their white wine, don't they? M&S and Waitrose too. No cheap paint stripper."

Neil counts ten bottles. There's no sign of the champagne that Jonathan says he was promised, though.

Dave regards the immaculately groomed houses. "Wonder how she found the money to live in a place like this? Or hire a helicopter for the day."

Neil has asked himself the same question. Daisy can't be much older than him. "Bank of Mum and Dad?" he ventures.

Daisy wears another long, floral frock. Her red hair is pinned up, wisps framing her face. She greets Neil and Britt warmly, shakes Dave's hand and offers them all coffee. Would they like to try her new Nespresso pods? It's a single origin blend from Peru.

When she leads them to the eat-in kitchen at the rear, Neil smells alcohol on her breath. Yet Daisy seems as keen to drink coffee as they are. She seats the detectives on high stools by a breakfast bar, on which she places four steaming mugs.

Britt takes a sip. "Rich, isn't it? I like that. Your house is lush, by the way."

"It needs a lot of work," Daisy says. "Gail has been super-helpful with design ideas. I don't know what I'll do without her."

Perhaps she hasn't heard about the rescue on Farigg, or that a man and woman are helping the police with enquiries. Sherry is keeping communications low key, after all. But it may be that Daisy expects Gail to go to prison for a very long time.

Neil checks out the coffee, decides regretfully that this is another machine he needs but can't afford, and studies Daisy.

She smiles at him. "How can I help you?" she asks.

"Presumably, you're aware that Nick Masterson died exactly two weeks ago? On a Thursday afternoon. Where were you at the time?"

She gasps, clearly thrown by the question. Good.

"I don't know how that's relevant to anything," she says stiffly.

"We're conducting a murder inquiry, and we're trying to eliminate as many people as possible," Neil says. He's sure he's hit a nerve. She was up to something that day, but it would be the greatest gift ever if she confessed to murdering Nick.

He rarely enjoys such good fortune, though, and Daisy's silence tells him no admission of guilt is imminent.

"It will help us a lot if you'd explain what you were doing," he says.

Her eyes harden. "I was with a friend."

"And your friend will confirm that to us?" Neil is careful not to inject innuendo into the term, although he can guess what kind of friend this is.

"I suppose so," Daisy spits.

"Could you write down contact details, please? We'll be discreet. Tell them it's for elimination purposes."

Slightly mollified, she fetches a pen and a sheet of smooth cream paper. She prints the name and telephone number with a flourish.

"Thank you. We'll be in touch with this Alex Jones." Neil passes the note to Britt. "Now I'd like you to tell me about your movements last Friday."

Daisy shrugs. "Same as usual. Dropped the kids at school, came home and cleared up. Washed my husband's shirts. Made a pie for supper."

She sounds more confident now. Nonchalant.

"You didn't, by any chance, take a helicopter ride with a few friends?"

Daisy's mouth falls open. Her eyes bulge as they shift focus between Neil and Britt.

"I don't know what you mean," she says.

"We have information to suggest you travelled to the Inner Hebrides island of Farigg," Neil says. "That's all. Remember anything about it?"

"I want a lawyer," she snaps. "Hang on while I call my brother."

Neil nods to his colleagues. "Do you need privacy?" he asks Daisy.

"Yes." She hurries out of the kitchen.

Neil overhears a muffled, one-sided conversation.

When she returns, Daisy's face is flushed. She scowls. "It turns out my brother isn't my lawyer after all," she says. "He tells me he can't act for me. Conflict of interest or some such rubbish. Anyway, you might like to ask him who paid for the helicopter. From now on, I'm making no further comment."

# CHAPTER 60 NEIL

## Day 19 - Friday

Michael Gill's office boasts a view of The Gherkin, its glittering façade catching the sun as clouds float behind it. Although he's working at a desk when Neil and Britt arrive, he suggests they all sit on a pair of leather sofas by the window. A girl with a plummy voice brings coffee.

Neil holds the cup to his lips to disguise a yawn. He caught the red eye train this morning, the only saving grace being that it was direct from his local station. Luckily, tiny Yatton is on the line to London.

Their surroundings are a palace compared with Bridewell. Gill's career is evidently in the stratosphere, way above ordinary mortals. In the cutthroat world of City law firms, he can't have succeeded by caring much about others.

Refreshingly, the lawyer is willing to talk. The words 'No comment' don't enter his vocabulary. He doesn't request a solicitor. Of course, he's qualified in the field himself, although he points out that criminal law is not his area of expertise. Corporate work is his speciality, he tells them, and it has made him a multi-millionaire despite Nick Masterson's depredations. Why would he risk all that to kidnap his stepfather?

Neil coughs to cover his surprise. He hasn't mentioned either kidnapping or Jonathan Smyth. "You tell me," he says.

"Well, I wouldn't." Gill runs a manicured finger over his smooth chin. He proceeds to throw Daisy under the bus. Whatever went wrong, it was nothing to do with him. Oh, and his reference to kidnapping was a figure of speech. He wouldn't dream of suggesting any such event took place.

The gist of his account is that he paid for his sister to enjoy a private helicopter flight as a treat. She was upset after his mother's funeral. A little R and R would do Daisy the world of good, he thought. He borrowed the aircraft from a friend, found a sympathetic pilot, and left her to it. Although he can't quite remember, he may have suggested Daisy take a few mates. No, he has no idea who went with her. And it's not his fault if the trip turned out badly.

"What do you think of Jonathan Smyth?" Neil asks.

Gill doesn't bat an eyelid. "I try to avoid him, to be frank," he says. "At school, he was a bit of a geek. Didn't fit in. In spite of that, we rubbed along reasonably well. But I never felt he was the right man for my mother. I can understand her marrying again, but she needed a more mature person. Somebody her own age."

"You thought he was after her money?"

Gill laughs, not unpleasantly. "You said it, not me."

"Who inherits her estate?"

Gill shakes his head. "Well, he will, of course. It doesn't bother me. I'm not short of cash. My sister may feel differently, but you'd have to ask her."

Everything he says is plausible. Scrutinising the calm, urbane lawyer in his well-cut suit, Neil suspects a jury would believe every word.

Yet Gill isn't finished. As Neil rises to leave, the lawyer adds, "I understand you guys in Bristol are looking into Nick Masterson's death. I may be able to help."

Neil's outstretched hand returns to his side. "What would you like to tell us?"

"My wife's uncle is Chief Constable of a Home Counties police division," Gill replies. "If your boss wants a few tips on running a murder investigation, he has only to ask. I'd be happy to facilitate a meeting."

# CHAPTER 61 LACEY

## Day 20 - Saturday

It's the call Lacey has been dreading. She's still lounging in bed, enjoying a rare lie-in, when she picks up her phone for a little doom scrolling. That's when she discovers it's been switched off since yesterday morning. She did a late drop last night, and went straight to bed afterwards. Her life is so glamorous. Not.

There are five missed calls from an unknown number. As she stares at the screen, the same number rings her.

Detective Constable Brittany Billinge asks Lacey to pop into Bridewell Police Station this morning, if she doesn't mind.

The unspoken subtext is that, if she does mind, they will find ways to compel her to attend an interview. Lacey sighs. They agree on a time.

Slightly less than two hours later, she arrives on foot. She rents a studio flat in the city centre at the trendy Wapping Wharf development. Naturally, she stopped at her local coffee shop for breakfast: an espresso and a pain au chocolat. In fact, she treated herself to a second pastry to calm her nerves. The taste of butter clings to her lips. It comforts her.

She has been paid in full by now, and Michael Gill rang her yesterday to promise a bonus if he stayed out of trouble. Lacey didn't recognise that number either. It must have been a burner phone, which means he's worried. However, she is too. If there's any suggestion she left unwilling passengers behind, she could lose her licence. No, she will say that Jonathan and Gail wanted to stay on Farigg.

Of course, the rotors were running, so she may not have heard them properly. But her client, Daisy, assured her that was the case.

Lacey has practised her story so often than she almost believes it.

# CHAPTER 62 NEIL

## Day 20 - Saturday

It's a small group at the briefing this Saturday afternoon: Sherry, Neil, Britt and Dave. As ever, Dave is the Action Manager, ready at his keyboard to update HOLMES for completed tasks and ensure that new ones are captured. First, he's eager to tell them what he's discovered about Daisy.

"Keep it short, Dave," Sherry says. "We can't hold Gail in custody much longer unless we charge her. So, start us off."

"Daisy Gainsborough is an alcoholic," Dave says.

Neil smirks. Why is he not surprised?

"Alex Jones is her addiction coach. She's confirmed Daisy was with her all afternoon on the day Nick Masterson died."

That's a curveball. Neil had assumed Alex was male. His smugness evaporates.

"This is in Bishopston, two miles from Harefield Road. You'll recall there was a window of two hours between Jonathan Smyth turning up at the Mastersons' house, and Gail calling the emergency services. Alex had Daisy in sight the whole time, give or take five minutes. Further corroboration — Alex showed me that the meeting was booked and paid for via an online calendar. They emailed each other about it, both in advance and afterwards. Daisy can't be the killer."

Dave winces, and Neil realises his colleague dislikes Daisy. Welcome to the club. The woman has wasted their time.

Sherry moves on to that very point.

"Daisy may not be a killer," she says, "but she's a liar. She accompanies Gail and Jonathan to Farigg, then tells us they've run off together and she doesn't know where Gail is. Hmm."

"The Farigg episode stinks," Neil agrees. He'd experienced a brief burst of euphoria when Police Scotland found the missing couple. That's long gone. He's been kicked into touch by the usual round of conflicting statements. The only common ground is the identity of the helicopter passengers, and the assertion that they were all happy campers.

He suspects Daisy isn't the only liar.

"How did you get on with Tamara Kaczmarek and Lacey Lewis?" Sherry asks.

Neil shrugs. “Tamara didn’t answer Britt’s call. Lacey—”

“Hold on,” Sherry says, “You left a message, right, Britt?”

Britt nods.

“Try again. See if City have information on her whereabouts. If not, she lives in the Met area, doesn’t she, so we can get them to bring her in. Anyway, Neil, you were saying about Lacey?”

“Want to watch the interview?” Neil offers.

Sherry glances at the clock. “Summarise it for us. The transcript was uploaded, no?”

Dave, their faithful scribe, is already clicking his mouse. “Yes,” he confirms.

“Lacey Lewis was just the pilot,” Neil says. “A mere taxi driver. That’s it in a nutshell, wouldn’t you say, Britt?”

“Exactly that,” Britt agrees. “Michael Gill asked her to fly the crate — it’s called a Squirrel, two seats in the front, three in the back, boot for luggage. They didn’t take luggage, because it was just for the day. Four friends on an outing. Michael paid, but he wasn’t with them. He told Lacey to do whatever his sister, Daisy, wanted. Lacey hardly spoke to her, or the other passengers, because she was just the pilot.”

“She told us she didn’t notice tension between the passengers,” Neil points out. “But she also couldn’t hear the conversation in the rear seats, which were occupied by Daisy, Jonathan and Gail, in that order. The helicopter was noisy. Passengers in the back were miked up on a separate circuit.”

“Okay, she didn’t spot any hostility. What about closeness between Gail and Jonathan?” Sherry asks.

Britt splutters, almost losing a mouthful of coffee. She grins. “You got a robust response to that one, didn’t you, Neil?”

Neil laughs. “The short answer is no. But there’s history. Jonathan was Lacey’s fiancé, until she dumped him for making a pass at Gail three years ago. According to Lacey, Gail wasn’t interested.”

“A lot can change in three years,” Sherry says.

“True,” Neil acknowledges, “but Lacey didn’t think there was anything between them, and she wasn’t best pleased that I asked. Even when they demanded to be dropped on Farigg—”

“So, the couple were definitely on Farigg at their own request?” Sherry asks.

"That's what Lacey maintains, but she didn't hear it from them direct. As Britt said, Lacey claims she took orders from Daisy. When Daisy said Jonathan and Gail wished to stay on Farigg, Lacey didn't question it. She'd dropped people off on Farigg before. Scientists."

Sherry wrinkles her nose. "I bet they took luggage. Did it occur to her that Jonathan and Gail were poorly equipped to stay behind?"

"Apparently not," Britt says.

"To recap," Sherry says, "We can hold Gail until 7pm tonight, and Jonathan until 3pm tomorrow. But we don't have enough to charge either of them with murder. Barring a last-minute confession from one of them, we won't get it in time. There's a chance of a child neglect charge sticking in Gail's case, though. By her own admission, she didn't make proper arrangements for her kids to be collected from school last Friday. A tentative agreement with an alcoholic friend isn't good enough. Neil, can you charge her now, please? Then you can go home. You've put in enough hours."

"Want me to minute that?" Dave asks.

"Just the action, please. And our next steps, which will be questioning Gail and Jonathan's known associates. I want them quizzed in more depth. Neil and Britt, you can start tomorrow with the neighbours…"

# CHAPTER 63 GAIL

## Day 20 - Saturday

My cell is as empty as my emotions. If I allowed myself to feel anything, I'd be a blubbering heap on the cold lino floor. My kids must be a hundred times more worried and scared than I am, though. I can't afford to think about that either.

I'd go crazy.

There's a click. I shudder under the gaze of the eye that's appeared through the spyhole. By itself, it seems disconnected from humanity. It could belong to anybody. And whoever they are, they're observing me coldly. Judging me.

The solid metal door clanks open.

I stand up, hope surging as I remember the duty solicitor said the police couldn't keep me here much longer. At last, I'll be reunited with Mary and Tom.

Neil Slater and Brittany Billinge march in. A lump rises in my throat. They're not smiling. Neil Slater's jaw is set and his brow furrowed. The vibe is dark. Disturbing.

"How are my children?" I demand.

"Safe and well," Neil Slater says. "I have news you may not wish to hear—"

"What have you done with them?" I fall back onto the hard, vinyl-covered mattress, lights dancing in front of my eyes.

"Your children are fine," his colleague soothes.

"You may wish to have a solicitor present," Neil Slater says. "Britt can call one in if you like."

Brittany Billinge nods. "Just say the word."

"Thanks, but there's no need."

Their news can't be important. My kids are all right, and nothing else matters.

"Very well," Neil Slater replies. As if quoting from a script, he begins, "Gail Masterson, I am Detective Sergeant Neil Slater, and this is Detective Constable Brittany Billinge. You are aware of your right to legal advice, and you have been offered it…"

Sighing, I hardly listen as he goes through the preamble. How can they possibly say I murdered Nick? I wasn't even there.

"I am charging you with child neglect, specifically for contravening Section 1 of the Children and Young Person's Act 1933."

My head spins. Not murder, but neglect. Nobody collected the kids from school, because Lacey flew off without me. But I can't tell the police that she wasn't supposed to. I can't admit that I drugged Jonathan and kidnapped him.

Will I lose my children forever?

# CHAPTER 64 NEIL

## Day 21 - Sunday

Showy pale purple blooms festoon the Jukeses' front garden walls. A heady scent tickles Neil's nostrils.

"Lush." Britt sniffs appreciatively. "What's that shrub called?"

"Wisteria. It's early."

"Trust you to know, being on the property ladder."

While he and Gemma are on the first rung, Harefield Road's inhabitants have climbed considerably higher. It's a happy accident for the Jukeses. As teachers, they didn't earn huge salaries, but they bought in Clifton during a golden age when the houses were cheap. Now only Ponzi schemers and trust fund kids can afford it.

Britt rings the doorbell.

Maggie answers. She wears a pink cotton apron, on which the words KITCHEN BOSS are spelled out with white buttons. It looks home-made.

Maggie blinks a couple of times, probably a sign that she didn't expect them. "Hello. Neil and Bethany, isn't it?"

Britt has whinged often enough to Neil about folk stumbling over her name, but she replies without annoyance. "Brittany. May we come in, please?"

Maggie's smile appears forced. "Of course, but I've told you everything I know, and Perry has too."

"It would help us to go over it again, in case we've missed anything," Neil says. "The tiniest detail can make a difference."

"Then do come through. You'll have to excuse me, as I'm cooking Sunday lunch. Would you mind if I answer your questions while I prepare the meal? Or I can fetch Perry from his shed."

"We'll talk to you first, if we may." Neil imagines that won't take long, then she can work her culinary miracles undisturbed. An appetising smell of roast beef has set his mouth watering. Since his vegan wife took control of their kitchen, he misses his old carnivorous ways.

Maggie pulls out two chunky pine chairs from beneath a matching farmhouse table. "Shall I pop the kettle on?" she asks.

"Yes, please."

Like the rest of the house, this room is homely. The golden wood furniture blends well with bright yellow walls, while a cream Aga pumps out heat as well as delicious aromas. It would be stuffy without the breeze gusting in through an open window.

Britt switches on her laptop. Meanwhile, Maggie makes coffee with an air of brisk efficiency, setting it in front of them with a plate of chocolate digestives.

"Perry's favourites," she says. "He likes to treat the little ones next door. I suppose you know we haven't seen them for a week? Dreadful. Gail would never be cruel to them, I can tell you that much."

Neil deflects the challenge, which he's sure is intentional. "Could you tell me more about your neighbours' relationships with their children?" he asks.

"As I said before, he — Nick — was hardly ever there. When he was, he wasn't interested. Didn't play with them much. Shouted. Gail, on the other hand," Maggie sets down her chopping knife, "she couldn't do enough for them."

She wipes tears from her eyes, and begins slicing apples. As she works, she describes a paragon who never has a cross word for her youngsters. Her narrative tallies with Ruth Cluff's, but it doesn't change the fact that Gail abandoned her children to fly to a remote island.

Maggie slides the slices into a glass dish, adding spices and a sprinkle of white powder from a jar.

"Stevia sweetener," Britt reads. "You don't use sugar?"

"I'm careful with my diet," Maggie says. She tops the mixture with crumble and places the dish in her Aga.

"I'm sorry," she says, her back still turned, "I have to inject myself now, and you may not want to watch. It's best to look away, if so."

"We can give you privacy." Neil motions to Britt to stand up. He points to the utility area, an alcove with a glazed door to the garden.

"It's only in my stomach. Insulin. I appreciate some people are squeamish." Maggie pats her chubby belly.

Neil stops stock still. His breath hitches. "You're a diabetic?"

"Type 2," Maggie confirms. "It comes with age, and, well, I didn't help myself by piling on the pounds. They diagnosed it twenty years ago. The injections are an everyday routine, something I do before a big meal."

"Actually, I wouldn't be squeamish about that." Britt grins. "I was afraid you'd be jabbing your bum when you told us not to look, but everyone's got tummy fat, haven't they, Neil?"

"Speak for yourself. Some of us hit the gym."

"Anyhow, I don't mind sticking around," Britt says.

Maggie unscrews the cap of a plastic cylinder, attaches a disposable needle and fiddles with a dial at the other end. Then she lifts the front of her jumper and stabs herself.

The jab only takes a few seconds.

"That's your insulin pen? May I hold it, please?" Neil asks.

"Sure." Maggie removes the needle and throws it into a miniature garbage bin on her worktop. She hands the pen to Neil.

He examines it and finds the batch number. "I'd like to take a photo."

"Go ahead."

"Do you keep a supply of these?" he says, reaching for his phone to snap the image.

"A few," Maggie says.

Neil keeps hold of the pen. "Were you aware that Nick Masterson was a diabetic too?"

Maggie nods. "Type 1, though. A different variant."

"And you have the Mastersons' spare keys, don't you?"

The glazed door opens. Peregrine hurries into the kitchen.

"I know what you're trying to do." Peregrine, red-faced and scowling, points a finger at Neil's chest. He doesn't quite touch it. "You can stop right now. Maggie had nothing to do with Nick's death."

Neil steps back. "Let's have a chat. Could we perhaps go to your shed?"

Maggie gawps at her husband. She's quivering. "Perry, what are you talking about?"

Peregrine sags. "I killed him, dear. I'm sorry. Truly I am."

"But you… you don't even kill spiders." Maggie turns to the detectives. "Tell him to put an end to this nonsense. Please. He isn't well, you know."

"I'm afraid it's true," Peregrine says. "You know we wanted to buy Noah a car? Pay for Kate's school? Go back to that lovely hotel in Devon… We can't, because he took all the money."

Britt says gently, "You may want to have a solicitor with you when you talk to us, Peregrine. We're going to have to take you down to Bridewell, I'm afraid."

"No." A tear trickles down Maggie's cheek. "At least let him stay for his lunch. It's nearly ready, and when will he have a proper meal again?"

Peregrine straightens up. "She's injected her insulin," he says fiercely. "She needs to eat."

Britt opens her mouth to speak, then stops. She looks at Neil with an enquiring expression.

Neil feels the couple's eyes upon him too. He imagines Maggie removing food from the oven after they've gone. She will be distraught, lacking in appetite, and at risk of slipping into a hypo.

It would be highly irregular to agree to her request. But just this once, he's going to let compassion trump the letter of the law. Anyway, they'll end up waiting for a patrol car to take their suspect in.

"You've got thirty minutes," he says. "And I'm afraid I'm staying with you."

He does, after all, have a duty to bring Peregrine to justice. In the heat of the moment, suppose the old couple made a suicide pact? If he left them for five minutes, he might return to find them unconscious with insulin pens beside them. So he asks Britt to fetch beer from the shed. They watch as Peregrine enjoys the last meal he will eat as a free man.

There are times when Neil wishes he did a different job.

# CHAPTER 65 NEIL

## Day 21 - Sunday

Unlike many visitors to Bridewell, Peregrine has no need of the duty solicitor's services. His own lawyer, Dev Singh, is already sitting in the reception lobby when Neil and Britt arrive. Two minutes later, a uniformed constable follows with their prisoner.

"How are you, Mr Jukes?" Dev says cheerily, standing up and shaking Peregrine's hand.

"Could be better," Peregrine mumbles. "Got a terrible headache."

"Been overdoing it in the garden?" Dev says. "Never mind, we'll sort that out. DS Slater, isn't it? I'll need to have a conference with my client. Could you arrange for some water and paracetamol too, please?"

"The meeting room's booked, Dev," one of the desk civilians says. "And I'll call a medic to bring painkillers."

Dev beams at her. "Proactive or what? Thanks, Tracy."

Dev is a familiar figure at the police station, respected if not loved. If there's a loophole, Dev will find it. He's been in the game for decades. Of course, he's well-known among the criminal fraternity too. Neil wonders how he and Peregrine are acquainted.

Dev answers the unspoken question.

"Did he tell you that he taught me physics?" he says to Neil. "Informed me it wasn't my forte and I'd never pass the GCSE. I worked my socks off and got an A. Put me right off it, though." He laughs. "What could I do? I had to study law."

Client and solicitor are escorted to their meeting room by one of the uniformed police, who summons Neil and Britt thirty minutes later.

Dev raises an eyebrow to them. "I have advised my client to provide a prepared statement rather than engage with you," he says. "However, he is keen to talk to you instead. Take it away, Mr Jukes."

Despite his evident disappointment, Dev remains bright-eyed and smiley. He occasionally places a sympathetic hand on Peregrine's arm as the old man gives a full account.

Peregrine has a meningioma. Neil has never heard of it, but it turns out to be a growth pressing on the brain. Although classed as benign, it is increasing in size and obstructing the flow of cerebrospinal fluid away from the brain. There is no scope to operate.

Peregrine's life expectancy is three to six months. That's barely time to process the murder case through the courts, even if Peregrine pleads guilty, which he intends to do.

He explains that Gail's injuries were the last straw. Peregrine is old school: you don't hit women.

Already upset at the theft of his nest egg, the old man donned his gardening gloves, picked up his neighbour's keys and prepared his wife's insulin pens. He opened the Mastersons' front door carefully, and slipped inside. The sound of Nick shouting at someone only increased his resolve. He crept towards the source of the noise.

"Nick's back was turned," Peregrine says. "He didn't even see me. But he felt the first jab all right."

The old man winces. "He turned round to take a swing at me. I didn't think… I mean, it was such a large dose, I expected him to be go under at once. But he didn't. In that moment, I thought I was a goner."

Evidently he was wrong about that too. "What did Jonathan Smyth do?" Neil asks.

Peregrine grimaces. "Jonathan? He was out cold," he says, clearly puzzled.

"I thought you said Nick was shouting at him?"

"No, I didn't. He was arguing with the tree surgeon," Peregrine replies.

Neil tenses. This is the first time anyone has mentioned the presence of another person. "Tell me more about him," he says.

"Her. A young lady. Very pretty," Peregrine says. "Standing in his office. Or should I say, being shaken roughly by Nick. He had hold of her arms, and she was screaming. I think she was grateful for my intervention. As I was for hers."

"What did she do?"

"Hit him with a rugby cup. She grabbed the ears and swung it at his legs, like this." Peregrine motions with his right hand.

"And then what?"

"Nick fell down. He started to scream. The tree surgeon said he'd stop soon. She told me to get out."

Peregrine glances at Dev, who nods.

"I took to my heels. Went back to my garden. Kept busy. But first, I stabbed him with the other pen. Just to make sure."

"What happened to the insulin pens?"

Peregrine tilts his head to one side. "I don't understand the question. Obviously, I dropped them. So it would look like they were his, and he'd done it himself."

"Jonathan Smyth's fingerprint was found on one."

"Well, I don't know how. As I told you, the guy was out for the count."

"May I suggest," Dev says, "that you locate the tree surgeon as quickly as possible. My client will, of course, give you every co-operation in building an e-fit. It would be helpful if you could arrange for that today, as I intend to apply for bail tomorrow morning."

"And I'm confident we'll oppose it," Neil says.

Dev doesn't betray a jot of concern. "As you wish. Yes, I'm aware it's not usually granted in murder cases. But Mr Jukes is not your average murderer."

# CHAPTER 66 GAIL

## Day 22 - Monday

The waiting room of the Bristol Magistrates' Court is like a bus station, with extra security measures. Sitting beside a security guard with my hands cuffed, I watch a stream of people move in and out: police officers, prisoners, sharp-suited lawyers, anxious mothers and wives.

I freeze, jaw slackening. My heart speeds up. Peregrine shuffles in, his hands similarly restrained.

"Peregrine!" I can't catch his eye, but risk calling to him anyway. "What are you doing here?"

He looks away. "I'm sorry, Gail," he mumbles.

"What happened?"

His guard gives me a black look.

"You'll find out soon, I suppose. I'm afraid I… I killed Nick."

Kind, gentle Peregrine did what? He can't have.

"Forgive me. I shouldn't have done it. And I should have owned up. I never meant to get you into trouble."

I gawp at him, unable to find my voice. It's impossible to believe.

My solicitor nudges me in the ribs.

"Gail." Her voice is soft, urgent. "We're up next."

I sense Peregrine's eyes on my back as I allow the guard to lead me away.

In the courtroom, I have to sit in the dock, a low bench boxed in with glazed partitions. It feels like a goldfish bowl. DS Neil Slater, standing nearby, stares at me before abruptly turning to speak to the woman next to him. She wears a dark dress and jacket with matching six-inch stilettos. Despite the boost to her height, she barely reaches his shoulder.

Facing me on the other side of the room, three magistrates sit, elderly, suited, and surly. Their section of the chamber is elevated above the rest, a nod to the power in their hands. They tower over the lawyers, police officers and court officials conversing in the middle.

An usher calls the court to order, then a clerk quizzes me to confirm my identity. These are easy questions, yet I find myself trembling. So much rests on this hearing, as is clear when the charges are read. I have neglected Mary and Tom, contrary to the Children and Young Person's Act 1933.

Throughout my children's lives, I've tried to do a better job than my own parents. Even Nick was way ahead of the monster who crushed all the kindness out of him. Yet none of that matters. The criminal justice system focuses on failure, not success.

The clerk asks how I plead.

"Not guilty," I announce, with a breezy, fake confidence. Out of sight of the magistrates, I wring my hands together to stop them shaking.

That's my part over for now. My heart races in my ribcage as my solicitor, Ellie, applies for bail.

I have learned that the woman in high stilettos is the prosecutor. She argues stridently that this is a serious case, and there's a risk I'd snatch my children at the first sniff of liberty. But Ellie's softer tone is what seems to make the magistrates listen. Their eyes follow her as she explains that I've just lost my husband at a young age. I love my children deeply, but as a law-abiding citizen, I will comply with whatever bail conditions are imposed.

My heart beats even faster as I strain to hear their decision.

"Mrs Masterson. We have considered bail. It is granted on the following conditions. You may attend supervised contact sessions, but will not otherwise attempt to get in touch with your children. You will surrender your passport. You will remain at your home between the hours of 9pm to 9am. You will report weekly to Bridewell Police Station."

It's not completely good news, but Ellie has taken care to manage my expectations. Light-headed, adrenaline draining away, I say, "Thank you."

Perhaps that is not the done thing. The magistrates frown. But my handcuffs are removed, and I follow Ellie out of the courtroom.

Neil Slater taps my shoulder. "Gail, do you have a moment? Can you tell me if you employ a female tree surgeon?"

"Definitely not." I peer at him. "Why?"

"A hunch," he says. "I'd like you to see an e-fit image."

Ellie glares at him. "Neil, we can arrange an interview later."

"It will only take a moment. Do you know this woman?" He thrusts an A4 sheet at me.

I recognise her instantly.

"That's Tamara," I tell him.

# CHAPTER 67 TAMARA

## Day 23 - Tuesday

Still rubbing her eyes, Ruby is unimpressed by her dawn wake-up call.

"I've got a job interview later. How could you?" she hisses, as if it's Tamara's fault that the police rang the bell at 5.45am. Thankfully, Ruby woke up. She looked out of the window, saw the officers, and let them in. They told her they'd have used their steel battering ram otherwise.

Tamara received a rude awakening. These are the bruisers from the Met, not the gentlemanly types in the Square Mile. She's hardly had time to dress before they're searching the house, causing maximum inconvenience to its inhabitants. Then she's carted off to Brixton in a squad car.

"I'll put your stuff outside," Ruby yells as Tamara leaves.

She's been arrested on suspicion of perverting the course of justice. Tamara isn't sure if the charge relates to Nick's death or Jonathan's one-way trip. At the Brixton custody suite, she learns that it will be hours before she finds out. Detectives from the Avon and Somerset force are travelling to London to speak to her. She's left to get what sleep she can in a sparsely furnished, brightly lit cell.

It's noon by the time she's brought to an interview room. A camera winks at her from the wall. Tamara yawns at it. DS Neil Slater and DC Brittany Billinge introduce themselves. They ask if she wants a solicitor. Are they kidding? Of course she does.

The duty solicitor, Tariq, is duly produced. He's an Essex boy, but she won't hold it against him. She knows as well as anyone that you don't need a posh voice to be sharp. When he informs her that she should tell the police nothing unless she's absolutely sure it will help her case, she nods.

The interview begins. Tamara confirms her name and address, although she suspects Ruby won't welcome her back.

Neil Slater takes the lead. He begins with the day when Nick died. She's hardly going to forget her ill-fated expedition to find samples of his DNA. At least she succeeded in that. Naturally, she's admitting none of it. She tells the detective she was in London all day, as she's mentioned to the local police.

"You did go through that with my City colleagues," Neil Slater says, "and gave them a list of recruitment agents you'd visited. But they were unable to verify this with the agents concerned."

Tamara shrugs. "I may have seen different agents that day, then. There are so many that it becomes a blur."

"If you had visited Bristol, how might you have travelled?"

She sees the trap. If she divulges a preferred mode of transport, that's where the police will seek evidence first.

"I'd hire a car," she says.

"May I see your driving licence?"

"It's at home," she lies, breath quickening. It will be a simple matter for him to discover she doesn't possess a licence.

"Who would you hire the car from?"

Tamara scrabbles for the name of a rental company. Her bosses usually ask for limousines with a chauffeur; they're not keen on driving themselves. "Hertz," she replies.

"I believe you also went to Bristol for a funeral," Neil Slater says. "How did you travel then?"

Tamara purses her lips. This man thinks he's so clever. "Not 'also'. It was my first time in the city," she says.

"And how did you get there?" he repeats.

She hesitates. The silence stretches out like elastic. If she tells them, they'll be crawling all over the previous week's CCTV at Victoria Coach Station.

"No comment," she says finally.

He changes tack. "How did you feel about Nick Masterson's death?"

"Upset." She wasn't, of course, but she's on safer ground with this line of questioning. "It's terrible that he was murdered," she adds.

"What makes you think it was murder rather than suicide?"

Tamara rolls her eyes. "Seriously? You're conducting a murder investigation, and you ask me that?"

"She has a point," Tariq says.

"Sorry, I'll move on." Neil Slater leans forward. "What's your relationship with Gail Masterson?"

Tamara evades his gaze, unsure where he's leading. "Businesslike," she says. "I worked for her husband."

"As a tree surgeon?"

She frowns, wondering if he's crazy, before remembering her lie to the old man. The police must have spoken to him.

Tamara's chest tightens. Is he claiming she's a killer? She'd imagined they'd never find him. He'd committed the perfect murder, after all, so perfect that it wouldn't have appeared to be homicide without her help. It was easy to press Jonathan's fingertip onto the insulin pen.

Still, the old man didn't see her do it. And who's really going to believe he encountered a tree surgeon in Nick's study?

She plays it with a straight bat. "I was Nick's PA," she says icily.

"And how close were you and Nick Masterson?"

"We worked well together," she says.

"Are you pregnant with his child?"

She inhales sharply. Talk about going for the jugular. Tamara considers a denial, but he's obviously heard what happened at the funeral.

"Yes," she says.

"Do you have a financial interest in his death?" Neil Slater asks.

"No." How would they prove it, after all?

Brittany Billinge speaks, making Tamara jump. The girl is so quiet that Tamara forgets she's there.

"You wouldn't happen to have taken out life insurance, would you?" the detective constable asks in her soft West Country lilt. "I mean, as the mother of his child, you'd have an insurable interest. And most policies don't pay out if there's a suicide in the first year."

Under the table, out of sight, Tamara's hands ball into fists. "No comment," she says.

Neil Slater sighs. "We can do this the hard way or the easy way, Tamara. Rest assured that we'll get to the truth. We'll take witness statements, contact banks, look at CCTV. Would you like a short break to talk to your solicitor?"

"That would be a good idea," Tariq says.

# CHAPTER 68 GAIL

## Day 100 - Wednesday

In high summer, my old stone house is a refuge, shady and cool inside. When I answer the doorbell, a blast of dry heat hits me. Sun in my eyes, I squint at the visitor.

The man holds out a bouquet, a lavish selection of white blooms. I spot roses, hydrangea and cosmos. No daisies, which may be intentional.

"Jonathan." I try to sound thrilled. It's no mean feat when I neither expected nor hoped to see him again.

He smiles. "Gail, how are you doing?"

"Not bad," I stutter.

"Are you going to let me in? At least to put them in water for you."

He's made it hard to refuse politely. I offer coffee, warning him to beware of children running around at his feet. Mary and Tom are back from school, flitting about between house and garden.

We traipse through to the kitchen in silence. I glance furtively at him. His hair has grown over the bonxie's gash, and I don't spot any scars. He's been lucky.

"Let me find a glass vase. The flowers are gorgeous, and wow! The scent of those roses is out of this world."

"They're a sign of new beginnings, according to the florist. My thank you gift. You saved my life, after all. I would have brought a present sooner, but my solicitor advised me to steer clear. You know, because I might be called as a defence witness? Then I heard the charges had been dropped…"

"Grudgingly," I point out. "But yes, the CPS realised they wouldn't get a conviction, I think."

"How are the kids?"

I take a deep breath. "It was wonderful getting them back. Of course, they were clingy. People say that children take everything in their stride, but you and I know that's not the whole truth. Each experience leaves a mark."

"You're right," Jonathan says. "Hey, now you have a chance to build more good experiences for them. And over time, the bad ones will fade."

"Fair point." I appreciate he means well, but Jonathan's parenting expertise is limited to a toxic relationship with adult stepchildren.

In his defence, Daisy is a piece of work. Sadly for my kids, I've had to encourage them to make new friends. It was difficult. But I'd already decided to cut Daisy out of my life, even more so when Ruth Cluff explained they'd charged her with wasting police time. My 'bestie' had alleged Jonathan and I had run away together. I wonder if she always intended to leave me on Farigg?

I've warmed towards Ruth Cluff, our Family Liaison Officer. She suggested I check whether Nick had life insurance. Because he did, I can continue to live in this house. I'm going to redecorate, however: slowly, room by room, so the children don't notice his influence gradually fading.

He'll never be entirely gone, but I hope it's the best of him that endures in Tom and Mary, and in Tamara's unborn baby. I haven't yet told my two that a little brother or sister is on the way. It's another challenge to overcome. Meanwhile, I've asked my solicitor to send Tamara a letter offering my help with childcare.

Given everything she's done, we won't become friends. I have to remember that Tamara is also Nick's victim, though. There will be a support network for her if she goes to prison.

Arranging the flowers in a crystal vase, I switch on the kettle. "Is instant okay, Jonathan? Maggie next door has given me scones, too."

He frowns. "Is she coping?"

"As well as can be expected. Her husband's dead, which isn't great for her. The only mercy is that she was able to nurse him at home. The funeral's next week."

There have been too many funerals recently. Matilda's. Nick's. His mother's. Fortunately, her brain was so scrambled that she didn't know Nick had trashed the family firm. Or that he'd died because of it.

It's strange. I hated Jonathan when it seemed he'd murdered my husband. Yet I can't feel the same hostility towards Peregrine. He was a kind man. A good man.

Not like Nick.

I plate up four scones, halving them and adding butter and jam. The kids will enjoy a treat as well. Meanwhile, Jonathan makes small talk about the weather and the free festivals in Bristol during the summer.

I fidget.

I'm not sure why he's here.

Tom races in from the garden, a whirling dervish. "Mum, we dug up the treasure. Come and see."

"Later. I've got a visitor. Say hi to Jonathan."

"Hi," Tom announces, eyes glazing as he sees the newcomer is an adult. He'd undoubtedly prefer a child, someone who can join in his pirate game.

"How about a scone, Tom? Fetch Mary if you think she'd like one."

"No, she wouldn't. But can I have two, please?"

"Nice try, Tom. Please can you ask her."

He dashes away, shouting, "Mary! There's a scone, but you don't want it, do you?"

Jonathan finishes his, leaving not a crumb on his plate. "Thanks, Gail. A pleasant change from gruel. Well, I'd better be going."

"I hope all's well with you?" Now, I feel guilty that I didn't ask.

"I think so. We got the business back on track." His face darkens. "I miss Tilly so much, though."

"Be kind to yourself," I urge him.

"I will. Actually, I'm sort of seeing Lacey again. As a friend for now, but who knows? We always had a lot in common. A couple of geeks."

"Fair enough."

He looks askance at me. "You think it's too soon?"

"I'm not judging you." It's a white lie. Considering he claimed to be besotted with his wife, I'm surprised.

Jonathan sighs. "I asked myself what Tilly would say. And I remember how she refused to live in the past. She'd want me to move on. And she made me into a better person — the kind of person Lacey deserves."

"What does Lacey think?"

He looks sheepish. "We haven't really discussed the future."

"Good luck with it." I squeeze his arm.

"You too," Jonathan says. "Take each day at a time. You're looking well."

"Thanks."

He undoubtedly means I've put on weight. It's no disaster.

Slowly, I'm coming to terms with the end of my life with Nick. Unlike Jonathan, I'm in no hurry to enter another relationship. But when I do, it will never again be as someone else's appendage. I'm worth more than that.

"By the way," I say before I shut the door on him, "if it works out with Lacey, I expect an invitation to your wedding."

He laughs. "I'll get it in the post."

The children run back inside as I'm clearing the crockery.

"Look!" Tom's cheeks dimple with a broad smile. He dumps a handful of shiny gold discs on the kitchen table.

"What are those, Tom?" I pick one up, immediately noticing its weight. It feels too heavy to be a toy. A coin of some sort, then? Examining it, I see a pretty image of a running deer under the word KRUGERRAND.

A memory triggers. Someone mentioned Krugerrands once.

"It's Granny's treasure. I buried it under the tree." Tom beams up at me.

"There's more," Mary says. "I bet there's a hundred. You can't count that much, Tom, can you?"

He sticks his tongue out. "Can too."

My mind races. I remember now: Nick, just in from London, distraught that his Krugerrands were gone.

They must be valuable. I pick up my phone and start Googling.

A single Krugerrand is worth two thousand five hundred pounds.

How many are there? The coins on the kitchen table are a fraction of Nick's horde.

They could change our lives.

I stare at them for a long time. Then I pinch myself. Breathe in and out slowly. Recall that it's not just about us. I must report the find to the liquidators of Nick's business, who are salvaging what they can for the unlucky investors. These aren't faceless institutions. Nick ripped off the financially unsophisticated. Ordinary folk. Pensioners like Maggie.

"Why don't you show me?" I suggest.

Tom takes my hand. "Come on."

I duck underneath the apple tree's branches, laden with fruit. Below, the family-size ice-cream tub is still half-buried. Tom has removed enough earth to take off the lid.

"There." He points to the glittering gold inside.

"Let's count all the coins together, Tom," I say. "And then we should give the treasure back to its owners. Because sometimes pirates steal things, don't they? And stealing is wrong."

Tom hesitates. After a moment, he nods. "All right then."

"I'll help you count, Tom," Mary offers. "Look, one, two, three…"

Together, we agree there are a hundred. I help the children carry them into the kitchen.

Tom and Mary reward themselves with scones. I ruffle their fair heads, feeling that life can't get much better than this. I'm so lucky to have my precious children. They will always come first.

I used to think that wasn't so for my parents. But I judged them too harshly. If it hadn't been for the skills they taught me, Jonathan and I wouldn't have survived Farigg.

I'm planning a long holiday later in the summer. The kids will finally meet their grandparents in Tierra del Fuego. It's time to broaden their horizons.

And mine.

oo0O0oo

Thank you for reading **Lies Between Friends.** At last, Gail is reunited with her children and reconciled with her family. She can finally build the bright future she deserves.

If you like a dark psychological thriller wrapped around a murder mystery, you'll love **Lies at Her Door**! It's also set in Clifton, and features Neil Slater at the start of his career.

**She forgot about her childhood friend… until his body is found under her garden. Can she prove she didn't commit the decades-old murder?**

oo0O0oo

## SPREAD THE WORD

Again, thank you for joining Gail as she throws off the chains of her toxic marriage. If you enjoyed the book, do help more readers meet Gail. Please take a minute to review **Lies Between Friends** on Amazon and Goodreads. Even a shoutout on social media would put the story in front of bookworms who will love it. **Your recommendation is the key that unlocks Gail's story for others.**

ooo0ooo

## FIND OUT MORE

AA Abbott is a British author of psychological thrillers about women finding strength in the face of danger. Discover AA Abbott's other books, enjoy freebies and subscribe to her newsletter on her website, aaabbott.co.uk. You'll also find details of large print, dyslexia-friendly, audiobook and ebook editions. There are notes for book groups too: great for starting a conversation!

oooOooo

## SOCIAL MEDIA

Meet AA Abbott on Facebook, Instagram, Threads, Bluesky and X as @AAAbbottstories.

ooo0ooo

Printed in Dunstable, United Kingdom

68419406R00129